T0199107

CONQUER THE DARKNESS

She forced herself to continue. "Once I was taken to the Oracles I only became more determined to bury my emotions." She needed him to understand. "My people were depending on me to fulfill my duty. I couldn't risk being distracted."

"That's what I am?" His fingers drifted along her jaw and down her neck. "A distraction?"

"At first," she murmured, tilting back her head as his hand wrapped around her throat. It wasn't threatening. It was a gesture of delicious possession. "A very sexy, occasionally charming distraction."

His eyes darkened, the heat in the room ratcheting up several more degrees.

"Sexy," he growled. "I like the sound of that."

Rainn swallowed a groan, her gaze skimming over his hard, chiseled features, and down the muscular chest that was emphasized by his tight T-shirt. Sexy was actually an understatement. He was...well, she didn't know what was sexier than sexy. All she knew was that he was a loyal, gorgeous male who came complete with a wolf.

What could be better?

Books by Alexandra Ivy

Guardians of Eternity
WHEN DARKNESS COMES
EMBRACE THE DARKNESS
DARKNESS EVERLASTING
DARKNESS REVEALED
DARKNESS UNLEASHED
BEYOND THE DARKNESS
DEVOURED BY DARKNESS
BOUND BY DARKNESS
FEAR THE DARKNESS
DARKNESS AVENGED
HUNT THE DARKNESS
WHEN DARKNESS ENDS
DARKNESS RETURNS
BEWARE THE DARKNESS
CONQUER THE DARKNESS

The Immortal Rogues
MY LORD VAMPIRE
MY LORD ETERNITY
MY LORD IMMORTALITY

The Sentinels
BORN IN BLOOD
BLOOD ASSASSIN
BLOOD LUST

Ares Security
KILL WITHOUT MERCY
KILL WITHOUT SHAME

Historical Romance
SOME LIKE IT WICKED
SOME LIKE IT SINFUL
SOME LIKE IT BRAZEN

Romantic Suspense

PRETEND YOU'RE SAFE
WHAT ARE YOU AFRAID OF?

YOU WILL SUFFER
THE INTENDED VICTIM

And don't miss these Guardians of Eternity novellas

TAKEN BY DARKNESS in YOURS FOR ETERNITY
DARKNESS ETERNAL in SUPERNATURAL
WHERE DARKNESS LIVES in THE REAL WEREWIVES OF
VAMPIRE COUNTY
LEVET (ebook only)
A VERY LEVET CHRISTMAS (ebook only)

And don't miss these Sentinel novellas

OUT OF CONTROL
ON THE HUNT

Published by Kensington Publishing Corporation

Conquer the Darkness

Alexandra Ivy

LYRICAL PRESS
Kensington Publishing Corp.
www.kensingtonbooks.com

LYRICAL PRESS BOOKS are published by

Kensington Publishing Corp.
119 West 40th Street
New York, NY 10018

All Kensington titles, imprints, and distributed lines are available at special quantity discounts for bulk purchases for sales promotion, premiums, fund-raising, educational, or institutional use.

Special book excerpts or customized printings can also be created to fit specific needs. For details, write or phone the office of the Kensington Sales Manager: Kensington Publishing Corp., 119 West 40th Street, New York, NY 10018. Attn. Sales Department. Phone: 1-800-221-2647.

Lyrical Press and Lyrical Press logo Reg. U.S. Pat. & TM Off.

First Electronic Edition: December 2019
ISBN-13: 978-1-5161-0844-2 (ebook)
ISBN-10: 1-5161-0844-2 (ebook)

First Print Edition: December 2019
ISBN-13: 978-1-5161-0847-3
ISBN-10: 1-5161-0847-7

Printed in the United States of America

Chapter 1

Mojave Desert

Ulric released a howl of sheer pleasure as he loped through the vast darkness. It'd been far too long since he'd had the luxury of leaving the glittering lights of Vegas to run across the desert. This week, thank the goddess, Chiron had returned to his elegant casino on the Strip.

That meant Ulric could finally shift into his wolf form and lose himself in the wild pleasures of the night. He ran, he hunted, he terrified a group of campers and bayed at the moon until his throat was raw.

All in all, a perfect night.

Dawn was nearing when he halted at the edge of the desert. Tilting back his head, he released a pulse of magic. A shudder raced through him before a shimmer surrounded his body. The thick, midnight-black fur disappeared, and his elongated muzzle started to shrink. In the space of a heartbeat he'd gone from a massive wolf to his human form.

Bathed in moonlight, he stood over six foot with the wide, muscled body that came from his long runs while in his wolf form. He also had the rabid temper of his animal, and the willingness to use violence when necessary. His skin was the creamy color of cappuccino and his eyes were golden and smoldered with an unmistakable power.

Running his hands over his smoothly shaved head, he wiped away the layer of sweat. The February air was cool, but he'd expended a considerable amount of energy during the night. Plus shifting always made him hot.

In a good, shivery way.

Primitive magic was always the best magic.

Stretching out his muscles, he moved to grab his jeans and black T-shirt that he'd folded on a flat rock. With a few efficient movements he was dressed and ramming his feet into a pair of military boots. Then, with a last glance toward the sky that was beginning to turn pink around the edges, he headed toward the city. Less than fifteen minutes later he was surrounded by civilization.

As usual, he took the most direct route to Dreamscape, indifferent to the fact he was strolling through one of the most dangerous neighborhoods in Vegas. What did he have to fear? Already he could hear the scrape of running footsteps. He had a badass vibe that sent both humans and demons scurrying out of his path.

A shame, really. The adrenaline was still pumping through his veins. He wouldn't mind the chance to knock one or two thugs on their asses.

Chiron, unfortunately, had strict rules on what Ulric could do to the customers, even if they were trying to cheat or being a drunken pain in his ass. It meant that he rarely had a chance for any fun. At least none that involved blood and screams of pain.

With a shrug of resignation, he jogged through a back parking lot and entered the towering glass and steel building through the kitchens.

Like all of Chiron's properties, this Dreamscape Resort was sleek, elegant, and designed to please the humans who were willing to spend a small fortune to avoid the horde of tourists that descended like locusts on the city. Only the high-end gamblers walked through the door or stayed in the luxury suites.

Ulric glanced toward the chefs who were sorting through the fresh ingredients they'd just purchased from the local markets before heading toward an opening next to the walk-in fridge. He entered a small, dark hallway and stood in front of the private doorway. He knew that Chiron would be making a last sweep of the gaming rooms before heading down to his rooms beneath the building. Although the vampire had a sun-proof office on the top floor, he always felt more comfortable when he was resting in his heavily fortified rooms buried deep in the ground.

On cue, Chiron opened the door and moved to stand directly in front of Ulric.

The vampire was not as large as Ulric. In fact, he was slender enough to look almost delicate in his expensive, tailored suit. His dark hair was cut close to his head and his features were finely chiseled. One glance in his black eyes, however, warned even the most thick-skulled creature not to screw with this male.

The temperature dropped by several degrees, but Ulric was accustomed to a chill in the air. He'd been with this vampire for over five centuries. Ever since Chiron had rescued him from the slave pits beneath the previous

King of Vampires' lair. The old Anasso had been addicted to blood that was tainted by alcohol and drugs, secretly holding humans and demons in dark caves to feed his nasty habit. Chiron had desperately tried to reveal the Anasso's treachery only to have his own master, Tarak, disappear and Chiron's clan banished.

Chiron had rescued Ulric and together they'd fled. For several decades they'd simply drifted from one place to another, both needing time to heal the wounds inflicted by the previous Anasso. Then, on a dare from Ulric, Chiron had established his first gambling club. It'd been an instant success and Dreamscape Resorts had been born.

Ulric loved the challenge. Chiron concentrated on the style and finances of the business, while Ulric dealt with the vast staff. Chiron had given him a purpose to keep living, along with a sense of pack.

But in the past three months, everything had changed.

Ulric didn't deal well with change.

Probably because it always sucked.

Easily sensing the strange agitation that boiled inside Ulric, Chiron tilted his head to the side.

"Everything okay?" the vampire asked.

Ulric shrugged even as the question pressed against his raw nerves.

Was everything okay?

It should be.

He had money. Security. Females if he wanted them. And a master who was as close to him as any brother. So why did he feel like a dark cloud was forming just over the horizon?

It was just the recent upheavals, he fiercely reminded himself. Chiron was mated to a witch named Lilah. Tarak was released from his prison. And the new Anasso, Styx, made a habit of traveling to Vegas. No doubt out of guilt that he'd refused to believe Chiron when he'd claimed the former King of Vampires was a whackadoodle.

Ulric trusted Chiron. Period.

As far as he was concerned, the rest of the leeches could sink back into the netherworld they'd crawled out of.

It was no wonder he was feeling a little antsy.

"Everything's better now that I had a chance to get out and stretch my legs," he assured his companion.

Chiron studied him for a beat, obviously aware that Ulric was hiding something from him. Then he shrugged. He knew Ulric wasn't a touchy, feely, share-every-emotion sort of dude. He was a growly, bitey, dangerously rabid sort of dude.

He'd talk when he wanted to talk.

"I don't think I've thanked you for taking care of things while I enjoyed my honeymoon," Chiron said, smoothly changing the direction of the conversation.

"It's what brothers do."

"Not all brothers." Chiron reached out his hand to lay it on Ulric's shoulder. "I appreciate your loyalty, Ulric, even when I forget to tell you."

Ulric felt heat crawl beneath his skin as he cleared his throat. Clearly being mated was making the vampire all mushy.

It was…unnerving.

"How's Lilah settling in?" Ulric asked, knowing it was the easiest way to distract his companion.

Chiron's features softened even as he released a rueful chuckle. "She's already making notes on how we can streamline our check-in process and more efficiently schedule the maid service. Plus, she has stacks of decorating magazines she's been thumbing through. I have a terrible fear we're in for a complete remodel."

Ulric smiled. He liked Lilah. He truly did. And she'd proven to be more than just a mate for Chiron. She had managed her own hotel for centuries. She was the perfect partner.

"If you wanted a mate who was happy fading into the background, you picked the wrong witch," he teased.

"True enough," Chiron readily agreed, a sappy expression on his face as he glanced toward a nearby elevator that led to his lair. No doubt Lilah was already down there waiting for him to join her.

Ulric paused, then spoke the words that had been on his mind since Chiron's return to Vegas.

"You know, now that you have Lilah to be your partner, it might be time for me to consider—"

"Stop right there," Chiron commanded.

"Why?"

"No one's moving anywhere," he informed Ulric, a hint of fang showing. "We started this journey together, and as far as I'm concerned we're going to finish it together. We're family." He narrowed his eyes. "You got it?"

Ulric held up his hand. He hadn't expected such a fierce reaction. "Yeah, I got it."

"Good." Chiron made a visible effort to soothe his flare of temper. "I'm headed to my lair. We'll talk more this evening."

Ulric nodded, turning away. Before he could leave, however, Chiron made a sudden sound of annoyance.

"Oh, I almost forgot."

Ulric glanced over his shoulder. "Forgot what?"

"Have you seen that damned gargoyle?"

A low growl rumbled in Ulric's chest. Levet was a three-foot gargoyle with fairy wings who was not only the bane of his existence, but a source of constant chaos.

"I kicked his thieving ass off the property when I caught him taking a joy ride in your favorite Porsche."

Ice abruptly coated the wall. "He stole my car?"

Ulric snorted. "Oh, he returned it. But only after he'd put a dent in the bumper and a long scratch on the hood. I have no idea where he went, or what happened."

Chiron's eyes glowed with a dark fire. "I'll kill him."

"Which is why I decided to have him vacate the property before you returned," Ulric admitted. "You've just started to form a relationship with your new Anasso. I didn't want you to do something stupid and be banished again."

Chiron snorted. "I've done just fine being banished, and if the cost of being back in the fold is having to deal with that aggravating lump of granite, I'd rather be in exile."

Ulric couldn't argue. Instead he watched in silence as Chiron stomped across the hallway and used the keypad to open the elevator. Then, as the vampire disappeared from view, Ulric heaved a faint sigh.

It was part envy, part regret for the inevitable change in his life, and part...what?

Damn. He didn't know. It was like having an itch he couldn't scratch. He gave a sharp shake of his head, forcing himself to walk down the narrow hallway to enter the main casino.

Despite the early hour, there were a few customers strolling through the vast rooms. A group of men wearing matching tuxedoes were clustered around a roulette table, while other gamblers were settled in front of the slot machines. On the far wall was a set of glass doors that opened into the high-limit section of the casino. That area was packed with guests no matter what time of day or night.

Strolling along the edge of the room, Ulric made a mental note to have the massive chandeliers polished and the silver carpets cleaned. It was the lull between the craziness of New Year's Eve and the crush of summer vacation. A perfect opportunity for some deep housekeeping.

Of course, Lilah might have a different opinion...

Ulric snapped his teeth together. What the hell was wrong with him? He was acting like a whimpering pup instead a grown-ass Were.

Lost in his baffling mood, Ulric barely noticed the svelte woman dressed in a long, backless black gown. Beautiful women in expensive clothes were a dime a dozen in this city.

It wasn't until he caught the faint scent of musk that he came to a screeching halt. Okay, maybe he didn't actually screech, but he did freeze in place as he sucked in a deep breath.

Disbelief exploded through him.

Over the years there'd been a handful of Weres who'd strolled through the casino or stayed at the hotel. Most, however, preferred the numerous demon clubs hidden on the fringes of the city. Why force yourself to behave in a civilized manner in front of the humans when you could literally let your animal out to play?

But none of them had smelled like pack.

Like family.

Narrowing his eyes, Ulric studied the female as she sauntered toward the front of the casino. If he'd been in his wolf form his hackles would have been raised.

It was impossible. His entire pack had been slaughtered over five hundred years ago. Still…

There was no denying that scent.

Unlike humans, Weres didn't use sight to recognize others. Anyone could change their appearance. Whether it was from aging, from magic, or mundane surgery, the outside shell was easily manipulated. But a person's smell…that remained the same.

Feeling like the earth was moving beneath his feet, it took a second for him to realize that the female had pushed open a side door to leave the casino. She paused, glancing over her shoulder as if sensing his fierce gaze. Then, with a faint frown, she was heading out of the building.

"Damn."

Shaking himself out of his stunned inertia, Ulric charged across the casino, thankful that most of the guests were tucked in their beds. Or perhaps they were tucked in someone else's bed. It was Vegas, after all. The only important thing was that he didn't have to toss customers out of his path as he stormed across the floor.

Bursting into the early dawn shadows, he glanced toward the waiting line of taxis that were pulled beneath the wide canopy. He scowled when he didn't instantly spot his quarry. Where was she? Then he caught a flash of movement out of the corner of his eye.

Whirling to the side, he watched as she moved to the edge of the sidewalk. His gaze skimmed over her pale, oval face that was framed by long hair that shimmered like crimson fire in the light spilling from the casino. Her features were bold, with a hint of sensuality in the curve of her lips and the smoldering dark eyes.

Ulric, however, didn't focus on her undoubted beauty. Instead he allowed her scent to settle deep in his soul.

Family.

The word whispered through his mind, stirring ancient memories that'd been locked away for centuries. He grimaced, aching regret clenching his heart as images cascaded through his mind. As if they'd been piled up, just waiting for the opportunity to be released.

He could see himself as a young pup, running through the open fields as he hunted rabbits. And spending the day dozing in the family cottage with his father standing guard. And being held in his mother's arms when he was afraid.

He swallowed the pain, forcing himself to concentrate on the female who was slowly turning to face him. He'd spent years building barriers around his memories; later he would deal with the bleak task of returning the damn things where they belonged. Nothing mattered in this moment but discovering the truth of the woman standing in front of him.

"Brigette," he breathed.

Her eyes widened, her expression stricken as she suddenly recognized him. "Ulric?"

"I don't believe it." His voice sounded harsh in the hush of dawn. "Are you real?"

She licked her lips. "I could ask you the same question. I thought you were dead."

"This is…" Ulric was lost for words, his gaze absorbing the high cheekbones and stubborn line of her jaw. Brigette had been younger than him, but her resemblance to his uncle was unmistakable. "A miracle," he finally managed to mutter, taking a step forward.

"No." She lifted her hand. "Stay back."

"What's wrong?"

Her eyes darted from side to side. Was she searching for someone?

"You have to forget that you've seen me."

Ulric snorted at the ridiculous command. "I'm getting old, but not that old. There's no way I'm forgetting that a cousin I believed slaughtered for the past five hundred years is alive and standing in my casino."

"Your casino?" She pointed toward the nearby building. "This belongs to you?"

"In part." He was too stunned to feel the usual pride in the empire he had helped to create. Right now, he was overwhelmed with the sight and smell of this female. "How did you survive?"

Her hand dropped, her shoulders slumping. "I'm not sure I did."

"Come back inside," he urged, barely keeping himself from reaching to grab her arm. She was clearly skittish. He couldn't risk scaring her away. "I have a personal suite where we can talk in private."

"I can't."

"Are you in trouble? Are you hiding from someone? I can help."

She shook her head, backing toward the curb. "Forget me, Ulric."

"Like hell. I've believed I was alone for centuries. I—"

"I understand," she interrupted. "I truly do. But it's too dangerous."

The sound of squealing tires momentarily distracted Ulric as a shiny silver Jaguar entered the circle drive. The car slowed as a side door was shoved open. Ulric instinctively braced himself, preparing for an attack. Instead, Brigette was leaping forward, disappearing into the car before it was squealing away.

"No," Ulric snarled in disbelief.

He stepped off the curb, his gaze locked on the back of the vehicle.

"Sir." A uniformed doorman abruptly appeared in front of him. "Do you need me to call security?"

Ulric turned his head, knowing that his eyes would be smoldering with the golden power of his wolf. "I'll take care of the situation."

Indifferent to the curious stares of the bored taxi drivers, Ulric ran after the Jag. Yeah, he got the irony of a werewolf chasing cars, but right now he didn't give a damn. Nothing mattered but keeping Brigette in sight.

They headed south for several blocks, Ulric falling farther and farther behind. When the car suddenly zoomed through a red light, there was a loud, angry blast of a horn and Ulric leaped toward a nearby corner as a whoosh of air washed over him. *Shit.* He'd almost been flattened by a bus.

Unnerved by the near miss, he watched as the taillights of the Jag disappeared around a corner. He was never going to catch the car. Did he risk changing into his wolf form? It was still dark enough to hide him from most prying eyes, but there was always the danger of...

Ulric stiffened, a prickle of awareness intruding into his fierce concentration.

He was being followed.

With a low curse, he pivoted on his heel and circled back to the hotel. He would track down Brigette after he'd dealt with his unwelcome shadow.

Avoiding the front lobby, Ulric headed toward the entrance just beyond the large dumpsters. It was an area he tried to avoid. His sensitive nose and rotting trash didn't mix. Halting in front of the heavy door that led to the storage room next to the kitchen, he abruptly spun on his heel to confront the female he'd sensed stalking him.

Rainn.

The rare zephyr sprite had appeared out of the desert twenty years ago and quickly earned Chiron's trust. Now she was second only to Ulric among the Dreamscape employees.

He scowled down at her.

Standing next to him, she appeared shockingly fragile with her slender curves and delicate features. Her hair was cut in a straight line at her shoulders and was as dark and glossy as polished ebony. Her wide eyes were pale, like a spring mist. Her skin was soft and dewy and her lips a lush, bow-shaped invitation.

Tonight, she had exchanged her usual business attire for a pair of black jeans and a black sweater that clung to her with growl-worthy results.

All in all, a tiny bundle of temptation with an inner core of pure steel.

A dangerous combination.

His scowl deepened. "Why the hell are you following me?"

Chapter 2

Rainn stood her ground despite the fact that Ulric's power was vibrating around her with a tangible warning. The Were might be a beast at heart, but he had full control over his animal. He wouldn't strike until he was sure she was a danger.

Which meant that the quicker she proved she was no threat, the less likely he would rip her open with his massive claws.

"I saw you take off from the hotel and I thought something must be wrong," she hurriedly assured him.

He narrowed his smoldering gaze. Did he sense she was lying?

"I don't need a babysitter."

Her lips twitched. Truer words had never been spoken.

"Let's go inside." She nodded toward the nearby door. "I want to talk to you."

"I'm busy now."

She watched as his gaze moved over her shoulder. He was already becoming distracted.

"With the red-haired Were?" she bluntly demanded.

He jerked. *Ah. That caught his attention.*

"This is none of your business," he snapped.

"It is if you're planning to do something stupid."

He made a choked sound, looking genuinely offended. "When have I ever done anything stupid?"

She held up her hand, ticking off his stupidity on her fingers. "The day you forced one of our customers to strip off his clothes and leave the casino naked."

"He wasn't a customer," Ulric protested. "He was the manager of a rival hotel who was handing out coupons to his all-you-can-eat buffet."

She touched her second finger. "And what about the night you decided to climb to the top of the High Roller and howl loud enough to attract the police?"

"It was a full moon. It always makes me a little…"

"Stupid?" she suggested in sweet tones.

"Giddy," he corrected, shaking his head as she touched another finger. "Enough."

"Hmm." She lowered her hand. "Tell me about the female."

"No."

Rainn ignored his sharp refusal. "She's a Were. Do you know her?"

He hesitated, clearly torn between wanting to toss her in the nearby dumpster so he could return to chasing his female, and his craving to share what was prompting his strange behavior.

"She's my cousin," he abruptly revealed.

Rainn's breath hissed between her teeth. *Great. Just great.* Her difficult task had just become damned near impossible.

"I thought your family were all killed by the Anasso who banished Chiron?"

"So did I." A vulnerable joy softened his features. "It's a miracle."

Rainn swiftly considered her various options. It didn't take long.

She had one.

"Or a trap," she warned in blunt tones.

Ulric sent her an angry glare. "A trap? What are you talking about?"

"I've had my eye on the female for hours."

"Why?"

Rainn headed toward the nearby door. "Follow me."

"I don't have time."

"It won't take long," she assured him, pulling open the door and stepping inside. She could only hope his curiosity would overcome his urgency to return to his hunt. "You need to see this."

"Fine," he muttered, following her through the maze of narrow corridors that at last led to the security office.

They entered the office that many people would no doubt find surprisingly small. They had over two thousand cameras spread throughout the casino, and fifty monitors lining the walls, but there were only three staff members keeping watch. Chiron preferred to have his guards on the casino floor, either mingling among the humans undercover as fellow guests or standing at the doors in full uniform.

"Out," Rainn commanded as she headed toward the hub of computers that powered the cameras.

The three guards were all curs, which meant they'd been bitten by a Were and weren't purebloods like Ulric. Still, they were all over six foot with the muscles of a steroid-addicted wrestler. The fact that they didn't hesitate to follow her orders was as much a testament to Chiron's respect for her authority as her own powers.

It was a knowledge that always warmed her heart, even as she tried to keep in mind that her reason for being in Vegas had nothing to do with earning a place in Chiron's clan. Even if that clan did include the gorgeous, outrageously sexy Ulric.

On cue, the male moved close enough to surround her in his luscious heat. Rainn swallowed, doing her best to ignore the scent of his primitive musk.

"What do you want to show me?" Ulric demanded.

Rainn squashed her shiver of awareness, concentrating on reversing the security video to the spot where the redheaded Were had made her appearance. Then she pointed toward a nearby monitor.

"This is your female entering the casino just after midnight," she said.

He leaned over her shoulder, his breath brushing her cheek. "Brigette."

Rainn hastily moved to the side. She couldn't think when he was touching her. "What?"

"Her name is Brigette," he explained, his gaze glued to the monitor.

Brigette. Rainn tested the name in her head. She didn't like it. It sounded…narcissistic.

"Okay," was all she said.

Ulric watched the female on the video as she sashayed through the front doors and made a slow circuit of the gaming rooms.

"She was alone," Ulric said, speaking more to himself than Rainn.

"Yes."

"Did she meet anyone here?"

"No, which was what captured my attention," Rainn told him.

He turned his head to study her with a suspicious expression. Could he sense she was lying?

"Not every beautiful woman comes to Dreamscape to meet a man." His gaze flicked down her body before returning to her face. "As you should know."

Rainn's breath caught in her throat. Was he calling her beautiful?

She clenched her hands. She had to focus on convincing Ulric that the female was dangerous.

"Guests come here to gamble, to drink, or meet with friends," she said. "Your supposed cousin spends over six hours wandering from one end of the casino to the other. She doesn't gamble. She doesn't drink. And she never talks to anyone."

"There's no *supposed* about it. She's without a doubt my cousin," he snapped, returning his attention to the monitor. "Maybe she was waiting for someone."

"She was," Rainn agreed. "You."

The air heated as Ulric struggled to maintain his temper. "Explain."

"Watch." Rainn reached out to fast-forward the video to the point where Brigette's bored expression was suddenly replaced by one of anticipation. "She has been wandering aimlessly until you enter the room. Then she suddenly stops, before she's crossing the floor to make sure that she's in your line of sight."

Ulric shrugged. "That's the most direct route to the door."

Rainn leashed her surge of annoyance. Ulric believed the female was a long-lost relative. Of course he didn't want to accept she might be luring him into a trap.

"Keep watching." Rainn pointed at the monitor. "She pauses, glancing over her shoulder in an obvious effort to attract your attention, then she lures you out of the casino."

Ulric snorted. "Lured me out so she could disappear?"

Rainn arched her brows. "Are you going to claim you don't intend to try and track her down?"

Ulric's features tightened. "That falls under the none-of-your-business category."

He couldn't be further from the truth. It was very much her business. It was, in fact, the purpose of her life.

"Did she tell you why she was here?" she pressed.

"She didn't have the chance. We only spoke for a couple of seconds." He paused, his jaw clenching. "I do know she was scared."

"Of what?"

"That's what I intend to find out."

"I knew it." Rainn gave a resigned shake of her head at the sight of his stubborn expression. "Stupid."

* * * *

Ulric pivoted on his heel, suddenly angry. He didn't know if it was because Rainn had called him stupid. Or because he knew she was right.

And in the end, it didn't matter.

He'd already made up his mind what he was going to do. Stupid or not.

Maybe it *was* suspicious that Brigette had been wandering around the casino. And that she'd left the minute he'd arrived. But there were probably a dozen explanations. She could have been waiting for someone who was late. Or she could have come into the casino to avoid someone searching for her. Or...

He released a frustrated growl.

There was one way to discover the truth.

Ask Brigette.

But first he had to find her.

"I need you to take over my duties for a few days," he told Rainn as he headed for the door. "I'm not even going to barter over your outrageous demands." The zephyr sprite had a habit of draining Dreamscape's coffers dry when she was asked to take on extra duties.

He didn't think it was the money. Or not entirely. She had to have a fortune tucked away. It was the game of bartering that she loved.

She followed him out of the security office. "Where are you going?"

"Family business." Ulric paused. Damn, it felt good to say that. *Family.* He allowed himself a second to savor the thought, then gave a small shake of his head. He was wasting time. "Tell Chiron I'll call him later."

Not waiting for Rainn to continue her argument, Ulric headed toward the stairs at the end of the hallway. Chiron had offered him the penthouse apartment, but Ulric preferred to be close to the casino. Opening the heavy fire door, he jogged up two flights of stairs and used the keypad to enter his corner suite.

The living room was designed with a sleek simplicity in shades of gray and black. Ulric hated clutter. In his life. In his mind. In his space. These rooms represented his love for precise order.

Or perhaps a fanatical urge to control everything around him.

Whatever.

Closing the door, Ulric crossed the pale gray carpet. He desperately wanted to hop in the shower. He didn't need his heightened sense of smell to know he was pungent after his sweaty run through the desert. At the moment, however, he had more important matters demanding his attention.

He took a seat at his desk, which was situated next to the glass wall that offered a view of the pool complex. It was a stunning sight, with the glittering blue water that was surrounded by lush vegetation and small fountains. The idea had been to create the sense of a garden of paradise for the humans. Ulric was surprised to discover he was equally enchanted.

This morning, however, he barely noticed the rosy bloom of the sunrise as it spread over the pools. Instead he opened his laptop and hacked into the account of a local car rental service that specialized in luxury cars. He'd recognized the small decal in the back window of the Jag as it'd zoomed away. A few seconds later he had typed in the license number he'd memorized and was able to determine the exact location of the vehicle. He smiled. Thank the goddess for GPS.

Then his smile abruptly faded. The car was parked just a few blocks away. Right in front of...

The Viper's Nest.

His shock wasn't a result of the fact that Brigette had chosen an establishment that catered to demons. If she was visiting Vegas, it was the most logical place for her to stay. No, it was at the specific choice of a club owned by a vampire. Most demon businesses were run by the fey, particularly imps who were capable of glamours, illusions, and spells designed to compel potential customers to return to their establishments over and over.

But the Viper's Nest was owned by Viper, the vampire clan chief of Chicago. And unlike the other establishments, it preferred sophisticated entertainment to primitive pleasures. Ulric had heard that it cost a small fortune just to walk through the front door, and that the current manager, a vampire named Javad, personally decided whether or not a guest could stay. Like a fancy country club, only with more fangs and less golf.

He'd always assumed that the glitzy place was filled with vampires. The cold-blooded bastards considered themselves the top of the food chain and rarely bothered to hide their disdain for rubbing elbows with the riffraff.

So why would Brigette choose that location?

Unless...Could Brigette be mated to a vampire?

The thought made Ulric's stomach clench with horror. It didn't matter that he was devoted to his master—who was a vampire. He didn't want his only surviving family member to be in the clutches of a bloodsucker.

Did that make him a hypocrite?

He shrugged. Probably.

He shoved himself to his feet and left his rooms, locking the door behind him.

Once in the hallway he paused. There was an itchy sensation between his shoulder blades, as if hidden eyes were following him. Was he being watched?

He glanced left and then right. Nothing.

Dismissing the strange feeling, Ulric hurried toward the staircase and bounded down the steps in one leap. A few minutes later he was out the back door and crossing the parking lot. He probably should have let the day manager know that he was leaving, but he had his phone with him if an emergency came up, plus Rainn was available.

A growl rumbled in his throat before he was fiercely shoving away the thought of the zephyr sprite. He'd already decided he wasn't going to be distracted by the female. Or her warnings.

Even if it meant he was waltzing into a trap...

He gave another growl, sending a parking attendant fleeing for the nearest door. He was a cunning predator who could kill most creatures with his bare teeth. Or one swipe of his claws. If this was a trap, he was going to make the demon responsible very, very sorry.

Of course, while he might be confident in his skills, he wasn't stupid. He wasn't going to blindly blunder into an ambush.

With that thought in mind, he jogged a dozen blocks to the north, doubling back several times to ensure he wasn't being followed, before circling back to his destination.

Once he had the club in sight, he paused in the shadows of a nearby house, carefully surveying his surroundings.

The area was nothing like the glittering Strip. Or even the aging glory of Fremont Street. This neighborhood was residential with a straight line of homes that had been built in the fifties. Once upon a time the lawns had been ruthlessly watered to keep them green and the picket fences had been painted white. Now an air of depression hung over the houses that had gone over the line of gracefully-fading to crumbling-into-oblivion.

On the south side of the block was a large empty lot where several houses had been burned to the ground. All that remained were charred foundations, rusting cars, and bags of rotting trash. Or at least that's what the casual observer would see. Ulric already knew that it was an illusion.

And next to the curb was the Jag that had squealed away from his hotel.

He peered around, looking for any hidden dangers. *Nothing.* Reassured that he was alone, he strolled forward, touching his fingers against the layer of magic that reflected a faint shimmer in the early morning sunlight.

Instantly the illusion of an abandoned lot disappeared, to be replaced by a five-story brick building with tinted windows. Ulric climbed the stairs and pushed open one of the heavy double doors.

Once in the front lobby, Ulric rolled his eyes. Yep, it was just as posh as he'd expected. Lots of marble, with a dozen fluted columns soaring toward a ceiling painted with dragons emblazoned on a star-studded sky.

There were a few leather sofas scattered through the long room, and in the center of the floor was a fountain with a golden statue of a male holding a massive sword over his head.

Ulric swallowed a sudden urge to laugh. Was that supposed to be Styx, the new Anasso? He'd met the King of Vampires during the search for Tarak—Chiron's former master. And while he couldn't claim to be BFFs with the male, he was quite certain that Styx would be thoroughly pissed at the sight of himself immortalized in gold and standing in a pool of water for the tourists.

Viper had a wicked sense of humor. Or a death wish.

He'd started to take another step forward when there was a blur of movement and a vampire was suddenly standing directly in front of him.

The female stood barely tall enough to reach his shoulders, with a delicate build. Her face was heart shaped and dominated by a pair of large brown eyes, while her blond hair had been cut short. She looked more like a pixie than a vampire, but Ulric didn't miss the power that vibrated around her.

His gaze briefly flicked over her slender body, which was covered in a little black dress that didn't leave much to the imagination. Not that he was interested. His only concern was in the silver dagger she held in her hand.

It was a weapon perfectly designed to kill a vampire. Or a Were.

Flashing a smile that emphasized her fangs, the female held out her hand. "Your invitation."

He scowled down at her. "Invitation?"

"This is a members-only club."

He curled his lips in disdain. The stench of leeches was thick in the air, making his wolf shudder in horror.

"Thankfully I have no desire to be a member," he told her.

"Then why are you here?"

"I'm looking for one of your guests."

The vampire narrowed her eyes. "We take the privacy of our guests very seriously."

"Understandable," Ulric agreed. He would be suspicious if someone strolled in off the street wanting information on a guest at Dreamscape. "I just need to get a message to her."

The female wasn't impressed. "Then call her."

"I don't have her number."

A sneer twisted the vampire's lips. "Trust me, if a woman wants to speak with you, she'll find a way to contact you. There's no need to hunt her down like a…" She deliberately paused. "Dog."

Ulric allowed a growl to rumble in his chest. He was trying to be polite. But he was going to find Brigette. Even if it meant tearing this damned place to the ground.

Starting with the vampire in front of him.

"If you won't take a message to her, then find someone who will."

The female stepped toward him, not nearly as intimidated as she should have been. "No."

"I'm not leaving until I speak with her."

The vampire flashed her fangs. "That's not your choice."

Ulric leaned down until they were nose to nose. He had his own fangs. And they were bigger.

"Run along, leech, and fetch your owner," he commanded. "I don't have time to waste arguing with you."

She hissed, her body tensing as she prepared to strike. But even as Ulric braced for battle, the temperature in the lobby dropped from cool to downright frigid.

"I'll deal with this, Candace." The voice was low and smooth as silk.

Ulric cautiously turned his head, his wolf rumbling inside him. The animal could sense danger even before the male walked through a nearby door.

He was as tall as Ulric, although his muscles were more chiseled than bulky. His dark hair was curly as it fell to brush his shoulders and his features were hawkish, with a bold nose and heavy brow. His skin was tinted with copper, no doubt from long years spent in the desert sun before he'd been turned into a vampire. His eyes were as black as the pits of hell and smoldered with the sort of power that could topple cities.

He strolled forward, and Ulric lowered his gaze to take in the male's bare feet before skimming over the casual black slacks and silk tunic that fell to his knees. It wasn't until the vampire turned his head that Ulric could see the intricate tattoo on the side of the male's neck.

Assassin.

This had to be Javad. The manager of the Viper's Nest.

"I can handle a hound," Candace protested.

The male kept his gaze on Ulric as he halted next to the female vampire.

"I don't doubt your ability, but this isn't just another Were," he said. "He belongs to Chiron."

Candace sniffed. "So?"

"The Anasso has spread the word that the Rebels are being welcomed back into the fold," the male explained, his expression mocking. "We're supposed to play nice."

Ulric folded his arms over his chest. "Chiron doesn't need your king."

Candace lifted her dagger, lunging forward. "Let me—"

"Go down to the gaming rooms," Javad interrupted. "I'm sure there's someone there who needs to be stabbed."

His voice remained soft, but it halted Candace in her tracks.

She sent him a sulky glance. "Promises, promises."

"Go."

Ignoring Ulric, the female vampire left the lobby, the icy scent of her anger trailing behind her.

Ulric sent Javad a wry glance. "She's feisty."

"Next time I won't stop her," the vampire warned in smooth tones. "Now tell me why you're barging into my club and creating an unpleasant scene."

Ulric leashed his wolf, which snarled at being given orders by a leech. Yeah, yeah. The irony of having a vampire as a master and all that...

"I'm searching for a female," Ulric forced himself to admit.

Javad lifted a dark brow. "I'm afraid this club doesn't offer those services, but there are plenty of places that do. I can give you the addresses if you want."

Ulric's fangs lengthened. Only the fact that he needed information from this aggravating vampire kept him from lunging at the male's throat.

Trying to keep you from doing something stupid. Rainn's words floated through the back of his mind and Ulric grimaced. Maybe he did need a babysitter.

"I'm looking for a specific female," he clarified in stiff tones.

"What makes you assume she's here?"

"The car she was riding in is parked in the street out front."

"Impossible," Javad said without hesitation.

Ulric frowned. Did the vampire assume he was lying? "Why impossible?"

"My guests are warned that they're to use our valet service. No exception." A cold smile curved Javad's lips. "Not unless they want to be locked in a room with Candace."

Ulric silently conceded that was a powerful incentive to follow the rules. He suspected Candace was a vampire who enjoyed causing pain. But Javad's confidence in his enforcer didn't change the fact that the Jag was sitting out front.

"Maybe this guest didn't get the memo." Ulric shrugged. "Or more likely, she wasn't afraid of your pet."

Javad paused, as if puzzled by Ulric's refusal to back down. Ulric hid a smile. How many creatures were suicidal enough to challenge the powerful vampire in his own establishment?

Ulric was going to guess: *one*. Him.

"Who is the female?" the vampire at last demanded. "Did she cheat the casino? Walk out without paying her bill?"

"My interest is personal."

"How personal?"

Ulric made a sound of impatience. "That's not your concern."

Javad simply stared at him, his expression inscrutable.

Ulric heaved a rough sigh of frustration. *Vampires.* They were as stubborn as freaking mules. He resigned himself to revealing exactly why he was at the Viper's Nest.

"What do you know of my history?" he asked.

Javad appeared surprised by the question. "Nothing more than the fact you've been Chiron's most trusted guard for centuries."

"Ever since he rescued me from the slave pens of your Anasso," Ulric said.

"Former Anasso." Javad was swift to correct Ulric, his black eyes shimmering with something that might have been disdain. "A dark time."

"Darker than you can ever imagine," Ulric rasped. "Your king destroyed my entire clan." His heart squeezed with a strange combination of joy and fear. As if he understood that Brigette might disappear as swiftly as she'd appeared. "Or at least that's what I believed for over five hundred years."

"And now?"

"This morning I discovered the daughter of my father's brother strolling through the casino."

"She survived the Anasso?"

"No," he firmly denied. "She wasn't in the slave pens. I assumed she'd been slaughtered with the rest of the pack during the attack."

"Did she tell you what happened?"

"When I approached her, she fled."

Javad's eyes narrowed, his expression revealing the same suspicion that Rainn had tried to ram down his throat. "You're certain it was your cousin?"

"Yes, I'm certain," Ulric snapped.

Javad ignored the heat that bristled around Ulric. "Why would she run from you?"

"That's what I'm here to find out."

Javad considered this explanation before giving a small shrug. "And she was driving the car that you claim is outside my club?" he asked.

"She wasn't driving, but it's the car she was in when she left the casino," Ulric assured him.

"Who was with her?"

"I couldn't see."

"Hmm."

The male's suspicion only deepened, and Ulric's limited patience reached its snapping point.

"Are you going to let me speak with her or not?"

"I can't." Javad lifted a hand as Ulric pulled back his lips to bare his lengthening teeth. "Easy, dog. I can't let you speak with your female because she isn't a guest at the club."

Ulric's anger abruptly faltered. It'd never occurred to him that the car would randomly be parked in front of a demon club.

"You're sure?"

Javad smoothed the cuffs of his embroidered tunic, a hint of arrogance etched on his hawkish features. "Our customers are carefully selected. If we had a female Were, I would know."

Ulric didn't argue. Hadn't Candace challenged him the second he'd walked through the doors? They clearly took the whole by-invitation-only thing seriously.

"Then why would the car be here?" Ulric spoke more to himself than the vampire. "Maybe the driver is a guest."

Javad considered Ulric's words before he slowly smiled. "I might have a way to assist you."

Ulric didn't need the warning that whispered through the back of his mind to know the male was plotting something. You didn't run a successful chain of casinos without being able to read people. Even if they were vampires.

"How can you help?" he forced himself to ask.

"I'll explain once we've negotiated a price," the male drawled.

"Price?"

Javad lifted his hands, gesturing around the large lobby. "I'm a businessman. Nothing comes free."

Ah. Extortion. He should have been expecting it.

"Are you related to Rainn?" Ulric demanded in dry tones.

"The zephyr sprite?" Javad asked.

Ulric jerked in surprise. This vampire was dangerously well-informed about Chiron and his various employees.

Something he needed to pass on to Chiron.

He squared his shoulders. He might not like being coerced, but Javad held the winning hand. If he was going to speak with Brigette, he had to pay the price. "What do you want?"

"A favor."

Ulric gave a sharp shake of his head. "That's too vague."

Javad considered. "Fine. It won't include anything that's harmful to your master, or against your morals."

"That's still vague," Ulric complained.

Javad studied him with his cold, black gaze. "It's as good as it's going to get."

His inner wolf snarled at the sensation of being cornered, but Ulric gave a slow nod. It wasn't unusual for demons to trade in favors rather than cash. When you lived for an eternity it was easy to accumulate money.

"But I get one refusal," Ulric insisted.

"Done."

Shoving aside the thought of being in this male's debt, he focused on Brigette. "How can you help?"

"Come with me."

Javad moved across the floor to press his hand against the marble wall. A second later a hidden door slid open. Ulric followed the vampire into the long room that was clearly the security office.

He glanced around, not surprised to find that it was even less high-tech than Dreamscape. Dealing with demons rarely entailed cameras or mundane alarms. It took magic and illusions and the occasional curse. Most of all, it took lethal guards who were willing to smash heads when necessary.

Heading toward the desk at the back, Javad waved the vampire guard out of his seat and tapped his fingers on a computer. One of the monitors mounted to the wall flickered, and the image of the outside street came into view.

Without warning, the air in the cramped space dropped to a temperature that would make Antarctica feel balmy, while pinpricks of ice dug into his flesh.

"Why didn't someone warn me about the car?" Javad demanded, his soft voice more terrifying than any amount of screaming.

The guard was a massive male with thick, ropy muscles, but he looked like he was hoping the ground would open up and swallow him. "The owner didn't come into the club," he babbled. "We didn't want to attract attention by moving it."

Javad's nostrils flared. "Like a car that cost more than any house in the neighborhood doesn't attract attention?"

"I'll—"

"Leave the room until I'm done," Javad cut in, watching the guard scurry out the door. Once they were alone, Javad gave a click of his tongue. "Good help is so hard to find."

The icy darts continued to press against him, but Ulric refused to rub the pain from his arms. There was no way in hell he was going to reveal that the vampire was hurting him.

Ah, the male ego was a gloriously absurd thing.

"Preaching to the choir," he muttered.

Javad unclenched his fists, the ice in the air fading. Once again in control of his temper, he let his gaze return to the monitor.

"I did a sweep of the area less than half an hour ago," he told Ulric. "So the car couldn't have been there for long."

Ulric nodded. "It was in front of Dreamscape half an hour ago."

Javad reached to touch the keyboard in front of the computer. The image on the monitor skimmed backward until the moment the Jag appeared in the street.

"There," Ulric said.

Javad reached to touch another key and the video moved forward. In silence they watched as Brigette climbed out of the car, strolling around the back of the vehicle.

Ulric leaned forward, absorbing the sight of his cousin. A ridiculous flare of relief washed through him. He hadn't imagined the female. She was real. And she was, without a doubt, his cousin.

He watched as she paused on the broken sidewalk. She appeared tense. Was it fear? Impatience? Annoyance?

Impossible to determine.

His attention was distracted as the driver's door was pushed open and a figure climbed out of the car. He hissed in frustration as he realized the creature was covered from head to toe in a heavy robe.

The thick material made it difficult to determine more than the fact that the form appeared to be shorter than Brigette. Meaningless. A large number of demons tended to be smaller than Weres. Fey, goblins, brownies…and of course, humans.

Brigette leaned toward the robed figure, as if listening to what the creature was saying. Then, even as Ulric waited for the two to head toward the Viper's Nest, the robed figure lifted an arm and a portal suddenly appeared in the middle of the street.

A few seconds later the two had disappeared.

"Shit," Ulric muttered, charging toward the door.

"Where are you going?" Javad demanded.

"I want to check the car," Ulric said, heading out of the office. "They might have left something inside."

Leaving the club, Ulric slowed as he approached the Jag. He hadn't forgotten Rainn's accusations. He was going to make damned sure he didn't rush into an unseen danger.

Sniffing the air, he tried to determine the species of the robed figure. It had to be fey to create a portal, but he couldn't catch more than a dull, oddly burnt scent. Was the creature capable of altering his odor?

He shrugged, stepping close enough to the car to peer through the window. At first, he couldn't see anything. The sleek interior was empty. But as he pulled open the passenger door, he caught a glimpse of a shimmering bead stuck to the floorboard. Reaching out, he searched under the seat. Nothing. He pushed his hand next to the console.

He felt a brush of something soft against his fingertips. Grabbing the satin material, he pulled it out to discover a black, beaded shawl.

He lifted it to his nose, easily catching Brigette's scent. But there was something more beneath the female musk. A heather perfume laced with the hint of salt.

Home.

Ulric straightened, pulling out his phone to scroll through his contacts. When he found the one he wanted, he typed a quick text.

Henrick, get the jet ready.

Chapter 3

Rainn covertly made her way to the private airfield that was hidden in the depths of the desert. Chiron wasn't the sort of vampire to endure the red tape that bogged down human airports, plus he'd had modifications made to his jet that would never be allowed by the FAA. The most obvious change was the fact that the main cabin was sun-proofed. There were no windows, the door could be sealed and locked from inside, and there was a hidden trap door in the floor that led to a compartment that was magically protected in case of a crash during the daylight.

The alterations hadn't diminished the comfort of the cabin. The plush seats were wide and sturdy enough to sit a grown troll in comfort. There was also a wide-screen TV, a bar, and a fridge stocked with blood. At the very back was an opening to the private bedroom and attached bathroom, complete with a shower.

Now Rainn stood next to the bar, wrapped in her magic. She wasn't precisely invisible, but she could bend the air around herself to reflect the surroundings. It had not only allowed her to leave Vegas unnoticed, but she'd managed to slip past the imps who served as the flight crew.

Her breath caught as she felt a small tingle of...not precisely fear. More unease. She didn't need windows to sense that Ulric was climbing the steps to enter the jet. The male was a force of nature. As soon as he entered a room, he filled it with the raw power of his wolf.

It'd been almost overwhelming when Rainn had first started working at Dreamscape Resorts. Her people were creatures of mist and magic. When they were required to move through the world, they did so with the delicacy of a butterfly. It wasn't until it became necessary to strike against evil that they recalled their warrior nature.

At least, that's how they were now.

She'd heard stories that in the past they'd rampaged through the world with the callous brutality of an enraged orc. Fearless.

That thought allowed Rainn to stiffen her spine as Ulric entered the cabin and she felt the jet start to roll down the runway and then pick up speed before there was a blast from the engines and they were surging into the air.

This was her destiny.

Another tingle inched down her spine. More unease, she told herself, even as her gaze clung to the sight of the pureblooded Were.

He was a spectacular specimen as he strolled forward with the powerful grace of a predator. His sleek muscles were emphasized by the black T-shirt that was stretched over his massive chest and the jeans that clung to his long legs. In the muted light of the cabin his eyes smoldered with a pure golden fire, revealing the wolf that prowled just beneath the surface.

The sensations that were prickling down her spine suddenly had less to do with unease and a lot more to do with lust. She swallowed a sigh. Ulric was a gorgeous, obscenely sexy male. It would be weird if she didn't feel a bit lusty. At least that's what she told herself each time the damned Were strolled past her.

Consumed by her ridiculous thoughts, Rainn allowed herself to be momentarily distracted. A terrible mistake. Without warning, Ulric lunged forward. She gasped, unable to avoid the fingers that wrapped around her throat as she was thrust against the paneled wall. Her magic faltered, and Ulric's eyes widened with confusion. Obviously he'd sensed he wasn't alone in the jet, but he hadn't realized who was there.

With a snarl he snatched his hand away, almost as if he'd been scalded.

"What the hell are you doing here?" he rasped.

Could she bluff? She gave a mental shrug. It was worth a shot. "I told you, I'm worried you're going to do something stupid."

"Try again."

His rough tone rasped against her temper, but she knew she appeared completely calm. Her people could manage a Zen expression no matter what was happening. Even when being confronted by a furious Were.

With a tilt of her chin she allowed herself to inch closer to the truth.

"Okay. I think you're going to do something stupid." She held up a silencing hand as he released a low growl. "Plus, I sense this is a trap."

He stilled, suddenly wary. "Sense what is a trap?"

"The female you're chasing."

His breath hissed between his clenched teeth. "When I left the casino, I was chasing the female through Vegas. How did you know I would need the jet?"

She shrugged. "What does it matter?"

"You were spying on me."

She flattened her lips. "I was watching your back."

"Spying."

"Don't put words in my mouth."

He glared at her, his eyes glowing with the power of his inner wolf. "Start answering my questions before I throw your very fine ass off this plane."

The heat of his body surrounded her. It was as much a warning as the large fangs she could see as he pulled back his lips.

Rainn swallowed a sigh. Why couldn't her destiny have included a dew fairy? Or even a human she could mentally manipulate? No, she had to have an aggravating, stubborn, savagely fascinating Were.

"Very well," she grudgingly admitted. "I followed you."

"Why?"

"I told you the truth. I'm trying to protect you."

He scowled. "I've gone into dangerous situations before without needing you to hold my hand. Why now?"

The jet veered sharply, nearly sending Rainn to her knees. "Can we sit down?"

Ulric slammed his hands on his hips, hovering over her as if he was about to pounce. Was he trying to intimidate her? Maybe. Or more likely, he didn't even realize what he was doing.

"Are you going to answer my questions?" he demanded.

She rolled her eyes. "Do I have a choice?"

"No."

"Then let's make ourselves comfortable." She moved to perch on one of the cushioned seats. "It's a long story."

Ulric turned to grab a bottle of whiskey off the bar. "I think I'm going to need this," he muttered, not bothering with a glass as he plopped in a chair across from her and took a deep drink. At last he waved a hand in her direction. "Tell me."

Rainn tapped the tips of her fingers against the arm of her chair. She didn't have a rule book for performing her duty. But there were certain traditions. And keeping secret her purpose for being in Vegas was one of them.

But she knew Ulric well enough to realize that he would make her task impossible unless she could convince him to trust her. Especially now that he believed his family had miraculously been returned from the dead.

"What do you know of my people?"

He frowned at her abrupt question. "You're rare. Reclusive." He gave a lift of one shoulder. "I've never encountered a zephyr sprite before you walked into the casino twenty years ago."

A wistful smile touched Rainn's lips. She missed her family. Every single day.

"Most of us remain our entire lives in our hidden lairs in the desert," she admitted, not adding they often burrowed deep underground. Many never, ever ventured out of their tunnels. "Unlike other demons, we aren't predators. We thrive in an atmosphere of peace and quiet."

Ulric arched a brow. "So you chose to come to Vegas to work for a vampire?"

She held his gaze. "It wasn't my decision."

Her answer clearly caught him off guard. "Someone sent you?"

She licked her lips, a genuine fear whispering through her. "The Oracles," she breathed.

"The Oracles?"

Ulric made a choked sound of shock. No wonder. The ultimate rulers of the demon world might remain shrouded in mystery, but no one doubted their immense power. In fact, most wise creatures avoided even speaking their name at all.

Like Beetlejuice.

"Once every century or so, a zephyr child is born with a mark." She lifted her arm, tugging up the sleeve of her sweater. Then, leaning forward, she revealed the black mark on her inner wrist that was shaped like a small triangle with wavy lines in the center. "Like this."

Ulric studied the symbol. "What is it?"

"At some point in our distant history, our king made a deal with the Oracles to help keep the zephyrs hidden from the world." She didn't reveal why they'd been forced into hiding. There were some secrets too awful to share. "But like all bargains that are made among demons, the Oracles demanded a price for their protection."

Ulric glanced up. "You?"

"Yes."

A swift, unexpected anger tightened his features. "You're a slave?"

"No. It's not like that." Was he remembering his own brutal existence in the slave pits of the Anasso? Probably. She lightly touched his hand.

"When we're sent to the Oracles it's with the understanding that we will be given a task that has to be completed."

"What sort of task?"

"To battle against evil." She flinched as she said the words. They always sounded so...corny.

She half expected Ulric to laugh. Instead he glared at her in disbelief. "Chiron isn't evil."

"Of course he isn't," she agreed, deliberately pausing. "But he's not the reason I was sent to Vegas."

Ulric looked confused. "Then who—" With a low roar, he jumped to his feet. "Me?"

She hid her smile at his outrage. She hated the shadows that darkened his eyes when he was recalling his brutal past. Now they were filled with a golden fire.

"Sit down," she said, heaving a sigh as he continued to glare at her. "Please."

He hesitated, obviously in no mood to concede to her request. But, perhaps recalling she could be almost as stubborn as he was, Ulric took another deep drink of whiskey before reluctantly settling back in his seat.

"Answer the question," he snapped. "Am I the reason you were sent to Vegas?"

"Not exactly."

"What the hell does that mean?"

The cabin was smothering hot as Ulric's temper continued to seethe, but Rainn didn't bother to use her powers to cool the air. As a zephyr sprite she had the ability to manipulate the elements. For now, her only interest was in easing his suspicions.

"Obviously, you've never had to deal with the Oracles," she muttered.

"I haven't had the pleasure."

Pleasure. She grimaced, eyeing the half-empty bottle of whiskey. Just the memory of the Oracles made her want to drink.

"Not so much a pleasure as a lesson in terror," she informed him.

A portion of his anger faded. "Did they hurt you?"

She shivered. Despite knowing since birth that she carried the Oracles' mark, she'd still been petrified when she'd been yanked out of sleep to discover a strange creature standing in the middle of her bedroom. At first she'd assumed it was a young human girl. The stranger was short and slender with delicate features. But then she'd caught sight of the strange oblong eyes that were a solid black and shimmered with an ancient power. Oh, and the sharp, pointed teeth.

This was no human.

Rainn had parted her lips to scream when the creature had lifted a gnarled hand and the world had gone dark.

"No, I wasn't hurt, but I was snatched from my bed and taken to a barren stone cell. I waited in the darkness for weeks before they at last called me to a huge cavern where the Oracles were seated behind a long table." Rainn shivered, not ashamed to reveal how frightened she'd been. "The power contained in that room…" Another shiver. "It nearly crushed me."

Ulric appeared properly horrified. "You met with all of them?"

"It wasn't really a meeting." Rainn had a vivid memory of being led by a shrouded form out of her cell and through a twisting maze of tunnels. The silence had been oppressive, grinding down on her like a physical weight. "I was brought and commanded to kneel. That's when I felt them touch my mind."

"They speak telepathically?"

Rainn considered her answer, relieved when the jet reached a smooth cruising speed. She wasn't a big fan of heights.

"It's hard to explain, but they implanted a vision," she at last said.

Ulric studied her for a minute. Was he trying to decide whether to ask the question hovering on his lips?

Knowledge was not always bliss.

Curiosity, however, was a curse that was more powerful than common sense.

"A vision of what?" he demanded, the words seemingly wrenched from his lips.

"Of you."

His jaw tightened, as if she'd just confirmed his worst fear.

"Me?"

"I could see you in Vegas," she admitted. "You were walking through the doors of Dreamscape Resorts."

He took another drink, nearly emptying the bottle. Not that he was drunk. A Were's metabolism was in constant hyperdrive. He could drink Nevada dry without getting more than a mild buzz.

"That's it?"

She slowly shook her head. "I could see a shadow behind you."

The bottle dropped from his hand, his eyes narrowing. "Someone was following me?"

"It was more a warning," she struggled to explain. "That's why I came to Vegas. To stop the shadow."

"By spying on me?"

Her breath hissed between her teeth. "I haven't been spying on you. I've been waiting for the evil to reveal itself."

"And?"

The air prickled with an unspoken warning. Did he have a premonition of what she was about to tell him?

"I sensed something when I caught sight of your female," she forced herself to tell him.

"*Something?* That's a little vague, isn't it?"

The heat went from smothering to suffocating. A trickle of sweat inched down the curve of Rainn's back.

"Look, the Oracles didn't give me a manual," she snapped. Did he think she enjoyed having her head stuffed with images she didn't understand and a weird spidey sense of evil? Or perhaps he thought it was a real chuckle to be expected to fight that evil with nothing more than her powers. Powers that weren't exactly created for battle. "They didn't even speak to me. They branded your image in my brain and sent me away with the warning that the entire world was depending on me. I'm doing the best that I can."

He blinked, as if caught off guard by her sharp reprimand. Not that he was willing to concede defeat. Even as his anger faded, his features hardened into a stubborn expression.

"Brigette isn't evil."

Rainn had to bite her tongue. His naïve refusal to admit the female Were might be anything but his long-lost cousin who just happened to stroll into his casino was wearing on her nerves.

"Perhaps not," she conceded, "but it surrounds her."

"Which is all the more reason I need to find her."

"Just don't…" Her words trailed away. Ulric was male. Extremely male. Which meant telling him not to do something would only ensure that he would do it.

"What?" he demanded.

She hedged. "Be blinded by your need for a family."

"I'm not blinded." He lowered his gaze, as if trying to hide the vulnerable need that darkened his eyes. "I just want to know what happened."

"Fine," she said, knowing she'd pushed him far enough. "I'll be along to watch your back."

His jaw tightened, but he didn't argue. Nothing less than a miracle.

"Chiron won't be happy when he discovers that we're both gone," he groused.

"I left a voice mail on his phone that we were taking his jet," she said. "I'm sure he'd rather have me here to protect you."

He made an exasperated sound. "I don't need protection."

She shrugged, not wasting her breath by arguing. "Plus, Chiron has a mate to help him run the resort now," she continued, as if he hadn't spoken.

"Yeah." Unexpectedly, Ulric's hands clenched. "I suppose he does."

She studied him in confusion. "Does it bother you that…"

Her question went unasked as there was a sudden sound of a door opening. Moving as one, Ulric and Rainn surged to their feet, both of them turning toward the front of the cabin.

There was no one there. In fact, the cabin door was sealed tightly shut.

Then, the scent of granite filled the air and a tiny gargoyle climbed out of the hidden compartment built beneath the floor.

"Levet," she breathed in surprise, watching as the demon spread his wings, which were nothing like the leathery wings of most gargoyles. Instead they were a dazzling shimmer of gold and red and blue. Of course, there were a lot of things different about Levet. Including the fact that he was barely three feet tall and possessed the strangest belief that he was a Knight in Shining Armor.

Over the past weeks she'd become accustomed to seeing him waddling around Chiron's private offices. And, if she was honest, she'd secretly enjoyed watching how easily the tiny demon could piss off both Chiron and Ulric.

"Why is this heap of metal moving?" Levet complained, his gaze moving toward Ulric, who was regarding the creature with a horrified expression. "Oh. It is you." Levet reached up to rub one of his stunted horns, his expression petulant. "You interrupted my nap."

Ulric sliced his hand through the air. "Who else is hiding on this damned plane? Elvis?"

Levet sucked in a sharp breath, his wings fluttering. "He's alive? I knew it!"

"Arg."

Ulric pivoted on his heel and stormed to the back of the jet. Disappearing into the private bedroom, he slammed shut the connecting door. Rainn heaved a sigh.

This evil-fighting gig wasn't nearly as fun as it looked in the movies.

Chapter 4

Ulric barely waited for the plane to touch down before he was storming through the cabin to jerk open the door.

After Levet's unwelcome appearance, he hadn't been in the mood to listen to the creature's endless chatter. Instead he'd headed into the back room and stretched out on the bed. He'd been exhausted after his long run through the desert and the emotional turmoil of his morning. The last thing he wanted was seven hours trapped with a yapping gargoyle he wanted to choke. Plus, he suspected he was going to need to be at full strength to deal with whatever was waiting for him.

He was a male who liked to be in control. Of everything. But in the past twelve hours he'd had his fundamental belief in his past revealed as a lie. First had been the shocking revelation that Brigette was alive. And then he'd discovered that he was the featured star in an Oracle vision that warned of an impending evil.

He wasn't sure which was bothering him the most.

A scowl marred his brow as his heart gave a sharp lurch. If he was being honest, he'd admit that it was Rainn's betrayal that hurt the most.

Not surprisingly, he'd desired Rainn since her arrival in Vegas. She was gorgeous, clever, and exotically mysterious. Lust-worthy on an epic scale. But it'd taken a very long time for him to learn to trust her. Now that his faith had been shattered, he felt as if something important had just died deep inside him.

Melodramatic...but there it was.

The jet rattled over the runway of the small airfield on the coast of northern Wales. This remote area wasn't built for such a large plane, but Ulric had ordered the pilot to land as close to his old lair as possible.

They at last came to a lurching halt and Ulric impatiently waited for the outer door to open. Behind him he could sense Rainn move to stand a few feet away.

After what felt like an eternity, the outer door released, and the steps began to automatically lower. Ulric didn't wait for them to reach the ground. With one powerful leap he was landing on the rocky soil next to the runway. A second later he felt a breeze as Rainn used her power to touch gently down beside him. He glanced over his shoulder, pointing a finger at the gargoyle who was about to follow them. "You. Stay here."

"But—"

"This isn't a debate," Ulric snapped.

The gargoyle pouted. "Hash brown, you are not the boss of me."

Ulric snapped his brows together. "Hash brown?"

"I think he means hashtag," Rainn said in her soft, annoyingly calm voice.

Ulric threw his hands in the air. "How have you survived so long?"

"My winning personality." Levet pulled his lips into what Ulric assumed was a smile. "It's a gift."

"More like a curse." Ulric sent the creature a warning glare. "Stay here."

Levet's wings drooped. "Mangy hound."

Ulric stepped toward the jet. "You—"

"Shouldn't we be searching for your female?" Rainn hastily prevented a childish squabble.

Ulric cursed beneath his breath before turning to jog away from the plane.

"You might want to grab my clothes if you don't want me prancing around naked. And try to keep up," he warned Rainn as he kicked off his boots, then shed his garments before he released a burst of magic to shift into his animal form.

He could not only move faster as a wolf, but he wasn't bothered by silly things like regret or duplicity or even anticipation. There was nothing but the spongy ground beneath his feet, the salty wind that was blowing from the ocean, and the distant smell of home.

Angling toward the cliffs that dropped dramatically to the rocky shoreline below, he tried to ignore the female who easily kept pace beside him. Something that was next to impossible considering her soft, misty scent that teased at his senses.

Dangerously distracted, Ulric barely noticed the fog that was rolling in around them. Or the strange way the ground had gone from soggy to crumbly. As if it was disintegrating beneath the weight of his body.

It was the silence that at last had him slowing his pace. His homeland had always been isolated. That was one of the reasons his father chose this particular spot. But it hadn't been desolate.

Unnerved by the howling emptiness, Ulric changed back to his human form.

"Shit," he breathed, revulsion crawling over his skin as his gaze skimmed the tumble of stones that used to be sturdy buildings.

Rainn moved to stand next to him, handing him his clothing. "Where are we?"

"My home." Ulric quickly dressed, anxious to have something covering his bare skin. It wasn't modesty. He was a werewolf. Being naked was more natural than being clothed. But he didn't want the nasty air brushing against him. "Or what used to be my home."

Glancing over the pockmarked ground that was a sickly gray color, she looked like she wanted to back away from the decaying village.

"I assume it didn't look like this when you were here?"

"No." His gut twisted. He wanted to throw up, but he refused to allow himself to mourn the destruction of his childhood. Not now. "Damned humans. They ruin everything," he rasped.

Rainn sent him a startled glance. "The destruction wasn't caused by humans."

"How do you know?" Ulric demanded, not hiding his suspicion.

Granted, he'd expected the place to be in disrepair, but it looked like it'd been coated in nuclear waste. What else could cause a corruption that'd spread deep into the earth?

"The wind speaks of evil," she whispered.

"The wind?"

"Open your senses," she commanded.

Ulric growled in frustration. He was a wolf. His senses were always in hyperdrive. Then, a breeze rippled past him, brushing over his skin like a spider web. "Magic."

She grimaced. "Evil."

"Yes," he agreed, sniffing the air. It was oddly stagnated. As if it'd been trapped in the fog for centuries. "I can't determine a species."

"Neither can I." With a visible effort, Rainn forced herself to move forward, her expression distracted, as if she was using her powers to search the area. "Which should be impossible."

He followed, instinctively needing to protect her from the thick pulse of danger in the air. Immediately he was angry at himself.

"And people claim that I'm arrogant," he muttered.

"You are," she assured him, brushing her fingers through the fog. She released her breath on a low hiss, recoiling from the thick mist. "But mine isn't arrogance. You can conceal footprints or use magic to mute your scent, but you can't disguise your movement through the air around you."

Was she joking? Ulric stared at her in genuine amazement. "You can tell everyone who has been here?"

She shook her head. "Not if they were just passing through. But I can tell if they had a lair here. Or if they used magic," she explained.

Ulric tried not to look impressed. He was supposed to be sulking, not admiring her skills.

He gestured toward the fog. "Can you sense anything?"

"It's not precisely fey." She paused, then released a grunt of frustration. "The only thing I know for sure is that it's old. Really, really old."

Ulric nodded, not pressing her for information she couldn't give him. At some point he intended to discover who or what was destroying the land his father had loved, but for now he was more interested in finding Brigette.

Unfortunately, the fog was muting his senses.

With a rare caution, Ulric inched his way over the brittle ground. It crunched like honeycomb beneath each step and he had a horrifying fear it might suddenly collapse. He didn't want to know what was lurking underneath the bleak wasteland.

At last reaching the center of the decimated village, he squatted down to brush the dirt away from a stone foundation.

"Ulric?" Rainn crouched down beside him.

Ulric breathed in deeply, welcoming her soft, misty scent as it wrapped around him. It somehow managed to combat the creepy smog that shrouded the area.

"This was our cottage," he told her, his voice thick with an ancient pain.

"Your parents?" She touched the foundation, her eyes closing as she concentrated on the stone beneath her fingertips. "Yes," she at last breathed. "Along with your sisters." She paused before she released a low moan. "Oh."

He studied her delicate profile, unable to squash his flare of concern. "What's wrong?"

"I can feel the pain. The sadness. It's imprinted in the stone." She slowly opened her eyes, sending him a puzzled glance. "Why are you so faint?"

"I don't understand."

"Your essence isn't as strong as the others," she clarified.

Ulric flinched. Her words had touched a nerve he'd tried to forget over the past five hundred years. After all, it was bad enough to have his pack slaughtered while he was hauled off to the slave pits of the Anasso. But to accept that he had wasted precious time with his family because of his stupid pride…well, that hurt more than everything else combined.

"I spent several years in London," he said, his voice rough.

She arched her brows. "A werewolf in London?"

A wry smile curved his lips at her deliberate attempt to lighten his mood.

"Something like that. My father…" His smile faded as the words caught in his throat.

"Go on," she urged.

He glanced around, his regret combined with a near unbearable sadness.

"My father chose this location for his clan because it was isolated. Peaceful." He shook his head. "He was a scholar, not a warrior."

"While you were a warrior, not a scholar?"

"Exactly. I became restless," he said, remembering the nights he'd run over the distant dells to release his pent-up energy. He was a young male who wanted a thrilling adventure. He dreamed of bloody battles and claiming his place as leader of his own pack. Or perhaps fighting the vampires who were spreading across Europe. Now, he felt an aching sense of loss for the beautiful homeland that was forever destroyed. "I didn't appreciate what my father had created."

He felt something brush his shoulder. Her fingers? Or a breeze she created with her magic? Either way, it was a comforting gesture that allowed him to gather his composure.

"None of us do," she assured him. "Not until we actually leave home."

Ulric studied her delicate features, wondering if she missed her family since coming to Vegas. Then, he quickly slammed shut a mental door on his curiosity.

He was still in sulking mode.

Instead, he allowed his thoughts to drift back to his flight from the village after a particularly heated argument with his father.

"I intended to travel back to the Continent to find one of the packs who were vying for dominance. I arrogantly assumed they would welcome me as a soldier, and eventually as their leader," he admitted. "Instead I stayed in London."

"A female?"

Was there an edge in her voice? Jealousy? No, that was silly.

He shook his head. "Regret. By the time I reached the city I'd realized that I didn't want to leave my home or my clan."

His confession seemed to catch her off guard. "So why didn't you go home?"

A good question. It'd taken only a few months in London to make him realize the place was a cesspit. The humans happily dumped their filth in every gutter, allowing it to contaminate their surroundings. And worse, the thick coal smoke coated him in black dust each time he stepped out of his cramped rooms in the back of a bakery.

"My pride demanded that I spend at least a few decades fending for myself," he said with a shrug. "Probably not a bad thing. I learned how to live among the humans. And how to fight without the protection of my pack. Things that helped me to survive."

"Was there a specific reason you did finally return to this place?"

"My mother tracked me down." A genuine smile curved his lips. He'd been drinking in a local pub, looking for a fight, when his mother had strolled through the door. She shoved aside the human males who'd tried to grab her as she'd marched toward Ulric and pinched his ear to pull him out of the pub and down the street. He'd nearly cried with relief. He was going home. "She was worried about my father."

"Was he ill?"

"No, but he'd become obsessed with some scrolls he'd discovered hidden in a burrow," he said. "She was concerned he was focusing too much on his studies and not enough on his pack."

"What kind of scrolls?"

Ulric shrugged. "I'm not sure. By the time I arrived he'd sealed the burrow and was back to his old self. Less than a year later we were attacked by the vampires."

Turning her head, she glanced around the annihilated village. "Did they do this?"

Ulric's hands clenched. He'd barely realized they were under attack before a large troll had smashed in his head with an iron mace.

"I was knocked unconscious and hauled onto a goblin ship before the battle was over, but even if they had destroyed the village, they don't have magic that could have lingered for over five hundred years."

A female voice floated through the fog. "Welcome home, Ulric."

* * * *

Levet perched on the edge of the cliff, his brow furrowed as he listened to the waves crashing against the rocky beach below.

He'd waited in the jet all of five minutes before he'd decided to follow Ulric and Rainn. He had only a vague idea of what was happening. It had something to do with the dog chasing after a member of his family that he'd thought was dead. And Rainn's insistence that she be allowed to protect him.

It really didn't matter to Levet. He knew beyond a doubt that he would be needed to save the day. It was what he did.

Besides, it was a lovely night to be out walking. Or at least it had been until the fog had rolled in and he'd found it oddly difficult to follow Ulric's scent. Now he perched on the cliff and allowed his mood to sour with every passing second.

Why should he try to help Ulric? The jerky jerk-face had tossed him out of Chiron's casino. Then he snapped and snarled because Levet had chosen to take a nap in a stupid jet that no one was using. Where was he supposed to sleep? The street?

He wasn't an animal. Indeed, he possessed a well-developed desire for the finer things in life. Expensive champagne. Silk sheets. Fast cars.

Ulric should have apologized to him. It was his nap that had been interrupted. Not to mention the fact that he'd been hauled from the bright lights of Vegas to this remote, foggy location.

He was the victim.

But instead, the Were had been foaming at the mouth as if he was rabid. And maybe he was. There was an animal inside him, after all. Who knew if he had been vaccinated?

Levet heaved a sigh, his magnificent wings drooping.

It wasn't like him to be in such a…what was the word? Funk? *Oui*, that was it. A funk. And he couldn't lay the entire blame on the Were.

He had wings. If he disliked his surroundings he could fly anywhere he wanted to go. London. Or Rome. Or even Paris. He abruptly grimaced, a shudder racing through him. Not Paris. Levet had been kicked out of the Gargoyle Guild centuries ago, and his one trip back to the City of Lights hadn't gone as well as he'd hoped. He preferred to stay far, far away. At least for now.

Non. His true annoyance was that he knew exactly where he wanted to be, but his pride wouldn't allow him to acknowledge that he was missing the ogress who'd deceived and manipulated him.

Inga.

He clicked his tongue in annoyance. He wanted to block the female from his thoughts. What was that human saying? Out of sight, out of mind.

Unfortunately, it wasn't so simple with the ogress. She had something about her…

"Are you lost?" a voice asked from the swirling fog.

Levet considered the question. Was he lost?

"I do not think so," he finally decided, turning his head to watch the stranger emerge from the mist. "Who are you?"

"You can call me Zella."

Levet tilted his head to the side. The female appeared to be human, with a chubby face and eyes that seemed too big. Her skin was wrinkled, and her tarnished silver hair was pulled into a knot on top of her head. She had a round figure that was bent at the shoulders, as if she was carrying a heavy load.

She walked toward Levet, her gray gown brushing the ground and a smile on her face that was supposed to look kind. Levet, however, wasn't fooled. Her dark eyes were as hard as the agates he'd found in the pits of the netherworld.

"You are not human," he said.

"No."

"Fey?" Levet sniffed the air, trying to identify her scent. There was something moldy about it. Like the scent of a freshly opened crypt. He wrinkled his snout. "*Non*, not fey."

"I'm quite unique," Zella assured him. "At least in this world."

Ah, that Levet understood. He pushed himself to his feet and spread his delicate wings that shimmered despite the nasty fog. "As am I."

She didn't bother to admire his magnificent form. Instead she narrowed her hard eyes. "You traveled here with the werewolf?"

Levet sniffed. The female obviously had no ability to recognize perfection. Even when it was standing directly in front of her.

"Not by choice. I was low-jacked." He furrowed his brow. That wasn't right, was it? "Tall-jacked?"

The woman scowled before waving her gnarled hand in a dismissive gesture. "And he left you here all alone?"

"I do not care." Levet flapped his wings, pretending his feelings weren't hurt. "I had no wish to go with the ill-tempered beast anyway."

Zella studied him in silence. Was she deciding whether or not to eat him? Probably. He was quite tasty.

"Never fear, you can come to my home," she assured him.

Levet instinctively stepped back, nearly tripping over his own tail. "That is very kind, but...um...I have places to go, people to see."

The dark eyes sparked with terrifying flames. "I'm afraid I'm going to have to insist," she told him.

Levet glanced down in amazement as bands of fire wrapped around his body. "What are you doing?"

"I preferred for you to come along nicely," Zella told him. "You might prove to be useful, but if you fight me I will not hesitate to kill you."

Levet struggled against the bands. The fire didn't hurt. He was a gargoyle, after all. But they were forcing him toward the strange female.

"Where is Ulric?" he demanded.

Zella shrugged. "I'll deal with him once I'm sure all the loose ends have been tidied up."

So Ulric and Rainn hadn't been captured. He tried to take comfort in the knowledge.

"Let us not be hasty," he said. "I am certain we can come to an understanding."

"The understanding is that you come with me or die," she informed him. "Simple."

"What if I leave and forget all about you?" Levet suggested. "It is not as if I care what happens to Ulric. The oversized dog has a nasty temper and a habit of biting first and asking questions later."

The flames in her eyes flared, as if she could sense his lie.

That was…unfortunate.

"A shame," she rasped. "You would have been interesting to study."

"Oh, I am *très* interesting," he hastily assured her. "I am brave and strong and handsome, with a pair of stunning wings…" Levet's words trailed away as he was suddenly distracted by a chill behind him. What was it? A vampire? Impossible to know for sure. The fog had become so thick it felt more like solid stone than mist. He gave a shake of his head, returning his attention to Zella. "Plus I am the savior of the world." He continued his list of his awesome virtues. "More than once."

Zella muttered a word that Levet didn't understand, although he had a feeling it had something to do with stupid gargoyles.

"You have wasted enough of my time."

The bands of fire tightened, but even as he was being hauled toward the female, a hand reached through the fog to grab him by one stunted horn.

He tucked his tail and squeezed his eyes shut as he was yanked through a barrier of magic that nearly ripped the tough hide off his body.

"Arg."

Chapter 5

Ulric muttered a curse as he glanced over his shoulder. While he'd been distracted by his painful memories, the fog had thickened to the point it'd muffled the sound and scent of any approaching intruder.

How the hell could he be so sloppy? He'd not only put his own life at risk, he'd endangered Rainn.

The thought had barely formed when Rainn was stepping in front of him, her hand pointed toward Brigette as the female appeared out of the fog.

A sharp wind ripped through the air, sending dust flying and Brigette stumbling backward. So much for Rainn needing his protection. He reached out to lightly touch her shoulder.

"Rainn, that's enough," he murmured.

She sent him a warning glare. "Look at the fog."

He glanced toward the thick wall of mist behind Brigette. "What about it?"

"It's not moving," she said, her attention locked on Brigette, who was struggling to regain her balance. "It's a spell."

The female Were peeled back her lips to reveal her extended fangs, but she managed to keep herself from shifting. "She's right, but the magic isn't connected to me," she said, speaking directly to Ulric.

"Rainn." Ulric tightened his grip on the zephyr's shoulder, then turned her to face him. "I want to speak with Brigette."

"I'm not stopping you."

He swallowed a sigh. He knew she was going to be pissed when told her what he wanted. What he didn't know was why he gave a damn. "In private."

"No."

"It's not your decision."

She narrowed her eyes to stubborn slits. "It's my duty."

"Just…" He shook his head in resignation. "Stay here. I promise I'll remain in sight."

She didn't appear particularly pleased by his grudging concession. "I don't like this."

"I have to know."

The nasty dirt swirled around his feet as Rainn struggled to control her temper. Her expression, however, remained as calm as ever.

"Fine."

Walking forward, Ulric focused on Brigette. Or at least he tried. There was a part of his brain that was relishing Rainn's protective attitude.

He told himself that the strain of the past hours had rattled his brain. He was a big, bad wolf. He didn't need protection. But nothing could dislodge the ball of warmth in the center of his chest. Just as nothing could diminish the sensations that were niggling through him, stealing his powers when he needed them the most.

With every passing second, Rainn was becoming more and more his obsession.

He clenched his hands, halting in front of the female he'd thought was dead. She'd changed her clothes from the slinky black dress to a thick robe that blended into the fog, and her fiery hair was dulled by the murky atmosphere. Her familiar scent, however, remained the same.

"Why did you run from me?"

She stepped toward him, laying her fingers on his arm. "I didn't want to put you in danger."

"What danger?"

She turned her head, her gaze skimming over the fog. "I can't tell you."

Annoyance slashed through him. He was trying to be empathetic, he really was. After all, he had no idea what Brigette had endured over the past centuries. Still, he'd traveled halfway around the world to find her. He wasn't in the mood for puzzles.

"Are you being held against your will?"

She leaned against him, as if it was hard for her to stand. "Please, Ulric, don't ask."

He heard Rainn make a sound behind him, but he kept his gaze on Brigette. One female at a time.

"Okay." He studied her pale face. She appeared terrified, but oddly her scent was more…determined than frightened. "Can you at least tell me how you survived?"

Her eyes filled with tears. "I'm ashamed to tell you."

"Brigette," he urged in a soft voice.

"That night…" She stopped to clear her throat. "The night we were attacked, I'd been in trouble with my father. I can't even remember why he was angry, but he'd forbidden me from leaving the lair. Of course, I was too rebellious to accept my punishment."

Ulric had a sudden memory of Brigette storming through the village, screaming at the top of her lungs when she didn't get her way.

"I recall you were always…" He searched for the proper word.

She finished for him. "I was a brat."

"So what happened?"

"I shifted and ran as far as I could," she said. "I just wanted to challenge my father's authority. It wasn't until I realized I was getting close to a vampire's lair that I turned back. That was when…"

"Please tell me."

She shivered. "I could see the flames from miles away. I thought perhaps the storage house had caught fire. My father was always complaining that it was dangerous to keep the hides we cured in the same building as the firewood. It wasn't until I was near the village that I could see the horde of demons slaughtering our people."

She abruptly buried her face in his shoulder, quietly sobbing. Behind him Ulric heard Rainn snort in disgust.

Ulric lifted his hand to awkwardly pat the back of Brigette's head. He didn't deal well with crying females.

"You must have been terrified," he soothed.

"I was a coward," she said in a choked voice. "I'll never forgive myself."

"Why not?"

"Instead of rushing forward to help my family, I turned my back and searched for a place to hide."

"So?"

She lifted her head to regard him with a fierce regret. "I should have fought. I should have died with my family."

The same awful regret echoed inside Ulric, but he refused to let it show on his face. "What good would that have done?"

She blinked away her tears. "That's what pack does."

"It takes more courage to go on living," he said in harsh tones. "Trust me, I know better than anyone."

She released a shaky breath, seemingly pleased to be distracted from her terrible memories. "How did you survive?"

"I was knocked unconscious during the battle." He couldn't keep the self-disgust out of his voice. "When I woke, I was locked in a cage on a goblin ship."

"They kept you alive?" An odd expression rippled over her face. Almost as if he'd answered some unspoken question.

He shrugged. "Goblins might enjoy a good bloodbath, but unlike trolls and orcs they never forget their love for making a profit. They took me and a dozen other of our pack to the Anasso to feed his sick hungers." He wasn't embarrassed by his sharp shudder. No creature could spend time trapped in the dark, freezing-cold caverns with their food laced by poisonous amounts of opium and not have lingering nightmares. "I was lucky to be rescued by my master before I could become the Anasso's next victim."

"Did anyone else escape?"

"No." He glanced away. He didn't know why he'd been the last of the werewolves left in the slave pens, but Chiron had furiously demanded that he not blame himself. It was fate. Of course, that was easier said than done. "What about here? Who else survived?"

"It's just me," she said, crushing his vague hope that there might be more.

He continued to allow his gaze to search the annihilated village. "Why do you stay?"

She paused before leaning forward to whisper in his ear. "I have no choice."

"You're trapped?"

Her lips brushed his ear. "The only place I could think to hide was in your father's burrow."

He leaned back to send her a puzzled glance. "I thought he sealed it to protect the scrolls he'd discovered."

"I was…" She licked her lips. "Anxious enough to force my way past his barricades."

Ulric remained puzzled. His father had told him that he'd contacted a local witch to place a lethal curse on the entrance to the burrow. The older male hadn't revealed why he was so determined to keep his people away from the scrolls inside, but Ulric assumed he had a powerful reason.

He shook his head. What did it matter now? "A good thing, since it obviously allowed you to survive."

She grimaced. "Yes, but I wasn't safe."

"Tell me."

She squeezed his arm, as if offering a silent warning. "It's easier to show you."

"Where?"

"The burrow." She tugged on his arm. "Come with me."

* * * *

Rainn scowled at the tall, redheaded vixen who leaned against Ulric as if she was a fragile dew fairy instead of a powerful predator. And worse, she spoke in a trembling voice that was obviously earning Ulric's sympathy. She rolled her eyes.

How could Ulric be so susceptible? Okay, the female was his long-lost relative. And he was vulnerable from the drama of returning to his village, which had been brutally savaged. But she'd risked her sole purpose for existing by warning him that she felt an evil shadow around Brigette. Clearly she should have locked the stupid Were in a cage.

She heaved a harsh sigh.

It was an appealing thought. In fact, she'd had dreams of having Ulric locked in handcuffs and at her mercy, his body hard with desire...

Unfortunately, her magic couldn't overpower a full-grown Were. At least not long enough to shove him in a cage. And there was the knowledge that while Chiron treated her as a valuable member of his staff, he wouldn't be happy if he discovered she'd restrained his personal guard. In fact, she was fairly certain Chiron would destroy anyone stupid enough to force Ulric to do something he didn't want to do.

Chiron might be a vampire and Ulric a Were, but the two were as close as brothers. Besides, there was a reason Ulric had been in her vision. He had some role to play in her quest.

What that role might be was still a mystery.

Her eyes narrowed, and the air thickened around her as she watched Brigette grab Ulric's arm and tug him toward the nearby fog.

No. Hell no.

Tiny whirlwinds danced around her feet as she stormed forward. Enough was enough.

"Stop," she commanded, the sharp word echoing eerily through the thick air.

Ulric halted, glancing over his shoulder. At the same time, Brigette swiveled to send her a furious glare. If looks could kill, Rainn would've died on the spot.

"Tell your servant to stay here," the female commanded.

Servant? The whirlwinds were spraying tiny rocks and shattered bits of wood through the air. Hmm. Should she send them toward Brigette? A few bruises wouldn't truly hurt the bitch, and it might teach her a few manners.

"I'm no one's servant."

"This is Rainn," Ulric said, sending her a warning frown.

Brigette sniffed the air, curling her nose as if she'd caught a nasty scent. "Fey." She leaned against Ulric. "Why is she here?"

"She's my..." Ulric hesitated, as if not sure what to call Rainn. "My friend."

"There's no need for you to come with us," Brigette said, waving her hand toward Rainn.

Rainn moved to stand beside Ulric, bringing the whirlwinds with her. Brigette hissed as the shards of stone smacked into her legs. *Big baby.* "Ulric doesn't go anywhere without me."

"This is pack business," Brigette snapped. "Outsiders aren't welcome."

"If I don't go, no one goes," Rainn announced.

Brigette glanced toward Ulric. "Is she your friend or your boss?"

Ulric snorted. "I'm beginning to wonder."

Rainn folded her arms over her chest, her gaze locked on the female Were. "You can leave if you want, but Ulric is staying with me."

Rainn could hear Brigette grinding her teeth as she glared at Ulric. "Can't you get rid of her?"

He shrugged. "I've discovered it's easier not to argue."

Brigette flattened her lips as she glanced toward the fog. There was a long, uncomfortable silence. Rainn frowned. What was going on? Was the female waiting for something? A sign? A visitor? Perhaps listening to a voice they couldn't hear?

At last the female blinked and flashed Rainn a tight smile. "If you insist."

"I do," Rainn said.

Brigette turned, leading them through the fog that circled the abandoned village. "Follow me."

Walking next to Ulric, Rainn tried to ignore the strange vapor that clung to her skin like a wet rag. It was giving her the heebie-jeebies. Instinctively she moved closer to Ulric, ignoring his raised brows. Yes, she'd been bossy, and yes, it'd felt good. Really good.

She didn't like Brigette. More importantly, she didn't trust her. That shadow was still swirling around her. Until Rainn knew exactly what it meant, she was going to assume the female was at the center of the evil she had to battle.

Plus, she was treating Ulric with a possessiveness that set Rainn's teeth on edge.

Why?

Because...Just because.

She was going to let it go at that. No good could come from shuffling through her renegade emotions. Best to pretend they didn't exist.

Brigette walked ahead of them, her powerful strides a silent warning to Rainn that she could turn on them at any second. At the same time, Rainn allowed her gaze to skim from side to side, searching for any movement in the murky fog.

They crossed the shattered landscape, the ground crumbling beneath their feet as if it was sawdust. Rainn might have suspected the devastation had been caused by dragon fire. There were few weapons more cataclysmic. She'd seen entire mountains melted beneath the intense heat. But this wasn't the same. The ground wasn't scorched, it was rotting. And the narrow rivers hadn't been boiled to dry beds. Instead the water was a brackish green as it moved sluggishly toward the nearby cliffs.

Toxic.

The word whispered through her mind.

Yes, that was it.

As if the very earth was being poisoned by some unseen force.

She shuddered. If she'd been by herself, she would have used her powers to float above the ground. Just walking over the decaying dirt made her feel like she was being contaminated. Grimly she resisted the temptation. She couldn't risk depleting her powers. And if she was perfectly honest with herself, she would admit that she didn't want to look weak.

Not in front of Brigette.

They continued through the strange fog until a large mound suddenly appeared before them.

It looked like the sort of burrow created by brownies. Or perhaps a loam sprite.

As they slowed, Rainn studied the dead vines that lay over the mound like a decomposing shroud. Once, it no doubt had been covered in green grass and lush flowers, but now it looked like a forgotten tomb.

Without glancing back, Brigette reached to touch the burrow. A hidden door slid open and Rainn wrinkled her nose. What was that smell? Brimstone?

Where the hell was this female taking them?

As if sensing her burst of fear, Ulric brushed his hand down the curve of her back. Instant tingles of pleasure sizzled through her. The heat of his fingertips felt as if it was branding her skin, even through the thick material of her sweater.

The sensation banished her temporary anxiety. As if the knowledge that he was at her side gave her courage.

Perfectly normal, she hurriedly reassured herself. What creature wouldn't feel better to know they had a lethal warrior to help in case there was trouble? It also explained why she pressed closer to Ulric as they followed Brigette through the opening and down the steep staircase dug into the dirt.

A smothering darkness closed around them the deeper they went, the gagging stench nearly overwhelming.

Rainn at last broke the oppressive silence. "It wasn't like this when your father came down here, was it?"

"I don't know," Ulric admitted. "He never let anyone come in."

Rainn struggled to see through the gloom. "I don't like this. It feels like a trap." The words had barely left her lips when Ulric came to an abrupt halt. She turned back to study his tense expression. "What's wrong?"

He tilted back his head, sniffing the air. "My father."

"What about him?"

His nostrils flared, his eyes smoldering with the power of his wolf. "I can smell him."

"He's here?"

"No. It's more…" He shook his head in frustration. "An echo. As if his blood seeped into the very stone."

Rainn wrapped her arms around her waist. The air was smothering, but she felt chilled to the bone. "I don't understand."

"Neither do I," he rasped.

Chapter 6

Levet squirmed and sputtered as he was jerked through the fog and then rudely dumped onto the hard ground.

"Hey, I am a mighty warrior, not a sack of potatoes to be tossed around," he groused.

"I just saved your ass," a dark male voice chided. "You should be thanking me, not complaining."

"You bruised my *derrière*, not saved it." Levet rose to his feet, rubbing his tender backside as he tilted his head to glare at the vampire who was regarding him with a disdainful expression.

The male had strong barbarian features with faintly slanted dark eyes and a proud nose. His hair was long and as dark as ebony. He was wearing jeans and a plain T-shirt that was plastered to his muscular chest.

Tarak. Chiron's master, who'd been imprisoned by the King of the Mer-folk for the past five hundred years. As far as Levet was concerned, the ill-tempered leech could spend another five hundred years locked away.

"Do you want to go back?" Tarak demanded. "I'm more than willing to get rid of you."

"*Non.*" Levet's tone was sulky. Vampires were so rude. "What was she?"

Tarak glanced toward the fog, his annoyance fading as he considered the question. "I don't know. I could smell you and the female because you were at the edge of the barrier, but the fog is distorting my senses."

"Magic." Levet offered a wise nod of his head, then he sniffed the air. "Something's burning."

"Chiron's jet."

Levet glanced beyond the vampire to see a distant plume of smoke rising toward the star-splattered sky. His wings drooped. That didn't look good.

"What about the crew?" he asked.

"Dead." Tarak's voice was cold, but Levet could feel the male's tension vibrating in the air. "When Chiron awoke to discover Ulric and the zephyr sprite—"

"Rainn," Levet interrupted.

Tarak frowned. "What?"

"The zephyr sprite has a name. It is Rainn," Levet insisted. As a demon who was constantly called "gargoyle" or "annoying pest" or "get out of here before I kill you," he understood how easy it was to dismiss a creature by refusing to call them by name.

It was a matter of respect.

"Fine," Tarak snapped, clearly annoyed at being interrupted. Really, vampires needed to take lessons in anger management. "After Chiron discovered Ulric and Rainn had taken his plane, he tried to contact his crew. When they didn't respond, he reached out to me."

Levet tilted his head. "Why you?"

"My private lair is just north of here."

"Oh." Levet snapped his fingers, belatedly realizing that the faint scent of salt wasn't coming from the ocean. Instead it was wafting from a small cluster of trees. "Waverly."

Levet took a step toward Tarak's mate. Like most mer-folk, she had pale hair that was highlighted with hints of blue. Her wide eyes were the color of aquamarines and her skin looked as if it'd been dusted with the luminescent shimmer of a pearl. At the moment, however, she'd traded in her long, gauzy gown for a pair of jeans and a thick sweater.

"Stop." Tarak moved to stand directly in Levet's path. "Tell me what happened."

Levet came to a sharp halt. Not because the vampire had told him to. He didn't take orders from leeches. But because he was worried about Rainn. She seemed nice. Plus, the strange fog was making him feel icky. Something should really be done to get rid of it.

He would need assistance, even if it meant working with a vampire.

"I am not entirely certain," he admitted. "I was minding my own honey—"

"Honey?" Tarak interrupted.

Levet furrowed his brow. Hmm. What was that ridiculous word?

"Beeswax," he at last corrected himself. "Right?"

Tarak rolled his eyes. "Just get on with it."

Levet clicked his tongue. It was the vampire who'd interrupted him. He continued his story. "I was taking a nap in the jet." Tarak's lips parted as if to demand why Levet would be sleeping in the plane, only to snap shut. He'd obviously learned his lesson. "When I realized that we were in the air, I came out to discover Ulric and Rainn, but they were barely speaking. All I really know is that Ulric was chasing some female he thought was dead. A pack mate."

Tarak looked puzzled. "Chiron told me they'd all died."

Levet lifted his hands. Rainn had given Levet an abbreviated account of what was happening after Ulric had stormed into the private bedroom on the jet. "Rainn said that a female Were, who Ulric claims is his long-lost cousin, strolled into the casino before she suddenly disappeared."

"A trap," Tarak said without hesitation.

"That is what Rainn thought," Levet said. "Ulric, however, was determined to track her down."

Tarak slowly turned to study the heavy fog that seethed and churned like a living force. "Odd," he murmured. "I'd forgotten there was a werewolf village here. What happened to it?"

Levet shuddered. "Abomination."

"Yes." Tarak glanced back at Levet. "Where are Ulric and Rainn now?"

Levet waved a hand toward the fog. "In there."

"How did you get through the barrier?"

Levet considered the question. He hadn't actually thought of the thick mist as a barrier. But Tarak was right. It was there to keep creatures out. Or perhaps, to keep someone in.

"I did not go through it. It surrounded me," he said. "Just as it must have surrounded Ulric and Rainn."

"Or it was parted because something in there was waiting for them," Tarak said. Before Levet could offer his opinion, the vampire was continuing. "I heard a female threatening you. Who was she?"

Levet blinked. Tarak needed to be more specific. He had a lot of people threatening him. Then he abruptly recalled his recent encounter with the old lady who'd tried to hold him captive with her burning bands of magic. "Oh." His tail twitched around his feet. "I have never encountered a creature like her, but I suspect she is old."

"Aren't we all?" Tarak asked in dry tones.

"*Non.* Really old," Levet insisted. Although he could count his years in the thousands, there were creatures who had been around from the dawn of time. "That is why we do not recognize her magic."

Tarak didn't argue. A miracle, considering that he was a vampire. Instead he nodded toward the fog. "The barrier wasn't here when I built my lair several centuries ago," he murmured. "So did the female travel here to create this place? And if so, why here? Why now?"

Levet tilted his head to the side, the taste of the fog still lingering in his mouth. "It did not feel as if the female was forming the magic," he said, finding it difficult to describe the vibrations of evil that pulsed around the strange woman. "It was more that she was a creation of the magic that was seeped into the ground."

Once again Tarak surprised Levet by accepting his explanation without a dozen tedious questions. No doubt because magic was something beyond the comprehension of vampires.

"If it's an ancient demon who has somehow been awakened, we need to find someone who can tell us how to battle it."

He sounded as if he was talking to himself. As if it didn't occur to him that Levet had the ability to contribute to the solution.

Typical bloodsucker.

"Cyn might be of assistance," Levet said in a voice loud enough to echo eerily through the darkness. "He has a library stuffed with old books and scrolls."

Tarak scowled at him. At least until the name seemed to penetrate his thick skull. "Cyn." He narrowed his eyes. "Why is that name familiar?"

"He is the clan chief of Ireland," Levet said.

"Ah. The Berserker."

"*Oui*. Although his new mate is attempting to tame him." Levet gave a sad shake of his head at the thought of Fallon, the royal fey princess who was mated to Cyn. "Poor fairy."

"This is not his territory, but he might have heard rumors of any ancient demons that lurk in the area."

"I can take you to his lair." Levet's smile was smug. The last time he'd been at Cyn's lair he'd been thrust into the role of hero. A familiar position. At least for him. "I was a guest there not long ago."

Tarak rolled his eyes. "Guest or prisoner?"

"Prisoner?" Levet snapped his wings in outrage. "I will have you know that I was responsible for battling the Dark Lord and saving the world."

Tarak appeared remarkably indifferent to Levet's astonishing feats. "How far is his lair?"

Levet sniffed. Philly steak. No wait. Philistine. The vampire clearly had no appreciation for Knights in Shining Armor.

"Waverly can take us there through a portal," he said.

As if she'd been eager for an opportunity to join the conversation, Waverly hurried forward. She ignored her mate's glare as she gazed down at Levet. "I need to know where we're going."

"Easily done," Levet assured her. "I can place the location in your mind."

"Telepathy?" she demanded.

"Of a sort." He stepped toward the mermaid, lifting his hand. "Will you allow me?"

Tarak reached out to slap Levet's hand away. "No."

"Tarak," Waverly chastised her mate. "It's fine. I trust him."

Tarak muttered a curse. His fangs were flashing, and his hands balled into tight fists. Still, he didn't protest as Waverly leaned down to speak directly to Levet.

"What do you need from me?"

Levet once again reached out. "Take my hand and…" His words trailed away as he felt himself lifted off the ground. "Hey, I am floating," he breathed in delight. Obviously, Tarak's powers included telekinesis.

Waverly wasn't so delighted. "Tarak," she snapped.

Tarak hissed in annoyance. "I don't like this."

"I'm a big girl who can take care of herself, remember?"

The vampire hunched his shoulders as he caught sight of the anger burning in the aquamarine eyes. "I'm trying."

Levet was abruptly dropped to the ground. He hit with enough force to rattle his teeth. He stuck out his tongue, sending a raspberry toward the stupid vampire before he grasped Waverly's hand. "Shall we?"

Waverly nodded, closing her eyes as Levet opened a small door inside her mind. That was the only way he could describe how his magic worked. Then, calling up his memory of Cyn's lair, he shared the image with the mermaid.

Waverly sucked in a sharp breath, an expression of wonderment on her face. "I've got it." She created a portal before she held out her hand toward Tarak. "Are you coming?"

The vampire stomped forward. "I should have left that stupid gargoyle in the fog."

Chapter 7

The darkness was absolute as they headed down the steps, the heaviness of the earth seeming to swallow them. Ulric's wolf pressed against his skin, anxious to be released. Grimly, he battled back his animal. Right now he needed to think clearly.

Or at least, as clearly as possible.

His nostrils flared, absorbing his father's familiar musk. How was it possible? Granted, the older Were had spent endless hours in the maze of tunnels while Ulric was in London. His mother had told him that his father was obsessed with a treasure trove of ancient scrolls that he'd discovered down here.

But after so many years, the scent should have faded to a mere whisper. Instead, it seemed to be seeped into the very stone around them. As if they were echoing their memory of the old wolf.

A shudder raced through Ulric.

It had to have something to do with the thick air, he told himself. Nothing could escape from the choking darkness.

Another shudder started to race through him, only to be halted as Rainn reached out to grasp his hand. Immediately, a delicious warmth chased away the chill. Ulric arched his brows. Talk about a magic touch.

He didn't know if his intense reaction was a result of her innate talent or just a response to the feel of her soft, welcome touch. And right now he didn't care.

He squeezed her fingers, shoving aside his distraction with his father. He needed to concentrate on where Brigette was leading them.

It wasn't that he didn't trust his cousin. But…

He swallowed a sigh. Since entering his childhood village, he couldn't deny a gnawing sense of horror. He'd expected the place to be trashed. Demons rarely left behind more than rubble after an attack. They killed, they plundered, and they torched the place to the ground. And with his pack dead or captured, there was no one to return and rebuild.

But there was more wrong with the village than being pillaged five hundred years ago.

Evil.

The word whispered through the back of his mind.

Just a couple hours ago he'd been eager to dismiss Rainn's claim that Brigette was connected to her mysterious quest for the Oracles. How could a member of his family be evil? It was unthinkable.

And yet, with every step deeper into the burrow, the knot in the pit of his stomach twisted a little tighter.

Instinctively he tugged Rainn closer as the tunnel opened into a small cavern with a ceiling low enough to touch the top of Ulric's head. The gloom was even thicker in here, but Ulric could see a heavy wooden trunk that was open to reveal a collection of fragile scrolls. He could smell the age in the papyrus, and something else. Blood. Ancient blood. A low growl rumbled in his throat. These had to be the scrolls that had fascinated his father.

His gaze moved toward Brigette, who had halted at the back of the cavern. It was only then that he noticed the skeleton that was propped in a shallow alcove that'd been chiseled into the wall.

Ulric wrinkled his nose even as he heard Rainn's breath rasp between her teeth. As immortals, it was always unnerving to consider death, but that wasn't the cause of his outrage. Demons' physical forms naturally disintegrated if they died. Vampires turned to ash, fey creatures turned to sparkles that danced through the air, and Weres would burst into flames until nothing remained. It was a necessary part of their transformation back to the primeval spirit that created them. Only human bones would remain standing in the alcove like some gruesome tourist attraction.

"What is this place?" he muttered.

"A temple." Brigette waved her hand in a grand gesture. "*My* temple."

He studied the female in confusion. "A temple to what?"

"Magic." Brigette shuddered, a mysterious smile playing around her lips. "Can't you feel it?"

Ulric paused, reluctantly reaching out with his senses. A mistake. He'd already been acutely aware of the strange stench that clogged his nose, and the heavy air that pressed against him like a death shroud. But now he could feel the unseen tentacles that crawled through the cavern, brushing against his skin and leaving behind a trail of...

"Evil," Rainn whispered.

Brigette's smile evaporated as she pointed a finger in Rainn's direction. "You stay out of this," she snapped.

Ulric stepped forward, hiding Rainn from Brigette's view. "This isn't Were magic," he said.

She sucked in a deep, slow breath. "It's a gift from the earth."

He shook his head. No gift from earth smelled like decades-old garbage that'd putrefied into a noxious stew.

"Whatever this is, it doesn't come from nature," he said in disgust.

Brigette held Ulric's gaze, her eyes smoldering with a strange glow. It wasn't her wolf. He could barely sense her animal. As if it'd been leashed so tightly it was being strangled.

"It's power," she rasped.

"Blood magic," Rainn murmured, so softly the female Were couldn't hear her.

Ulric frowned, his attention focusing on the bones that were propped in the alcove. The hair on the back of his neck bristled. "What did you do to the human?"

Brigette offered a dismissive shrug. "Nothing. The skeleton was here before I entered the burrow."

An unexpected fury blasted through Ulric. As if it'd been waiting for the opportunity to explode.

"My father would never have done this. He was a male dedicated to peace."

"Of course our alpha didn't kill the human. That would have taken a backbone." Brigette looked disdainful. "I found the bones behind a pile of rocks. I thought they must be connected to the power that I could feel pulsing around me, so I hid them to keep your father from removing them from the burrow. He was too cowardly to understand the greatness that was beckoning."

"You mean he wasn't willing to trade his soul for power."

"I mean he was weak," Brigette hissed, holding up her hand. "Don't glare at me, cousin. I heard your arguments with your father. You felt as stifled as I did in this backwater."

Ulric's anger remained, but now it was directed at himself. He would give everything he possessed to take back the ugly words he'd hurled at his father.

"I was an arrogant ass," he muttered.

"No, you were right," Brigette insisted. "We were secluded from the world. I could almost feel the moss growing on me." Her jaw tightened. "It was even worse after you left. There was no one who could understand I was being slowly smothered."

"Why didn't you leave?" he demanded.

She sniffed, her hand lifting to cover her face as if hiding her tears. "My father was a traditional male. He considered me his property, to be traded to the highest bidder."

Ulric's brows snapped together. His uncle could be a stern, demanding male. And he might have held the opinion that his sons held more value than his daughters. But he would never have sold a member of his family. Not for any reason.

"Bullshit."

Brigette dropped her hand, revealing dry eyes and a mocking smile. "That might be a little overdramatic, but he did threaten an arranged marriage."

Ulric wasn't amused by her act of the abused daughter, although he did believe her this time. For centuries the Weres had struggled to have children. They'd tried everything to create a new generation, even trading sons and daughters to neighboring packs in the hope that an injection of new blood would be the cure.

He'd heard the new king, Salvatore, had managed destroy the malevolent demon responsible for their lack of pups. He hadn't, however, tested the theory.

"You could still have left," he pointed out. "You weren't being held prisoner."

"I thought about it. Instead, I started sneaking down here."

Ulric grimaced as he glanced around the gloomy space. It might please a vampire. They liked anything dark and dank. But werewolves preferred wide-open spaces where they could breathe fresh air.

"Why?" he asked.

"I wanted to know what your father found so fascinating."

He glanced toward the trunk. "The scrolls?"

She gave a dismissive wave of his hand. "I searched through them, but they were all a bunch of mumbo jumbo. Some sort of ancient spells."

He turned, glancing toward Rainn. "Can you sense who created them?"

The zephyr's eyes were a stormy gray as she allowed her magic to swirl through the air. Instantly the nasty tentacles clinging to his skin seemed to dissipate. Ulric released the breath he didn't even know he was holding.

"There are dozens of different species," she at last said. "Fey. Druid. Were." Her brows lifted in surprise. "Even dragon."

Ulric understood her surprise. Demons could barely get along with their own species, let alone other creatures. There had to be an epic reason for them to have gathered so much magic together.

"Why are they here?" he asked Brigette.

The female Were hesitated, then her jaw tightened with anger. "It took a while, but I eventually discovered that they were bound to the human's blood," she grudgingly revealed.

Ulric frowned. "How?"

"Sacrifice." Rainn was the one who answered his question, glaring toward Brigette. "This place isn't a temple. It's a tomb."

He didn't bother to chastise Rainn for her sharp, accusing tone. There was something weird going on. And it was becoming increasingly obvious it had some connection to his cousin.

He took a step toward Brigette. "Why were you down here if you couldn't read the scrolls?"

"Because I could feel the power," she said. "It whispered to me. Even in my sleep."

"What power?" he pressed.

Brigette waved her hand in a vague gesture. "I didn't have a name for it. I only knew that it promised me the opportunity to break the shackles that were keeping me from my destiny."

Her destiny? Ulric narrowed his gaze. Had the female Were always been so melodramatic? The truth was, he hadn't paid attention to her when they were younger. He'd been too self-absorbed.

Just one of his numerous failings in the past.

Now he studied his cousin with an unwelcome sense of dread lying heavy on his shoulders. "What happened the night we were attacked?"

Brigette glanced away. A sure sign she was about to lie. "You know as well as I do."

Ulric shook his head, his mouth dry. "It was no accident you happened to be safely hidden in this burrow when the horde overran the village, was it?"

Brigette tried to look outraged by the question, then abruptly she released a shrill laugh.

"Perhaps you aren't as stupid as your father."

Ulric stiffened. "What's that supposed to mean?"

Brigette flashed a taunting smile. "He caught me down here more than once. Thankfully, he was too obsessed with researching his precious scrolls to do more than warn me to stay away." She snorted. "As if he was my boss."

How dare she insult his father? Ulric latched on to his anger. It was easier than accepting that his only remaining relative was a psycho bitch.

"He was your alpha," he growled.

Brigette leaned forward, her heat adding to the oppressive sense of smothering in the tight quarters.

"He was a coward who had no idea how to lead," she sneered. "And my father was an even greater coward for following him."

"You thought you could be a better alpha?"

"Of course," she said without hesitation.

Ulric made a sound of disgust. "Then why didn't you challenge him? That's the way of werewolves."

"Because I found a better way."

"There is no other way—" Ulric swallowed his protest as he caught sight of the fevered glitter in Brigette's eyes. Was it caused by the strange power she claimed she could feel? It had to be. "My father sealed this burrow because of you," he breathed.

Brigette didn't deny the accusation. "One day he snuck up on me talking to—"

"Who?" he demanded as she cut off her words.

"Myself," she muttered. "The idiot thought he could keep me out with a stupid curse, but it was too late."

Ulric glanced around. She was lying. She'd been talking to someone. But who? It was impossible to hide someone in this space. Unless…

Had whoever, or whatever, she'd been talking to already escaped from the burrow? He balled his hands into tight fists. The thought made him want to smash something into itty, bitty, tiny specks.

"What did you do?" he demanded. She turned her head, as if unwilling to meet his accusing glare.

"What was necessary," she muttered.

There was a stir of the thick air as Rainn stepped beside him. "She's responsible," she said, her gaze locked on Brigette.

His expression was puzzled. "Responsible for what?"

"She destroyed your pack."

Ulric slowly shook his head. He had to accept that there was something wrong with Brigette. Something he wasn't sure could be fixed. But that didn't mean he could blame her for everything.

"She never left the village," he protested. "How could she have brought a marauding horde to this isolated spot?"

Rainn clicked her tongue. As if he was being unbearably stupid. And maybe he was. He was still trying to wrap his brain around the fact that in less than forty-eight hours, he'd found a long-lost cousin, followed her to his destroyed village, and was now being forced to accept that this wasn't going to be the sweet, soul-healing reunion he'd been aching to enjoy.

His brain felt like it'd been stuffed with wool.

"You were gone from here for years," Rainn pointed out. "How do you know she didn't travel to find demons who would help her?"

His lips parted, but before he could argue that no self-respecting Were would ever align themselves with a bunch of nasty orcs and trolls and goblins, he was struck by a sudden thought.

"The shrouded form," he murmured.

Rainn glanced around. "Here?"

"No, in Vegas. Brigette was traveling with a companion who was wrapped in a heavy shroud. The two of them disappeared through a portal." Yet another blast of fury raced through him. *Gods.* He'd been so blind. "You were right. Her arrival was a trap," he said between clenched teeth. His gaze returned to Brigette. "Why such an elaborate ploy? Why not just talk to me at my casino? Or better yet, just call me?"

Brigette hesitated. Was she debating whether to try and pretend she was innocent? Then a smirk settled on her face. Clearly, she was delighted with her own cleverness.

"I needed you to follow me here," she told him. "If I had contacted you out of the blue and asked you to come, you might have been suspicious."

"Traitor." Ulric bared his fangs, but before he could lunge forward, Rainn was stepping in front of him.

"What purpose did you have in bringing Ulric here?" she demanded of the other female.

Brigette kept her gaze on Ulric, seemingly indifferent to his searing rage. Was she too stupid to realize he could rip her to shreds?

"Your father might have been a coward, but he was clever," the female mocked. "After I broke through the curse—"

"How?" he snapped.

Brigette frowned. "What?"

Ulric clenched his fists even tighter. Dammit. He couldn't allow his anger to cloud his mind. He needed to know what had happened to his pack. And Brigette was the only one who could tell him. "How did you break the curse?"

She scowled as if annoyed by the question. "I have powers."

Rainn snorted. "It must have been her partner," she taunted.

"Shut up." Brigette flushed, as if Rainn had struck a nerve. Then, sticking her chin at a defiant angle, she returned her attention to Ulric. "After the curse was gone, I assumed I would be capable of commanding

the magic that should be mine. It was only then that I realized your father
had layered a protective spell on the doorway."

"What doorway?"

"The doorway to the magic," she said, as if her words made perfect
sense. "He thought he'd outwitted me, but no one was going to stop me.
No matter what I had to do."

"You contacted the horde," he said, the words a statement, not a question.
Brigette shrugged. "I was more of a conduit."

Ulric released a slow, shaky breath. He couldn't deny the truth any
longer. This female had deliberately massacred her own family.

And for what? Power? Pride? His stomach heaved.

"Gods. Why not just kill the alpha?" he snarled. "Why destroy the
entire pack?"

"It's your father's fault. Everything is his fault. Including the death of
his precious pack." Brigette sulked as if she were a petulant adolescent,
not a full-grown Were.

Ulric's wolf surged against his skin, struggling to be released. It no
longer considered this female as his cousin. Or even pack. She was the
enemy that needed to be destroyed.

His human side was equally outraged. But he didn't allow himself to
lose sight of the fact that he still needed information. Something that would
be a lot more difficult to attain if Brigette was dead.

"You're batshit crazy," he muttered.

"It's true," Brigette hissed, tossing back her long, shimmering red hair.
"He must have realized I was becoming desperate and that I was plotting
to get him out of my way."

Ulric felt a pang of guilt. Why hadn't his father told him what was
happening? Didn't he trust him?

Then Ulric swallowed a sigh. In his youth, he'd been hot-tempered,
stubborn, and impulsive. How could his father have depended on him not
to overreact?

If he'd been the sort of son who was capable of…

No. Ulric slammed the door shut on his bout of self-pity. Later he'd
torture himself for his childhood arrogance. Right now, he had more
important matters demanding his attention.

"What did my father do?" he demanded.

Brigette's lips tightened. "He attached the spell to someone else."

Spell? Ulric furrowed his brow. She couldn't be talking about the curse.
She'd already said that she'd broken through that. So what magic was she
talking about? "What sort of spell?"

She shrugged. "A protective shell that encases the scrolls. I've tried everything to destroy them, but nothing has worked." She sent him a jaundiced glare. "And worse, he bound the spell to someone in the pack."

"Attached it to who?"

"I had no way of knowing." Her lips twisted into an ugly smile. "So everyone had to die."

"You," Rainn abruptly breathed, turning to face him. "It's attached to you."

"Yes," a female voice whispered behind them.

Chapter 8

Levet shivered as a sharp wind howled over the bleak landscape, tugging at his wings. Surprisingly, however, it wasn't a shiver of cold. Or even aversion.

It was sheer pleasure.

This isolated spot in Ireland might not be an exotic beach in the Bahamas, but the air was clean and crisp, and the rich scent of fertile soil was as sweet as any perfume. It emphasized the noxious atmosphere they'd just left.

There was something wrong at Ulric's old lair.

Something wicked.

He shook off the clinging sense of evil, turning his attention to the nearby castle.

To most people it would look like a crumbling pile of rocks. Just another forgotten ruin that dotted the landscape. But Levet was easily capable of seeing through the illusion to the massive structure that towered far above them. It was a forbidding fortress, with heavy stained-glass windows and a gothic vibe that would have made Dracula proud.

Not that Dracula was real. And he certainly hadn't been around during the gothic era…

Levet's scattered thoughts were brought back to sharp focus as the enormous wooden door opened to reveal a vampire.

Cyn. Clan chief of Ireland.

At six foot three, the male possessed a powerful chest and thick muscles that he'd acquired during his human years as a Berserker. His dark blond hair hung halfway down his back except for the front strands that he kept woven into tight braids that framed his face.

His features looked as if they'd been chiseled by an angry artist in blunt lines, with a square jaw and high cheekbones. His brow was wide and his jade-green eyes heavily lashed. At the moment he was wearing slacks with a cashmere sweater.

Almost as if he was a respectable lord of the manor, and not a lethal vampire.

At least until he parted his lips to expose his fully extended fangs.

"Stop there," Cyn warned.

Levet stepped forward, holding up his hand. "We come in pieces."

"What?" Cyn appeared momentarily baffled, then his eyes were widening in shock. "No. No, no, no."

"At least we know the creature wasn't lying," Tarak drawled as he stepped to stand next Levet. "Only a vampire who'd met the gargoyle could react with such genuine horror."

Levet sniffed. "I am a delightful creature. It is not my fault that leeches are inconsiderate brutes."

Tarak ignored his perfectly reasonable explanation for Cyn's lack of welcome. Instead he offered a cautious bow.

"I'm Tarak."

Cyn cast a glance over Waverly before settling his gaze on Tarak. "The one imprisoned by the mermaids?"

Tarak straightened, his expression tight. "And our beloved Anasso."

Cyn grimaced. "Point taken," he conceded. He folded his arms over his chest. "What are you doing here?"

"I'm seeking information," Tarak said before Levet could answer. *So rude.* "The gargoyle said you have an extensive library."

"My library is one of the best in the world," Cyn said. His words weren't a boast. Just a statement of fact. "What specific information do you need?"

"Gargoyle," Tarak said. "Tell him what we need."

Levet clicked his tongue in annoyance. Really, enough was enough. "I do have a name. It is—"

"Tell him what you know," Tarak interrupted, his eyes narrowed.

Levet muttered a curse. His feathers were thoroughly ruffled. Okay, he didn't actually have feathers, but if he did they would be sticking out all over the place. Where was the respect? The adulation?

He was, after all, a hero.

Giving a snap of his wings, he forced himself to ignore the lack of proper appreciation. He would be the bigger demon. In graciousness, if not in physical size.

Clearing his throat, he shared the few details he knew about Ulric and Rainn's journey to Wales, as well as the old woman who'd threatened to kill him.

"Describe the female," Cyn commanded. He was as bossy as Levet remembered.

Silently, Levet decided that anger management wasn't enough to make vampires fit for civilized society. They also needed charm school. Or perhaps a stake through the heart. That would help.

Feeling the vampire glares burning into his skin, Levet cleared his throat.

"She appeared to be an elderly human with silver hair and a wrinkly face," he told his audience. "At first I thought she might be a grandmother, and I hoped she would invite me to her house for some pot roast and yummy mashed potatoes. Oh, and pie. Apple pie." His stomach gave a loud gurgle in protest. "Speaking of pie, I do not suppose you have—"

"Focus," Cyn snapped. "Was she human?"

Levet scowled, but he forced himself to consider the question.

Closing his eyes, he concentrated on the memory of his brief encounter with the female.

Like he'd said, she'd appeared to be human. At least at first. Then she'd come nearer, and all he could sense was her incredible age. It'd weighed on him like a physical pressure.

Plus, there'd been her magic. He'd never experienced anything like it before.

"Perhaps at one time," he slowly concluded, aggravated with his inability to pinpoint the female's species. "In the very distant past."

"What is she now?" Cyn demanded. "A zombie?"

The vampire wasn't being sarcastic. Human wizards could truly raise the dead from their graves.

"No." Levet gave a decisive shake of his head. "She was alive, but I cannot say more than that."

"I thought you might have heard word of such a creature," Tarak said to Cyn. "Or perhaps possess a book that has legends about ancient magic in the British Isles."

Cyn waved his hand toward the rugged landscape. "This is the land of legends. We need to narrow down the possibilities of what species the female might be, unless you want to spend the next few years digging through my library."

"Her magic has created a thick fog around the area," Tarak said. "There's no way to get through the barrier to discover more."

"Perhaps I can help." A female voice drifted on the breeze, as soft as a summer mist.

Fallon, Princess of the Chatri. Oh, and Cyn's mate. Poor fairy.

Stepping out of the castle, she moved to stand next to Cyn. She was beautiful, of course. Her hair was a glorious tumble of rich gold brushed with hints of pale rose. Her eyes were polished amber with flecks of emerald, and her ivory features were perfect. She was wearing a pair of jeans and a thick sweater that emphasized her slender curves.

Cyn instantly wrapped an arm around Fallon's shoulders, pulling her tight against his side.

"This is my mate, Fallon," he said, his voice thick with pride. "You have a suggestion?" he asked her.

Fallon nodded, offering a shy smile. "I could try to scry for the werewolf. It might allow us to see through the fog that you described."

Levet's wings perked up. He had nearly forgotten Fallon's astonishing skill in scrying. She could locate and spy on anyone she wanted. Including the Oracles.

Hastily running his hands up and down his arms, he held up one claw in triumph.

"I have a hair if you need it to connect to the dog," he announced. His brows arched as he realized his companions were regarding him with confusion. "What? He sheds."

Fallon tried and failed to hide her smile. "It couldn't hurt," she assured him, waving a hand toward the nearby door. "Follow me."

Ignoring the warning glare from Cyn, Levet scurried up the steps and entered the castle. He found himself in the cavernous foyer that was paneled in polished mahogany with an open beam ceiling. Across the space was a massive stone fireplace blazing with an impressive fire.

Levet's dislike for Cyn lessened at the sight.

The clan chief might be an arrogant patootie, like all vampires, but he adored his mate. He never forgot to keep the lair warm and toasty for Fallon, despite his aversion to fire.

They moved past the sweeping staircase and through a narrow door that led down to the kitchens. Levet halted in the middle of the stone floor, watching as Fallon grabbed a wooden bowl off a shelf and filled it with water.

She turned to walk back to him, placing the bowl on the floor. "Drop the hair in the water."

Levet did as she commanded, and they all watched in silence as Fallon knelt next to the bowl and called on her powers.

Minutes passed, the air laced with the intoxicating scent of champagne. Fallon's magic. Levet sucked in a deep breath. *Yummy.*

Not as yummy as an ocean breeze…

Non. He sternly squashed the thought, peering into the bowl.

"There's the fog," he murmured, happy to be distracted.

Cyn moved to kneel next to his mate. His brows lowered at the sight of the thick, swirling mist that crawled along the steep cliffs. It didn't move as if it was being pushed by an unseen breeze. Instead, it churned and boiled as if it was a living force.

Cyn stated the obvious. "That's not natural." He studied his mate's profile. "Can you penetrate it?"

"I'll try," Fallon said, waving her slender hand over the bowl.

The fog grudgingly thinned, battling against Fallon's magic before it abruptly disappeared. In unison, they all gasped as they caught sight of the bleak destruction that was suddenly revealed.

Levet leaned closer, his wings drooping. He'd been vaguely aware there was something wrong as he'd sat on the edge of the cliff. But he'd been distracted by his annoyance with Ulric, and the fact that he'd been unable to follow his trail. Plus, he'd been on the very edge of the decaying landscape. At least until the fog had surrounded him.

Now he felt a heavy ball in the center of his tummy.

This was bad. *Très* bad.

He lifted his head, glancing toward Cyn. "What could do that?"

"Humans," the ancient vampire snarled.

It wasn't surprising that Cyn would leap to that conclusion. He'd recently had a very bad experience with the local druids.

Levet gave a firm shake of his head. "*Non.* It is not human pollution."

Cyn looked like he wanted to argue, then he snapped his fangs together. No doubt he was recalling Levet's exquisite ability to see past illusions and magic and even human spells.

Nothing could fool him, Levet assured himself. He wrinkled his snout. At least, not for long.

Cyn returned his attention to the bowl, his big body stiffening as if he had been hit by a sudden thought.

"You said the female was old," Cyn said, his gaze remaining on the bowl.

"Ancient," Levet corrected.

"Hmm." He straightened, his expression distracted. "There might be something."

"What is it, Cyn?" Tarak demanded as the larger vampire headed out of the kitchen.

Everyone scurried to follow behind the clan chief.

"Not long ago we battled an evil druid," Cyn said, leading them down a hallway and toward the back stairs.

"This is not the same magic," Levet protested as he struggled to keep up with Cyn's massive strides. Why did vampires have such freakishly long legs?

It was annoying.

Reaching the upper floor, Cyn carefully unlocked the heavy door that protected his private library. As if any creature would be stupid enough to try and steal from a powerful clan chief.

Cyn entered the library first, followed by Tarak and then Levet. The females were last, although it had nothing to do with being treated as inferiors. Vampires adored their mates. It would never, ever occur to them to see them as anything but true partners.

But the fairy princess and the mermaid were leaning close as they whispered together. Clearly they were delighted to meet one another.

Cyn crossed the antique carpet, not even glancing toward the towering shelves that held hundreds of leather-bound books. He pulled out another key from his pocket and unlocked a second door that opened into his large study.

Levet hurried inside, his gaze skimming over the satinwood furniture that Cyn had carved, and the arched, stained-glass window. His only interest was in the tapestry on the far wall. It was a scene of a glistening white unicorn standing in the center of a flower-filled meadow with a pretty virgin kneeling at his side, which had been created by the fey creatures who'd fostered Cyn shortly after he'd been turned.

The image haunted him. As if it had some deeper meaning, if only he could see it.

Not that he'd ever had the opportunity to actually study the tapestry. Cyn was fiercely protective of his books. The few times Levet had tried to sneak a peek in these rooms, he'd nearly been tossed through the window. As if he was going to somehow hurt the stinky old manuscripts.

Pfft.

"What are we doing in here?" Tarak asked, obviously puzzled why they hadn't remained in the outer library.

Cyn moved to touch a section of the wall. Instantly it slid open to reveal a hidden vault that was lined with shelves. Unlike the library, however, the scrolls, magical objects, and ancient books on the shelves were protected behind a thick layer of magic. "After we ended the threat—"

"After I conquered the Dark Lord," Levet corrected Cyn. Really, had the stupid vampire forgotten what had happened?

Cyn sent him a jaundiced glare. "After the druids were defeated, I did some research on human magic."

Levet stomped his foot. "You are leaving out my astounding contribution to saving the world."

"Hush," Cyn snapped.

Levet stuck out his tongue. "So rude."

Cyn snarled a curse before turning his attention to Tarak. "I wanted to discover the origin of their power."

Tarak stepped between Levet and Cyn. Not that Levet assumed the vampire was attempting to protect him. The leech was simply hoping to put an end to the squabbling.

"Did you discover the origin?" Tarak demanded.

"I'm not sure. There's a book that I was in the process of trying to decipher. It spoke of a long-ago battle that was waged in Britain. Most of it was gibberish, to be honest, and I eventually gave up," Cyn confessed, entering the vault and heading for the back wall. "I did get enough translated to know it referred to some sort of corrupted magic that was eroding the land until the demons gathered together to banish it. I think there was even a mention of a dank mist that might be the fog that is surrounding the werewolves' old lair…" His words trailed away, and his body stiffened. "Shit."

There was the sound of hurrying footsteps as Fallon entered the vault to stand next to her mate. "What's wrong?"

"Look." Cyn pointed toward the bottom shelf. "Charred."

They crowded together, the air in the vault dropping to a frigid temperature. No need to ask if Cyn was displeased by the vandalism to his secret stash.

Using his compact size to his advantage, Levet wiggled forward. The bottom shelf was lined with manuscripts bound in worn leather. Even at a distance they looked fragile enough to disintegrate at any moment. Which was, no doubt, the reason they were behind the magical barrier.

Only one of them, however, looked like a lump of old charcoal.

"I assume it wasn't like that before?" Tarak asked.

"No."

"When was the last time you saw it?"

Cyn balled his hands into fists, the temperature dropping another ten degrees.

"It's been a year, at least, since I was in this vault." He glanced toward his mate, who instantly reached to touch his arm. "I had better things to do with my time."

"Understandable." Tarak nodded, sneaking a glance at his own mate. Levet pursed his lips. He wasn't envious. He wasn't.

After all, he was a Knight in Shining Armor, meant to rescue any damsel in distress. Who wanted to be tied down to one female when he could be tasting the delights of demons around the world?

He heaved a sigh. The words didn't have the same resonance that they used to have.

With an effort, he focused his attention on the crispy manuscript, waiting for Cyn to regain command of his temper.

Eventually the vampire waved a hand toward the open doorway. "Nothing should have been able to get in here without me knowing," he said. "I not only have the vault protected by spells, but there's an electronic alarm system that I had installed several years ago."

Tarak gave an absent nod. "Is there another copy?"

Cyn paused, as if considering the question.

"Jagr might have one," Levet said.

The head of Styx's private guards had spent centuries in isolation, with only his massive collection of books to keep him company.

Cyn looked surprised. "The gargoyle is right," he said, as if shocked. "Jagr has a library that is close to equaling my own." Pulling a phone from the front pocket of his slacks, Cyn headed out of the vault.

Levet was forced to leap out of the way or be squashed beneath the male's heavy shoes.

Vampires not only had legs that were too long, they had feet as big as barges.

They returned to the study, watching Cyn as he spoke into the phone and then restlessly paced from one end of the room to the other.

Was he waiting for Jagr to check his collection? Probably. Quickly bored by the delay, Levet drifted toward the tapestry. It really was fascinating.

A few minutes later Cyn muttered a curse and shoved the phone back into his pocket. "Jagr's book was destroyed as well."

"How?" Tarak demanded.

"Charred the same as mine."

Tarak arched his brows in surprise. "This at least confirms we're headed down the right path. Someone doesn't want us to know what was written in that book."

Cyn didn't appear quite so ready to jump on the bandage wagon. Bandwagon?

"It could be unrelated, but I agree, it's worth looking into," Cyn said.

"So how do we find out?" Tarak demanded.

The two males discussed the various possibilities, but Levet tuned them out.

He'd had an uneasy feeling before. Now it was downright alarming.

He had no doubt that the books were connected to the weird fog, the eroding land, and the creepy mist. Which meant that this wasn't just about Ulric and Rainn. Or even a small patch of land in a remote area of Wales.

This was bigger and badder than he'd imagined.

Grabbing his tail, he began to polish it. That's what he did when he was anxious. Then, without warning, Waverly stepped toward Tarak.

"I might be able to help," she said, blushing at being the center of attention. She tilted her chin, meeting Cyn's curious gaze. "You have a very fine library, but my father's is even larger." The vampire flicked a brow upward at the claim, and Waverly hurriedly rushed on. "And more importantly, it's surrounded by a powerful spell that could withstand the magic of a dragon. If he has copy of the book it might have survived."

Tarak sent her a smile filled with pride. "It's worth a try. I'll go with you."

"No." She gave a surprisingly firm shake of her head. "Chiron will want you to stay here and try to rescue Ulric."

Tarak scowled, but before he could speak, Levet thrust his hand in the air.

"I will go."

Dead silence.

Levet squared his shoulders, prepared to fight for his right to search for the book. He was the most logical choice, after all. Not only was he familiar with the mer-folk castle, but the current queen, Inga, owed him a favor.

A BIG favor.

It was Cyn who at last broke the silence. "Actually, it's not a bad idea," he slowly drawled, glancing toward Tarak. "I might want to throttle the creature, but he does have a rare talent for sensing illusions. Most collectors will protect books that are rare or dangerous. It's quite likely to be hidden behind magic."

Tarak snorted. "You just want to get rid of him."

Cyn flashed his fangs. "Bonus."

Levet slammed his hands on his hips. He fully intended to inform the leeches of what he thought about their lame attempt at humor. But before he could speak, Waverly laid her hand on the tip of his wing.

"I'll take him to the castle," she said.

Tarak leaned forward, brushing his lips over his mate's cheek. "Don't be away long."

Levet interrupted the tender scene. "Choppy, choppy. You can kissy-face later."

He was suddenly impatient to be through the portal. And it had nothing to do with seeing Inga again. Or at least he'd have his tongue cut out before he'd admit how eager he was to be reunited with the ogress.

Chapter 9

Shock jolted through Rainn.

Nothing should have been able to sneak up on her. Nothing. Not only did she possess the heightened senses of all demons, but the wind whispered in her ear. It should have warned her that danger was approaching.

Gritting her teeth, Rainn slowly turned to face the intruder. Next to her, Ulric was already snarling in fury as the heat of his wolf filled the cramped cavern. One wrong move and he would snap.

She needed to remain calm.

Something that was easier said than done as she caught sight of the wizened old woman.

What was this creature?

Rainn sniffed the air. The female had aged like a human. Her face was wrinkled, and her hair had faded to gray. But she smelled like a...

Rainn wrinkled her nose. It was difficult to smell anything beyond the stench that filled the burrow. Still, she should be able to catch some scent. Especially if the female was a mortal. But there was nothing she could latch on to. The woman just smelled old. Really, really old.

It was almost as unnerving as the smile that curled the woman's lips as she studied Ulric.

She looked like the cat who'd found its bowl of cream.

That couldn't be good.

Ulric stepped forward. His body vibrated. No doubt he was struggling to contain his wolf. But thankfully he didn't immediately attack the stranger.

Until they knew exactly what sort of creature she was, they couldn't risk a direct assault.

"Who are you?" Ulric demanded.

The woman's creepy smile widened. "You can call me Zella, if you insist on a name."

Rainn pressed against Ulric's side. She told herself it was to prevent him from doing something stupid. Deep inside, however, she knew she was seeking his warmth. It helped to banish the fear that was threatening to cloud her mind. Now, more than ever, she needed to think clearly. "The more important question is *what* you are," she said.

The woman reluctantly glanced toward Rainn. "I am the key."

"Key? You're here to unlock the doorway?"

Zella scowled with impatience. "Your brain is too primitive to fully comprehend my vastness."

Rainn snorted. "There's nothing wrong with your ego."

"Every part of me is perfect," Zella said, seemingly incapable of understanding sarcasm. "That's how I was created."

Rainn's brows drew together. She couldn't put her finger on what was wrong with the woman, but there was something.

Was this creature responsible for the horde that had attacked the village? And for luring Ulric to the burrow? And more unnerving, was she responsible for the decay that was spreading over the land?

If that was true, she had to possess enormous power.

Ulric wrapped an arm around her shoulders. Did he sense her need for his touch? The thought was almost as alarming as the mysterious female.

Almost.

"I assume you're Brigette's companion," the male said.

"My partner," Brigette corrected in an overly loud voice.

No one bothered to glance at the forgotten female Were. She was a mere annoyance. It was Zella who posed the danger.

Zella shrugged. "She's my servant."

"Partner," Brigette insisted.

"Hush." The woman waved a gnarled hand and Brigette gasped in pain.

Rainn stiffened. Had Zella's eyes flashed with fire, or was it a trick of her uneasy imagination? The woman blinked and the flames were gone.

"I assume my servant revealed our disappointment when we discovered the destruction of your pack hadn't opened the doorway as we'd hoped?"

Ulric growled. Quickly Rainn poked him in the side with her elbow. A silent warning to keep a grip on his animal.

"What is the doorway?" she asked the woman. "And why do you want it open?"

"To release the llygrd."

Rainn grimaced. She didn't know what the llygrd might be, but she was betting it wasn't good. Then she had a sudden thought. "Did you come through the doorway?"

Zella pinched her lips together, as if she'd bitten into a lemon. "A fragment of my spirit managed to enter this world before I was halted."

Ah. A spirit from another dimension. That explained her "otherness." It also made Rainn's gut cramp with dread. Ulric pulled her closer, silently giving her the courage to continue.

"You used Brigette to bring the horde to this village?" Rainn demanded.

"Yes." Zella shot Brigette a dark glare. "They were supposed to kill the entire pack. It wasn't until they sailed away that it was obvious at least one had survived."

"Why didn't you follow the ships?" Ulric demanded.

"I am temporarily..." Zella tilted her head to the side. Was she considering her answer? Or searching for the words? "Restrained in my movements. I can spend short periods of time away from this area, but I quickly lose my powers."

Rainn breathed a small sigh of relief. If the spirit was trapped in this location, that might give them the time to find a way to kill her. Or at least keep her locked in this burrow.

Seemingly unaware of Rainn's inner thoughts, the woman gave another wave of her hand. On cue, Brigette screamed.

"My servant was convinced that her missing pack mate must have managed to escape during the attack. And that the Were was hiding in London." Hints of flame returned to her eyes. "She wasted endless years searching. It was only with my prompting that she at last traveled beyond England to discover the information we needed."

Rainn grimaced. She didn't want to know what sort of prompting Brigette had endured. She might hate the bitch, but Rainn sensed the female Were had suffered over the centuries.

Be careful what you wish for...

"How did you find me?" Ulric asked.

Zella nodded her head toward Brigette. "Tell him."

Cautiously, the female Were inched toward them. "I was in a demon bar in Madrid when I overheard two vampires discussing the new Anasso's proclamation that the Rebels were no longer banished." Brigette's expression tried to be mocking, but she couldn't hide her pallor. She was terrified of Zella. "I had no interest in the bloodsuckers' politics. Nasty creatures. But then one of them mentioned a Rebel who had a pet werewolf named Ulric, who lived in Vegas."

Ulric's breath hissed between his teeth. "That's when you decided to stage your elaborate charade?"

Brigette shrugged. "It worked, didn't it?"

Rainn turned back to Zella. "Now what happens?"

The creepy smile returned. "First, you die," Zella announced, glancing toward Brigette. "I don't know why you were brought down here in the first place."

"Ulric wouldn't come without her. And you told me to keep him alive until you were ready." Brigette pouted. "What else could I do?"

Zella clicked her tongue. "As usual you've created a mess that I must clean up."

Rainn was astonishingly calm, considering she'd been told she was about to die. Honestly, her greatest concern was that Ulric would snap and get himself killed. "I wasn't talking about me," she said, covertly gathering her magic. "What do you intend to do to Ulric?"

Zella glanced toward the male Were, her features tightening with a disturbing hunger.

"His death will break the spell and the doorway will open."

Rainn glanced back at the skeleton. "A sacrifice like the poor human?" she asked, more in an attempt to keep Zella distracted than any genuine interest.

The woman's eyes filled with flames, the stench of brimstone nearly gagging Rainn.

"It was because of that stupid creature I was trapped in the first place."

Tendrils of fire danced around the woman. Rainn's mouth went dry. Okay, then. Clearly she'd touched a raw nerve.

Rainn kept her expression smooth as she used her magic to wedge air into the tiny cracks that spiderwebbed the ceiling. The stone was a thick granite, but it had hardened over the years until it was brittle. Perfect for her needs.

She grimly concentrated on her task, thankful when Ulric turned Zella's attention to himself.

"You can't be sure that the spell is attached to me," he warned. "There were several of us on the goblin ship. Some were sold to the Anasso, and some were sent on to the slave markets. Maybe one of them has the blood you need."

Zella's eyes narrowed. Could she sense Ulric's lie? Rainn wasn't about to find out. With a last surge of power, she shattered the rock above them, sending an avalanche onto the woman.

Almost as if prepared for the collapse of the ceiling, Ulric grabbed her hand and charged past Zella even as the woman tried to reach out and halt them. A cloud of dust followed them into the tunnel, but miraculously the pile of rubble blocked the opening behind them. They'd made it out just in time.

Not that Rainn was stupid enough to believe the rocks would keep Zella and Brigette entombed for long. But it did give them a head start.

Racing up the stairs, Rainn was caught off guard when Ulric abruptly shifted into his wolf. Had he lost control of his animal? Or had it been deliberate?

She had her answer when they ran out of the burrow and Ulric placed his nose firmly to the ground. He was searching for something.

Jogging behind him, Rainn took the opportunity to study his wolf form.

He was massive, with a muscular body that moved with a liquid grace. His eyes were a dark gold and his midnight fur was glossy even in the darkness. As a human he was gorgeous. As a wolf he was…stunning.

A strange sensation expanded her heart. It felt like it was being stuffed with an emotion she didn't want to name.

Giving a shake of her head, Rainn concentrated on their surroundings. Who knew if there were other creatures like Zella lurking in the fog.

Ulric zigzagged past the ruined village. His pace never slowed, although Rainn could see his hackles rise as he passed the spot where his parents' cottage had once stood.

Where was he going? Following behind the wolf, who kept his pace slow but steady, Rainn was increasingly confused. They needed to get the hell out of there. Pronto. Instead, he was taking them to the edge of the steep cliff. If someone snuck up behind them, they would be trapped.

It wasn't until he started down a narrow pathway that she realized he'd managed to find a breach in the fog. She'd been so rattled by the encounter in the burrow she'd almost forgotten the mist around them wasn't natural. This was very likely their only escape route.

Rainn scrambled down the terrifyingly steep path, refusing to glance toward the razor-sharp rocks on the beach below them. A fall wouldn't kill her, she reminded herself. Immediately, her mind whispered back that it would hurt like a bitch.

She stumbled twice, scraping her hands and sending her heart into her throat. But she managed to reach the flat ground without breaking her neck.

She'd take that as a win.

Next to her, a shimmer of magic swirled around the large wolf. She halted to watch in fascination. She had a vague impression of limbs lengthening and a muzzle transforming into bold, male features. Then the magic disappeared to reveal Ulric standing upright in front of her. Completely naked.

Her gaze began an appreciative slide down his broad chest, only to be halted by the sight of blood dripping down his ribcage.

She reached out a hand. "You're hurt."

He glanced down, his jaw tightening at the sight of the blood. "I must have scraped against a rock."

"Shouldn't it have healed while you were in your wolf form?" Rainn had seen werewolves heal broken legs, stab wounds, and burns that covered their entire bodies. A mere scrape should have disappeared within seconds.

"It doesn't matter," he muttered.

Rainn leaned closer. The wound looked like someone had used their fingernails to score four deep gouges into his flesh. She sucked in a sharp breath at the memory of Zella reaching toward them as they'd escaped from the burrow.

"Was it Zella?" she asked, lifting her gaze to his face when he didn't answer. "Ulric?"

"She might have scratched me when we went past her," he grudgingly conceded.

Fear crawled down her spine to settle in the pit of her stomach.

"Why isn't it healing?"

Ulric made a sound of impatience. "I'll worry about it later."

"But—"

"Rainn, we have to get away from here," he said, cutting her off and nodding toward the fog that hovered at the top of the cliff.

He was right. "Okay."

With typical werewolf arrogance, he took the lead. Rainn didn't protest. He possessed a superior sense of smell even in his human form. That meant he'd be able to detect any approaching danger long before she could. Besides, she wanted to keep a close eye on him. Ulric might pretend everything was okay, but she didn't miss the pallor of his face, or the sweat that glistened over his naked body.

They crawled over the rocks that covered the beach, moving in silence. Rainn's feet were wet, and her sweater was starting to itch, but she barely noticed. She was so damned happy to be away from the Village of the Damned.

She could breathe fresh air. See the stars sparkling overhead. And feel the salty breeze brushing over her skin. It was nothing short of paradise.

Once they were far away from the fog, Ulric found a path that angled up the cliff. It wasn't as steep as where they'd come down, thank the goddess. And jogging to the top, they both turned toward the small town where the jet was waiting. The sooner they got out of there, the better.

"Wait." Ulric reached to grab her.

She sent him a worried glance. "Do you smell something?"

"Fire," he said, pointing toward the airport.

"Oh crap," she breathed, catching sight of the smoke billowing into the air. "It can't be a coincidence."

"No." Rainn didn't need to see the jet to know it was on fire. It'd been the only plane at the remote airport.

Ulric swore in a rough voice. "Until we know how many servants Zella has, it might be safer to go on foot. I don't want to stumble into a trap."

Rainn's gaze remained on the plume of dark smoke that was spiraling upward.

"What about the crew?" She sucked in a sharp breath. "Oh. And Levet. We need to see if they've been injured."

"We can't do anything for them now." Ulric turned to angle away from the distant town. The rolling meadows seemed to stretch endlessly toward the horizon that was turning pink at the edges. There had to be another town out there somewhere. Right? Ulric picked up speed as they hit a road carved into the mossy ground. "Once we're away from here I'll call Chiron," he promised.

Rainn squashed her pang of guilt. The fire might very well be the bait to lure them into a trap if they managed to escape the village. They wouldn't be able to help anyone if they died.

They made a wide circle around the fog that was continuing to spread outward. Instinctively they both crouched low as they scurried toward a nearby hill. The cresting sun threatened to expose their presence to everyone in the area. Including any humans.

But expecting Ulric to veer off the road, Rainn barely avoided ramming into his large form when he came to an abrupt halt.

"Now what?" she asked, glancing around in alarm.

He sucked in a deep breath. "Do you smell that?"

She sniffed. The rich scent of wild thyme and heather was laced with the ocean breeze. But there was something else. Something cold.

"Vampire," she whispered.

"Tarak."

"Chiron's master?" she asked in surprise.

Tarak had been released from imprisonment a few months ago. She hadn't met him, but she knew he'd been secluded with his new mate in his private lair.

Ulric nodded, bending down to touch a small imprint on the dirt road. "His trail is headed for my old village. Chiron must have sent him to look for us."

Rainn's heart clenched with fear. *Oh crap.* Had the vampire been sucked into the fog? She scanned the area, looking for any sign of the leech.

Then, she realized the cold scent was laced with the hint of salt.

"He was with the mermaid," she said, following the scent until it abruptly disappeared. "He left through a portal here." Her nose wrinkled as yet another smell teased at her nose. Then relief raced through her. "Oh, and the gargoyle. He's alive."

Ulric snorted as he straightened. "Of course the aggravating pest survived. He's like a cockroach."

Rainn ignored his sour words, glancing around the emptiness that surrounded them. "If they were here to help us, they're gone now." She glanced toward Ulric. "We need to put some space between us and Zella."

He offered a slow nod, his expression distracted, as if he was considering their limited options.

"Let's see if we can find Tarak's lair," he abruptly announced.

"Do you know where it is?"

"Scotland."

"That's a fairly large area to search," she pointed out in dry tones.

He shrugged. "It's on the northern coast."

She swallowed a sigh. As much as she wanted to urge him to find the nearest human city and hop on a plane back to Vegas, she knew it was a waste of breath. Ulric wasn't going to return home until he'd destroyed the spirit responsible for massacring his pack.

Besides, she wasn't here to worry about Ulric. Or his safety. She was supposed to be performing the task the Oracles had sent her to do. And she had no doubt in her mind that Zella was the evil she was supposed to battle.

Still, she needed an opportunity to rest and regain her strength before she returned to do her duty.

"I don't have the ability to make portals," she muttered.

It was a source of unending annoyance. Every other fey creature could easily travel from place to place. A zephyr, however, who was a master of the wind, found it impossible.

Ulric gave a lift of his shoulder. "Then we'll drive there."

She glanced around, once again noting just how isolated they were. "Drive?"

Ulric pointed toward a patch of grass that had been nibbled to the ground.

"There have been sheep through here recently," he said. "And where there are sheep, there are humans." He nodded toward the hills. "Let's find them."

Chapter 10

Levet stepped out of the portal that Waverly created inside the mer-folk castle deep beneath the ocean. He glanced around, ignoring the faint breeze as the portal closed behind him. He was far more interested in his surroundings.

Ah. Waverly had brought him to the empty throne room. It was a familiar spot that helped to orient him.

Of course, the last time he'd been there, the marble floor had been busted and there'd been a gaping hole in the wall where Riven, the former King of the Mer-folk, had tried to escape.

Now he noticed the repairs to the floor had been completed and the hole in the wall was at least closed. The exquisite mural of a vibrant coral reef and delicate fish, however, was still in progress.

His heart missed a beat. It had to be Inga's work. She was blessed with a breathtaking artistic talent.

His survey of the room was distracted by the sudden odor of a breeze blowing over the ocean. Almost as if the thought of Inga had conjured her scent. Then the ground vibrated beneath Levet's feet and he knew it wasn't a figment of his imagination.

Slowly turning, he faced the double doors. There was a strange sensation niggling in the pit of his stomach. What was it? Nerves?

Non. That was absurd.

Why would he be nervous? Inga had been the one to mess with his mind. She'd made him believe that he was her personal Knight in Shining Armor.

Granted, she'd been fleeing from Tarak, a crazed vampire, who she had helped to trap in a prison for over five hundred years, a voice whispered in the back of his mind. As well as Riven, who wanted her dead.

Still, it was rude to tinkle with his mind.

No, wait. Not tinkle. Tinker. *Oui*, tinker.

Which was why he'd walked away as soon as the spell had been broken, he grimly assured himself.

It had nothing to do with the fact that he believed she was a former slave who'd been abandoned by her family and forced to make her own way in the world.

A misfit.

Just like himself.

Instead it was revealed that she'd been ripped from the arms of her mother. And that her family had spent endless centuries trying to find her. Oh, and that she was the rightful ruler of the mer-folk.

While he was…well, he was still a misfit.

Nope. Nothing. At. All.

Squaring his shoulders, he held his wings at a proud angle as Inga burst into the room.

The current Queen of the Mer-folk didn't look like a mermaid. She'd taken after her ogre father, standing well over six foot, with the broad shoulders of a human weight lifter. Her hair was reddish and grew in tufts on top of her large, square head. Her features were bluntly carved, and her teeth were pointed.

Only her eyes, which were a misty blue, spoke of her mermaid mother, although they flashed red when she was annoyed.

She was holding a large trident called the Tryshu.

The ancient weapon was filled with a mysterious magic that chose the leader of the mer-folk. Only the true king or queen could hold the trident. Like Arthur's sword, only without the whole round-table thing.

Charging into the room, Inga came to a sharp halt. Her eyes widened and her nostrils flared, as if drawing in Levet's scent.

"I knew it. I could sense—" She abruptly clamped her lips together as if battling to hide her intense reaction to his arrival. Then, tilting her chin, she peered down at him. "How did you get here?"

Levet barely heard her words as his gaze ran over the female.

What was happening? Her red, fuzzy hair had been smoothed to lie flat against her head, and her outrageous muumuu dress had been replaced by a shimmering gown that hugged her large frame.

There was even something on her face. "Are you wearing makeup?" he abruptly demanded.

She blinked, a dark blush staining her cheeks. "What?"

Levet waddled forward, pointing toward the dark pink gloss he could see glistening on her lips. "I asked if you—"

"Answer my question," she interrupted, her brows snapping together. "How did you get here?"

Levet sniffed at her sharp tone. "I see you have become a true royal. They never have any manners."

"I didn't have manners before I became a royal."

Levet couldn't argue. The female was rude, impatient, and occasionally vulgar.

And to be honest, he liked her rough manner. There was a charming lack of sophistication about her.

"I suppose that is true enough," he agreed.

His words did nothing to ease her burst of annoyance. "Well? I'm waiting."

Her foot *tap, tap, tapped* on the marble floor. The ground trembled beneath the impact.

Levet shrugged. "Waverly brought me."

Inga's irritation vanished, her expression brightening with anticipation. "She's here?"

"*Non*. She had to stay with Tarak."

"Oh. Of course." Inga cleared her throat, pretending not to be disappointed. "I'm sure she's busy."

Levet's heart melted. Inga had spent centuries believing the mer-folk had sold her into slavery. Now she was desperate to bond with her family.

"She wanted me to assure you that she intends to visit very soon," he said in gentle tones.

"And Lilah?" she demanded, speaking of the human witch whom she'd considered her daughter for over five hundred years. "She's well?"

"Obscenely happy," Levet admitted. "A baffling circumstance, considering she is stuck with a leech."

Inga smiled, but it was strained. It was obvious she wanted Lilah to be happy, but it pained her to be separated.

"I'm pleased for her." Giving a faint shake of her head, Inga visibly focused on Levet. "Why are you here?"

"I need to search your library."

"Library?" An odd expression rippled over her face. Was it... disappointment? "What for?"

Levet stepped closer, breathing in her soft ocean scent. "Ulric and Rainn are stuck in a magical fog and all the books we need are toasty."

"Toasty?" Inga was momentarily baffled. "Do you mean toasted?"

Levet nodded. "That's what I said."

"Ulric." Inga tested the name. "That's Chiron's werewolf?"

"Oui."

"Who is Rainn?"

"A zephyr sprite."

"Are you serious?" Inga waited, as if trying to decide if Levet was joking. "I thought they were a myth."

"That is what most creatures assumed about mermaids," Levet reminded her.

She waved aside his comment. "Is the magical fog in Vegas?"

"Non. It's..." His words dried on his lips as a familiar demon swept into the room.

Non, not swept. He *swooshed* into the room.

Troy, Prince of Imps, was a large male with the sort of muscles that Levet secretly envied. He was wearing a strange pair of stretchy zebra-print pants and a fuzzy sweater that had a vee neckline that dipped to his belly button. His eyes were a vivid green and he had long, brilliant red hair that looked like a river of fire.

Oozing with sensuality, the creature halted next to Inga. "There you are, my love," he chided, waving a finger in her face. "Why did you disappear? I haven't finished styling your hair."

Levet flapped his wings in shock. The last time he'd seen Troy, they had been standing in the cavern beneath Lilah's hotel. "What are you doing here?"

Troy flicked a dismissive gaze over Levet. "Clearly I am the Master of the Wardrobe."

Levet scowled. "The bastard of the wardrobe? What is that?"

"Master." Troy flashed a condescending smile. "I fear you wouldn't understand. You don't have royal blood in your veins."

Levet slammed his fists on his hips, puffing out his chest. "I have an abundance of royal blood. I reek of nobility. As far as I am concerned it worth less than..." He snapped fingers.

Inga snorted. "Less than that if you ask me."

Levet furrowed his brow. "Then why are you allowing this—"

"Careful." Troy cut off his insult.

Levet scrunched his snout. Most male demons were pathetically predictable. Lots of growling and gnashing their fangs. *Oh, I'm going to rip off your wings. Oh, I'm going to grind you to rubble.* Troy...not so much.

He hid his potent magic beneath a mocking smile and outrageous flirtations. Levet was never quite certain what he might do if he was angered.

Still, the imp had no right to be doing anything to this female. She belonged...

He shut down the thought before it could form. Instead he glared at Inga.

"Allowing this imp to change you?" he demanded.

She folded her arms over her impressive bosom. "He's not changing me."

"Then why do you have paint plastered on your face?" He waved a hand toward the glittery dress. "And what is that you are wearing?"

She stuck out her lower lip. "It's a gown."

"It's not your style," Levet said.

She glanced away, the color on her cheeks darkening to crimson. "I have been informed that my previous dresses were not appropriate for the Queen of the Mer-folk."

Levet's tail twitched around his feet. He didn't care what the imp might do to him. If he'd hurt Inga's feelings, Levet intended to shrivel his manly bits to sour little grapes.

"Informed by who?" He pointed toward Troy. "This fool?"

A fruity scent swirled through the air as the imp took a sudden step forward. "I did warn you."

"Troy." Inga hurriedly moved between the two males. "I need a few minutes with Levet." She rolled her eyes when Troy continued to glare at Levet. "Alone, please."

There was a tense beat before Troy had regained command of his temper. He gave a faint lift of one shoulder. "Fine, I'll wait for you in your bedchamber." He strolled past Levet, offering him a taunting smile. "For the record, I was not the one to suggest that Queen Inga alter her style. I applaud originality." He reached the double doors, pausing long enough to blow a kiss toward Inga. *"Ciao, bellissima."*

Levet stomped his foot. "He stays in your bedchamber?"

Inga turned back to face him. "Do you care?"

"I..." Of course he cared. The female had been used and abused her entire existence. First by the ogres, who'd killed her father and sold her to the slavers. And then by Riven, who'd taken advantage of her desperation to be a part of the mer-folk. But he found the words impossible to say. He hunched his shoulders. "I do not trust him," he finally muttered.

Inga's jaw tightened. "That's all?"

"Why did he come here?"

"He arrived shortly after you left," she admitted. "He said he'd never met a mermaid before and..."

"And what?"

Inga glanced away. As if trying to hide her expression. "We were strolling down the hallway when we overheard a group of mer-folk who were standing on the balcony discussing the embarrassment of having me as their queen," she said, her voice carefully devoid of all emotion. "They said it was bad enough that I look like a monster without dressing like a human clown."

An anger blasted through Levet that was greater than any he'd ever felt before.

"Where are they? I will turn them into newts." He started stomping his way toward the doors. "*Non*. Newts are too good for them."

"Levet." Inga quickly stepped to block his path. "You thought the same thing. Even when you were under my spell you tried to change my appearance."

Levet came to a sharp halt. "Nonsense."

She arched her brows. "Are you saying that you don't remember offering to take me to Paris, so I could have new clothes designed for me?"

Levet was struck by the memory of saying those exact words. He cringed. Perhaps for the first time in his very long existence.

"Sometimes I am not so smart," he admitted.

"It doesn't matter," she muttered.

"It does to me." He inched toward her. How often could she be hurt before she shattered? He didn't want to find out. "You are perfectly fine the way you are."

She stiffened, a fragile vulnerability in her eyes, before she was sharply shaking her head. "Tell me about the book you need," she commanded.

Levet swallowed a sigh. Perhaps it was best to focus on his reason for being there. At least for now. Later he would devote the time necessary to assuring this female that anyone who desired to change her was a jerky jerk-face.

With an effort, Levet forced himself to recall the tedious lecture that he'd endured just before he'd stepped through the portal. "Cyn said—"

"Who's sin?" Inga interrupted in confusion.

"Cyn," Levet corrected. "The annoying clan chief of Ireland. A bad-tempered vampire who happens to have a very large library."

"Oh." She waved a hand for him to continue.

"Cyn said that the cover should be dark blue with gold trim. And there are markings on the front that look like two pyramids overlapping. And something else." He furrowed his brow trying to remember the exact word. "A Vidalia."

Inga blinked. "An onion?"

"*Non*. That cannot be right." Levet shuffled back through his memories. It was a difficult chore. When vampires opened their mouths it usually sounded like *yak, yak, yak*. "I believe it is some round metal thingy."

"A medallion?" Inga suggested.

"*Oui.*"

Inga abruptly headed across the long room, pausing to touch the wall behind the massive throne.

"Let's see if we can find it," she said, waiting for a portion of the brilliant mural to disappear.

Levet felt a tingle of excitement. A hidden door! He loved surprises.

Scurrying forward, he followed Inga into the narrow hallway. It was low enough that Inga had to stoop over, and so narrow Levet had to fold back his wings. The smell of salt was thick in the air and the darkness was heavy enough to be a physical pressure.

Levet's claws scraped against the marble floor, his tail twitching as they turned into one side tunnel after another. It was all so fantastic. He'd never suspected the castle possessed so many secrets.

At last Inga halted and tapped the Tryshu on the ground. A panel slid open and she disappeared from view. Levet reluctantly followed. He could have spent an eternity exploring the hidden passageways.

Then, following Inga through the opening, his disappointment was forgotten.

His eyes widened as he spun in a slow circle.

The room was as large as Styx's entire mansion. And that was saying something. It was shaped like an octagon, with shelves built into the walls. Overhead was a massive chandelier that started to glow as soon as Inga entered. The soft light reflected off the gold and pearls that crusted the domed ceiling. And in the center of the room was a marble fountain that spilled water into a shallow pool.

There was something very lush and sensual about the library.

Knowledge truly was sexy in here.

"Magnificent," he breathed.

"Yes. It is," Inga agreed. Her blunt features softened as she moved to stand next to the fountain. She reached out to allow the water to trickle over her fingers. "It almost makes it worth being Queen of the Mer-folk."

Levet's wings drooped. "Are you unhappy, *ma belle*?"

She held up the lethal trident that marked her as leader of the mer-folk. "I never wanted this."

Levet furrowed his brow. "What did you want?"

"A family." A wistful smile touched her lips. "A home."

"You have that now," Levet pointed out, confused by the hint of sadness in her voice.

"But at what cost?"

"Inga."

She jerked, as if realizing she was revealing more than she wanted.

"The rare books are through here. Stay close to me," she said crisply, marching to a space between two shelves. Levet followed, a portion of his delight fading at the loneliness he'd glimpsed in Inga's eyes.

"You don't have any security?" he asked, surprised when they walked through an arched opening into a much smaller space.

Inga shrugged. "You must be holding the Tryshu to penetrate the magic guarding this room."

"Ah." Levet shivered. He didn't precisely understand how the magic of the trident worked, but he did know that no one could touch it unless they were the true leader of the mer-folk. Which meant precisely one person could enter this room. "Formidable protection, indeed."

"You search those shelves." She nodded toward the plain wooden shelves on the far wall. "I'll look over here."

Preoccupied with the realization that Inga wasn't as happy as he assumed she would be in her new role as queen, Levet allowed his gaze to run over the books stacked in neat rows.

Which meant he nearly walked past the book that was tucked on the very bottom row. It was the shimmer of gold stitching in the binding that caught his eye. Bending down, he pulled out the slender tome.

A blue cover with two pyramids and a heavy medallion stuck into the thick leather.

"Voilà." He held the book over his head. "I found it."

Chapter 11

Brigette's palms were raw and bleeding. Digging through a ton of jagged rocks was hell on a manicure. And despite being a pureblooded Were, her muscles were starting to protest the manual labor.

Tired, filthy, and aching from head to toe, she wasn't in the best mood. Throw in the fact that Ulric had escaped, and her companion was watching her with a mocking expression, and she was close to snapping.

Where was the glorious destiny she'd been promised?

Arching her aching back, she glared toward the old woman, who was leaning casually against the far wall.

How many years had it been since she'd first snuck into this burrow? Six hundred? At the time she hadn't been searching for anything in particular. She'd been bored and frustrated and looking for a way to rebel without getting in trouble. She might resent the authority figures in her life, like her father and the alpha, but she wasn't stupid enough to believe she had the power to battle them. Not openly.

She had to content herself with working in the shadows to undermine their power.

She spread stories about the alpha, she encouraged fights and petty jealousies among the younger Weres. She attacked travelers stupid enough to pass by the village and risked exposing their pack to the humans.

Nothing seemed to matter. Not until she'd entered the burrow and the voice had whispered she could have everything she so desperately desired. Not only her freedom. But the opportunity to become the alpha.

Over and over she'd returned to the burrow, performing the tasks the voice had demanded of her. They were small at first. She brought small animals to offer as sacrifices. She removed a strange statue that'd been carved from a whale bone. And at last, she'd busted through the layer of rocks that had covered the skeleton. She'd been amazed by the sight. Not only because the bones were obviously an old sacrifice, but by the magic she could feel surrounding them.

Eventually Ulric's father had sealed shut the burrow, but it was far too late. At least for him.

By then she could touch the spirit's magic, allowing her to bust through the curse the alpha had placed on the entryway.

Still, it wasn't enough. She was hungry for more.

Always more.

That's when the old woman had appeared on a road outside the village. Brigette had first assumed she was a human traveler. But even as she'd crouched behind a rock and prepared to attack, the woman had wrapped her in bands of fire.

For hours the woman had held her captive, claiming she was the spirit of the burrow, a physical manifestation of the magic that had been whispering to Brigette for decades. She also claimed that Brigette had been chosen to share in a great reward just as soon as she helped Zella to fully enter this world.

Brigette didn't know exactly what the reward was going to be, but the woman assured her it would include enough power to rule her own pack. Perhaps enough to become Queen of Weres.

It was only when Brigette was blinded by her lust for rank and position among her people that the female had revealed the necessity of destroying the current pack. Zella had insisted that Brigette could never fulfill her destiny as a ruler as long as they were alive. They were the enemy that kept her from achieving her dreams of glory.

Later, Brigette told herself she'd tried to protest. How could she endure such a sacrifice? But deep in her heart she knew she'd done nothing to halt the carnage.

She'd been willing to destroy everything, including her own family.

It wasn't until after the massacre that she began to regret selling her soul to the devil.

Not only was the full force of the spirit still trapped behind layers of magic, but Brigette was compelled to accept that the freedom she'd been promised was nothing more than an illusion.

In fact, Zella had turned out to be a crueler bully than either her father or her alpha. And the worst part was that there was no way to form a new pack as long as she was at the mercy of the spirit.

No. The worst part was that she had lost the ability to touch her wolf.

It was almost as if the animal had turned its back on her human half, retreating farther and farther. Now she could barely sense the animal, let alone shift. It left a gaping hole in her soul.

Unfortunately, her regrets did nothing to ease her situation. She'd gone too far to turn back, which meant she had no choice but to discover which of the pack had survived so they could be sacrificed.

Her jaw tightened.

And she'd done it. She'd found Ulric and lured him to this spot. But instead of achieving her dreams, she'd once again been denied.

Glancing over her shoulder, she studied Zella with a sour dislike. "This would go faster if you would help," she pointed out.

Zella sniffed. "You forget who the servant is and who is the master."

Servant. The word rasped over Brigette's raw nerves. This wasn't the way it was supposed to be.

"The longer it takes me to open the passageway, the farther away Ulric will be when we do get out of here," she snapped.

Zella continued to look unconcerned. As if she hadn't noticed they were stuck behind a mountain of rocks while the sacrifice they needed was strolling away.

"He won't go far," Zella announced. "I destroyed his..." She paused. Although the woman had a remarkable grasp of the language, as well as the current culture, she occasionally struggled with the proper word. "Flying machine," she finally said. "And got rid of his companions."

Brigette frowned. They'd decided that she would be the one to lure her pack mate to the burrow while Zella made sure that no one lived to spread word about where or how Ulric had disappeared.

"The fairy can take them anywhere," she said between clenched teeth.

"She's not a fairy. She's a zephyr."

Zephyr? Brigette had never heard of them. "What's the difference?"

"She can't travel."

"You're sure?" Brigette immediately regretted the question as a fiery pain seared through her body. "Sorry," she rasped, shuddering as the agony slowly faded. *Shit.* She hated Zella. With the power of a thousand suns. For now, however, she needed her. "I just don't want to waste more time trying to hunt him down again," she muttered.

Zella sneered. "Unlike you, I don't allow my prey to escape."

Brigette glanced toward the massive cave-in that blocked the tunnel. "Do you think they're up there waiting for us?" she demanded in disbelief.

"I ensured that he will return no matter where he runs."

"What did you do?"

"I don't explain myself to servants."

Okay. That was it. Brigette didn't give a crap if the bitch could destroy her with a wave of her gnarled hand.

She wanted answers and she wanted them now.

Turning back, she glared at the woman. "You promised me I would be an alpha."

"You are."

"A leader without a pack?" Brigette hissed, waving her hand around the cramped burrow. "Stuck in this hellhole?"

Perhaps sensing Brigette was on the cusp of a complete meltdown, Zella straightened from the wall. "There's no need to chase after the Were," she assured Brigette.

"Why not?"

The wrinkled face tightened with annoyance, but Zella answered the question. "I can use my power to compel him to return."

Brigette widened her eyes. She'd spent the past five hundred years endlessly searching for Ulric, while being told over and over she was an utter failure, and Zella could have used her powers to bring him to the village?

If she'd still had command of her wolf, she would have ripped the woman to bloody shreds.

"Why didn't you do that before?"

Zella held up one finger. Brigette's nose curled as she realized it was coated with a dark red.

"I didn't have his blood." A terrifying smile curved the old woman's lips. "Now I do."

"So where is he?"

Zella nodded toward the pile of rocks. "Once you've cleared away the rubble and I've prepared the altar for the sacrifice, I will call for him."

Brigette frowned. Only an idiot would trust this woman. "I want what I was promised," she warned.

Zella released a sharp laugh. "Be assured, Brigette, you will get exactly what you deserve."

* * * *

Ulric slowed the ancient truck he'd "borrowed" from a human farmer. He'd also "borrowed" a pair of jeans and a flannel shirt along with a pair of boots that were a size too small. The seven-hour journey had been an agony. Not only had the vehicle jolted over the rough road with enough force to rattle his teeth. But it'd sent sharp pains from the wound on his side shooting through him.

Even worse was the suspicion that the crippling weakness that made it a struggle not to collapse into a weary puddle had nothing to do with his injury. And everything to do with the female seated next to him.

Thankfully, his memories of Chiron discussing the time he'd spent at his master's lair helped him to locate the castle on the edge of the cliff without having to backtrack too many times.

Pulling to a halt, he studied the sturdy structure that was obviously in the mad throes of reconstruction. There were newly restored walls that had been carved out of gray stone. And heavy shutters covering the windows. Plus, a pathway had been cleared over the moat and up the steep incline to the front door. But even with an intact roof, it had an air of abandonment.

It wasn't easy to sweep away five centuries of neglect in a few months.

Rainn glanced through the filthy windshield. "Do you think that's his lair?"

"Yeah," Ulric said.

He'd caught Tarak's scent as they turned onto the road leading to the castle. Plus the faint hint of salt that didn't come from the ocean. A mermaid.

Ulric pushed open the door of the truck and slid out. He grunted as a burning sensation crawled up the side of his body.

What the hell had the woman done to him?

He shook his head. That was a worry for later.

Rainn joined him, her gaze on the castle. "I don't think anyone is here."

Ulric sucked in a deep breath. Tarak's scent was muted, but it was impossible to determine if he was inside the castle.

"It's midday." He glanced overhead at the sun that was spilling a welcome warmth over them. Then he snorted. His years in Vegas had made him into a wimp. A brisk ocean breeze and he was shivering as if he was in the Antarctic. "He's probably tucked in some secure room below ground."

"Are we going inside?"

"No." Only a fool tried to enter a vampire's lair without his invitation. Who knew what sort of nasty surprises were waiting for them? "We need to find someplace to wait for nightfall."

Ulric glanced around the empty landscape. Their choices were limited. They could drive the truck to look for a local town. Or...

Suddenly he remembered a story that Chiron had told him long ago. He turned to walk toward the cliffs.

Rainn scurried behind him. "Where are you going?"

"Chiron lived here when Tarak first brought him into his clan," he said, walking along the edge of the cliff until he found the narrow path.

"That doesn't explain why we're doing the whole mountain goat thing again," she muttered, her voice strained as they headed down the steep, zigzagging trail.

He glanced over his shoulder, noticing her unexpected pallor. "Are you afraid of heights?" he asked in surprise.

She wrinkled her nose. "I prefer flat land."

"Why?"

She crouched low to the ground as she inched her way down the cliff. "When I was very young I used my magic to float for hours at a time. It was my favorite game."

Ulric kept his pace slow and steady. Not only because he didn't want to rush Rainn, but because his legs felt like noodles.

Damn. His weakness was accelerating.

"You could fly?" he asked, hoping to keep her distracted. Not only from her phobia of heights, but from noticing his stumbles.

She shook her head. "I could only float," she corrected. "But one day I was away from our hidden lair and I drifted too far. The wind caught me, and I was swept over a canyon. It would have been fine, but I hit a downdraft and before I knew what was happening, I plummeted to the ground."

Ulric winced. Rainn was always in complete command of any situation. It was difficult to remember that she was more fragile than most demons.

At least physically.

"Were you badly injured?"

"Yes." She grimaced. "And it took nearly a decade to fully heal. It was one of many times I wish I had the thick hide of a troll."

"You have your own powers," he assured her. "You rescued me in that burrow."

She shook her head, clearly not ready to discuss what'd happened. That was fine with him. It was going to take a while for him to process what he'd discovered.

Like a century. Or two.

"Where are we going?" she instead demanded.

"Before Tarak found him, Chiron lived in a cave for centuries," Ulric said. "When Tarak brought him here, he refused to sleep aboveground. Chiron told me that Tarak created a private bedroom for him in the caves beneath his castle so he could feel safe."

Near the bottom of the path, Ulric stumbled onto the rocky beach. He turned to grasp Rainn by her waist, gathering his waning strength, to set her gently on the ground next to him.

Together they headed toward the nearest cave carved into the cliff. It was empty, but Ulric crossed the cramped space to squeeze through a narrow crack. He hissed as his skin was scraped off his back. He was considerably wider than Chiron. Thankfully, Rainn had no problem following him into the tunnel that led deeper into the cliff.

They continued to travel in silence, both on hyperalert as they moved through the darkness. Ulric had allowed himself to be led into one trap. It wasn't happening again.

At last he climbed the shallow steps to enter a large cavern that had been dug into the hard granite.

Immediately a soft light filled the space, glowing from the crystals embedded in the ceiling. Magic? It had to be. The entire space looked as if it'd been a creation of fey enchantment.

There was a massive bed that had been hand carved out of driftwood, and heavy tapestries that lined the walls, with images of sundrenched meadows. There were delicate carpets to hide the hard floor, and trunks stacked in a corner. Ulric assumed they were Chiron's old belongings.

It was clearly a place that had been designed for maximum comfort.

Rainn moved forward, laying a tentative hand against the tapestry. "It's no wonder Chiron was so loyal to Tarak if he had this created for him."

"Yes." Ulric gave a slow nod, feeling a pang of guilt. How could he have ever been jealous of Chiron's devotion to Tarak? The vampire would never have been capable of offering Ulric a home if he hadn't been taught to care for others. "It's rare to have a master you can also call a brother," he said in rough tones.

Something in his voice must have alerted Rainn that he was struggling to stay upright.

"You need to rest," she said, reaching out to grasp his arm. "I'll keep watch."

"There's no need," he assured her.

She tugged him toward the bed. "We don't know how long it will take Zella and Brigette to dig out of the burrow."

Ulric willingly moved forward, flopping onto the mattress. It was that or collapse into a puddle of goopy exhaustion.

"The tunnel will flood with the afternoon tide," he reminded her.

Rainn frowned, busily crossing to the bottom of the bed to grab a blanket that was miraculously pristine. More magic.

"That won't stop them," she said, laying the blanket over his body.

He breathed a sigh of relief as he sank into the mattress. His body was starting to hurt. Everywhere.

"No, but the waves will erase our scent," he said.

"Okay." She straightened, her eyes growing misty.

A sure sign she was doing some sort of magic. Perhaps a web of air over the door. Or some invisible alarm system. That was fine with Ulric.

He wasn't offended. It wasn't that she didn't trust his judgment. She simply needed the security of her own magic protecting the hidden lair.

Reaching up, he grabbed her hand. The small movement wrenched his side, making him gasp in pain.

"I should go for help," she breathed.

The mere thought of her leaving the lair without him sent a jolt of panic through Ulric.

"No, I just need to rest." Before she could guess his intent, he gave a sharp tug on her hand.

She toppled onto the mattress, her expression annoyed even as she took care not to struggle against his grip. Was she afraid she would hurt him?

"You aren't this weak just because you're tired," she protested. "That woman must have poisoned you. I need to find someone—"

He interrupted. "There's actually another explanation."

She stilled, gazing at him in confusion. "What are you talking about?"

Ulric hesitated. He didn't want to tell her what was bothering him. Hell, he was trying to pretend that it was nothing more than a figment of his imagination.

But the fear that she might take off while he was sleeping meant he had to reveal the truth.

"What do you know about werewolves?" he asked.

"About as much as you know about zephyrs." She tried to tease. Did she sense the gravity of what he was about to tell her? "I know that Weres are born from pureblooded werewolves, while curs are humans who are transformed by the bite of a Were. Oh, and that you're short-tempered, impulsive, and arrogant."

He pretended to be outraged. "Short-tempered? I'm as mild as a—"

"Rabid dog?" she interrupted.

"I'm only rabid when someone pisses me off."

"Hmm." Her expression softened. "I also know you're loyal and fiercely protective of those you consider a part of your pack."

"That part is true."

Ulric carefully rolled onto his side so they were face-to-face. A mistake. He was instantly consumed with the acute awareness that seethed between them.

Sensations tingled through parts of him that shouldn't be tingled. At least not at this precise moment.

She was so...perfect. The pale beauty of her face. The misty gray eyes. The satin sheen of her dark hair. The fragile exterior that hid the steel beneath.

And that scent...He sucked in a deep breath, allowing it to sink deep inside him.

"Does this have something to do with your wound?" she demanded.

Unable to resist temptation, he reached out to brush a silky strand of hair from her cheek. "It does."

She froze, as if shocked by his light touch. "Ulric?"

His fingers skimmed downward, tracing the line of her jaw. "Werewolf females are strong. And when they are protecting their young there's nothing more lethal," he murmured. "But they don't have the same brute power of a male."

She studied him with blatant concern. As if wondering if he was slipping into delirium. "Are you talking about Brigette?"

"I'm talking about females in general."

"I thought we were discussing your wound."

He moved his hand to rest against the side of her neck. She was right. He did have a fever. He could feel it burning through his blood. But it wasn't the result of his wound. Or at least, not entirely.

"Rainn." His lips twisted with a humorless smile. "I'm making a disaster of this."

"I think you have a fever," she warned. "You should sleep."

Ulric swallowed a humorless laugh. The few times he'd considered this memorable moment, he'd assumed he'd have created the perfect setting. A romantic dinner for two. Candles. Expensive wine. Flowers piled around the room.

Instead they were on the run from a crazed spirit who was polluting the land. Hidden in a damp cave. And he was wounded and weak as a kitten.

Pathetic.

"I will rest," he promised. "But first you need to know what's happening to me."

She paused before giving a reluctant nod. "Okay."

His fingers traced the neckline of her sweater. It was soft, but not as soft as her pale skin.

"It's…" He faltered. How did you explain destiny? "Biology," he at last said, only to shake his head in frustration. That wasn't it. At least, that was only a small part of it. "Or perhaps it's magic," he amended. "Either way, it's a maddeningly wonderful thing."

She sucked in a sharp breath as his finger slid beneath the sweater to skim over the gentle swell of her breast. "Why is that?"

Ulric smiled. Her voice was unsteady as her heartbeat quickened. She wasn't immune to his touch.

"It ensures that when a male Were finds his true mate, he's incapable of forcing her to accept him," he murmured.

Her eyes darkened to smoke even as the scent of a spring rain spiked with arousal swirled through the cave. "How?"

He ran his fingers back up the curve of her throat. His fangs ached to be buried in her soft flesh. He didn't drink blood like a vampire, but his wolf was eager to claim this female. The primitive need to mark her was vibrating through his body.

"Until she accepts him, his power is leashed," he told her.

"So." She wrinkled her brow. "You think the wound is causing your body to think it has found its mate?"

Ulric swallowed his growl. Was she being deliberately obtuse? Surely she had to know that he was talking about her? Then, with an effort, he reminded himself that Rainn wasn't a werewolf. All of this was new to her.

"No." He firmly denied the suggestion that this was a trick of magic. "The weakness started before I was scratched."

She continued to study him in confusion. "Brigette?"

"Goddess, no!" he roared. Even if Brigette hadn't turned out to be a treacherous, evil bitch, he would never have felt the urge to mate with her.

They were family.

She blinked at his fierce response. "It can't be Zella."

"Enough," he snapped, thoroughly ruffled. If he'd thought this whole revelation of his mating urges had started off bad, it was now skidding toward complete disaster. "You know who it is, Rainn."

She sharply shook her head, her hands pressing against his chest. "No."

Ulric flinched. Then he groaned as the sudden movement tugged at his wound. He'd considered mortals to be incessant whiners. They always seemed to have some ache or pain.

Now he had a new appreciation for lesser beings who didn't automatically heal.

It not only felt like a hot poker was being shoved in his side, but it was draining with alarming tenacity what little strength he had left.

Forcing himself to count to ten, he managed to study Rainn with commendable calm. Yay, him.

"Why not?" he asked.

"I'm not a Were."

His gaze swept over her delicate features and down her slender curves that were instinctively arching toward his own. Her mind might try to deny the truth of his words, but her body was obviously less conflicted.

The knowledge sent jolts of sizzling pleasure through him. Even with the pain and weariness, his cock was hardening in anticipation.

Still, it wasn't enough. As much as he desired to roll her onto her back and sink deep into the moist heat between her legs, he wanted her heart. And her soul.

Nothing less would do.

"I know you accuse me of having more muscles than brains," he said in dry tones. "But I'm capable of recognizing that you're not a Were."

She flushed at his light teasing, but her expression remained tight with tension.

His fingers gently cupped her cheek, a dark dread spreading through his heart.

He hadn't expected her to squeal with delight at his confession. Well, he might have hoped for a squeal or two. But the panic in her wide eyes felt like a punch to the gut.

"Then how could I be your mate?" she demanded.

He pressed his lips to the center of her forehead, silently attempting to ease her anxiety.

"That's a mystery beyond my comprehension," he murmured, brushing his hand down the curve of her back.

"When did the weakness begin?" she demanded.

Ulric allowed his lips to drift over her temple and down to her cheek.

"During the flight to Wales," he admitted. "At first, I assumed I was weary from the run through the desert and then the shock of discovering that Brigette was still alive."

Her hands continued to lay against his chest, but they were no longer trying to push him away. Ulric was going to take that as a good sign. Right now, he was willing to cling to anything that could give him hope.

"I'm sure that was it," she hurriedly agreed.

"No, it only became worse when we reached the village."

"Brigette must have done something to you," she said.

"Impossible," he told her. "She doesn't have magic."

"Zella might be able to use her as a conduit for her powers. Or maybe—"

"Rainn." Ulric lifted his head, gazing down at her in wary confusion. "Why are you so anxious to dismiss the idea of being my mate?"

Her expression was impossible to read. She was better than a vampire at hiding her emotions.

"You've known me for twenty years," she said. "Why would it suddenly happen now?"

It was a legitimate question. Unfortunately, Ulric didn't have an answer. At least not one that made any sense to anyone who wasn't a Were.

"My wolf wasn't ready."

She waited, as if expecting him to continue. Ulric shrugged. That was all he had.

"And now it is?"

He laid his hand over hers, pressing her fingers tight against his chest. She might not be able to see his animal, but he could ensure that she felt the thunder of his heart and catch the musky scent that clung to his skin.

Inside, his wolf howled with hunger.

"Desperately ready," he admitted in rough tones.

Without warning, Rainn jerked her hands away. Her face had drained to a sickly white and her eyes were dull as slate.

"Ulric."

He resisted the urge to wrap her in his arms and tug her close. It wasn't his right. Not yet.

"Tell me what's wrong," he urged.

"I can't," she breathed. "I just...can't."

The dread solidified into a stark, riveting rejection. His wolf cringed inside him as something precious began to shrivel and die.

He'd heard of wolves being bonded with a partner who wouldn't or couldn't mate with them. It wasn't unusual for them to go into isolation. Or even will themselves to die.

Now he understood why.

As if sensing the soul-deep pain that was searing through him, Rainn parted her lips. Was she seeking to find the words to ease his agony?

Blessed goddess, the only thing worse than Rainn's rejection would be her pity.

"Shh." He pressed his fingers to her lips. "You don't have to say any more."

"Ulric."

Squeezing his eyes shut to avoid her shattered expression, Ulric halted his battle against the weariness. With shocking speed a darkness rose up to crash over him. As if he'd been holding it back by sheer will.

He was drifting into the welcome void when he felt something soft press against his lips.

A kiss?

His wolf whined in need, even as the man told himself he was being an idiot.

Rainn didn't want him.

He was alone.

For all eternity.

Chapter 12

Levet handed the book to Inga. It was tiny in her large hands, but there was something about it that made it appear bigger and heavier than it was. As if it was so important that it possessed its own aura.

He grimaced. Only a book with enormous power could do that.

"Can you read it?" he asked his companion.

Inga hesitated. She could obviously sense that it wasn't an ordinary book. Then, squaring the impressive width of her shoulders, she started to flip through the pages.

Her heavy brow furrowed in confusion. "It's a strange mishmash of languages." She tilted the book so Levet could see the various glyphs that had been sketched on the fragile parchment. "Look. This is harpy," she said. She turned to another page. "Here is troll." She searched toward the back of the book. "And these hieroglyphs are human."

Levet made a sound of surprise, pointing a claw at the flowing script with an elaborate border.

"That's gargoyle." He wrinkled his snout, barely capable of deciphering the words. "Really, really old gargoyle. I haven't seen such formal writing for thousands of years." Despite being a bunch of stodgy traditionalists, the language of the gargoyles had evolved over time. He lifted his head to meet Inga's steady gaze. "Why would a book be written by different species?"

"I have no idea," she admitted. "Maybe your vampire will have an explanation. You're welcome to take it to him."

"Non."

Inga looked confused. "Isn't that what you came here for?"

It was, of course. Okay, deep inside there'd been a secret, urgent desire to see Inga. But that was something he'd already decided not to ponder. Not when there was a more important reason for his need to visit this castle. After all, Ulric—and more importantly, Rainn—were in extreme danger. Plus, the nasty fog was destroying the land. What if it spread? Not even demons wanted to live in a toxic dump.

"*Oui*, but the reason I was sent here was because the other books had been turned to Cinderellas," he reminded her.

"Cinders," she corrected in absent tones.

"Exactly." Levet glanced around the small room. The layers of magic were a physical presence. "It is possible that removing the book from the protection of this space would leave it vulnerable to whatever destroyed the other copies."

"You're right," Inga instantly agreed. Levet inwardly preened at her readiness to accept that he was more than just another pretty face. He had brains and talent and nutty skills. "I suppose I could bring the vampire here," Inga continued, her tone reluctant. "But I need to warn my people. They're still jittery after Tarak killed their king."

Levet was puzzled. "I thought they were celebrating Riven's death. He was a nasty fish-man."

Inga gave an awkward shrug. The female might hate the previous king who'd used and abused her, but Levet sensed that she was still sensitive at the knowledge that his gruesome death at the hands of Tarak had led to her current position as queen.

It gave "climbing the corporate ladder" a whole new meaning.

"They were happy to have Riven off the throne, but they were disturbed to have him slaughtered by an outsider. And then I was chosen as their leader." Inga glanced down at her solid body stuffed in the stupid, gauzy gown. She sighed. "They've been very isolated down here. These changes are difficult for them to accept."

Levet sniffed. The mer-folk were idiots if they didn't adore their new leader.

"Then we will decipher it ourselves," he announced.

"Us?"

Why did she look surprised? Had she forgotten that he had single-handedly saved the world just a few years ago? Well, perhaps it had not been single-handed. Still, he and Inga could accomplish far more than any leech.

"We are both intelligent demons who have traveled throughout the world," he said.

She held out her arm, exposing the crude tattoo carved on her wrist. "I was a slave, not a tourist."

"Which only means that you had to adapt to all sorts of cultures."

She blinked, then a wry smile curved her lips. "I suppose that's true." With a determined step she moved to the corner of the room. Placing the book on the flat surface of a small desk, she waited for Levet to hop onto a chair so he could see.

"Do you smell that?" Levet demanded, reaching to touch the pyramids carved into the leather of the front cover.

She nodded. "Blood."

"Human blood."

Opening the book, Inga slowly turned the pages instead of flipping through them. There were several drawings. Most looked like a river that was painted a strange green. Like it was contaminated with an icky sludge.

She paused as they reached a page of sharp, angular glyphs. "This is ogre."

Levet leaned forward, catching Inga's cool, salty scent. It always refreshed him. Like a welcome breeze on a muggy night.

"What does it say?" he asked.

"Beware."

"Oh." What could scare an ogre? Levet shivered. He was fairly certain he didn't want to find out. "That is...ominous. What are we to beware of?"

Inga made a sound of frustration. "It doesn't really make any sense."

"Why?"

She jabbed her finger against a half circle with a dot over it. "This means birth." She moved to the next symbol, three wiggly lines. "And this means corruption."

"Birth of corruption?" Levet's mouth felt dry. Did it have something to do with the history of the ogres? Or the future? "Is there any explanation?"

"It's a warning about an evil." Inga glanced toward Levet, her expression bitter. "Which is ironic, considering it was written by an ogre."

Levet understood. Her father had been an ogre leader who'd been in love with her mermaid mother, but the rest of the tribe hadn't been happy with the relationship. They'd killed her father and sold Inga into slavery. Who wouldn't hold a grudge?

"Do you think they mean the Dark Lord?"

She shook her head. "The way it's written, it seems more like a taint than a physical creature."

Levet grimaced. "The woman I encountered was very real. Look." He pointed to the faint singe mark that lingered on his skin. The burning bands of magic had done more damage than he'd first realized.

Inga tapped her fingers on the desk, her brow furrowed. "I suppose the power might be capable of manifesting itself into a tangible form."

"Manifesting." Levet's tail twitched as he reached to turn the pages to the gargoyle section he'd glimpsed earlier. "Or infecting," he told her, pointing toward the flowing line of script.

"Yes," she agreed. "That makes more sense."

Levet wasn't sure any of this made sense. The creepy fog. The strange woman. The missing werewolf. "So is this evil infecting demons?"

Inga shrugged, pointing at a gilded design at the bottom of the page. "Is that the symbol for demon?"

"Non." The elaborate pattern of the design had simplified over the centuries, but Levet had no trouble recognizing it. "That stands for magic."

Inga jerked, her face paling at his explanation. "Infecting magic," she breathed.

"That doesn't sound good."

Inga shuddered. "I don't think it is."

Levet considered the strange fog that shrouded Ulric's old village. Was it feeding off the magic left behind by the werewolves? The thought made his tummy cramp. "Is there a way to stop it?"

Inga turned the pages, pausing to study the various languages and images before she was at the last chapter.

"The rest of the book is written in a language I don't recognize," she admitted.

Levet clicked his tongue. "Typical. We just get to the best part and *bam.*" He slapped his hands together. "We are left hanging."

"Now that is a shame," a voice drawled from behind them. "I never leave a female hanging at the best part."

Levet's wings quivered with a sudden burst of anger.

"You," he rasped, spinning on the desk to glare at the intruder.

Troy smiled, sashaying across the room.

Inga watched the imp with a lift of her brows. "How did you get in?"

Troy waved a languid hand toward the opening. "You left the doorway open."

"Oh." Inga grimaced, glancing toward the Tryshu in her hand. No doubt she was still trying to learn how to use the powerful artifact.

Levet didn't care how the imp had gotten in. He just wanted the aggravating creature to go away. "What are you doing here?" he demanded.

"I was bored. Plus, the queen has a full schedule." He flicked a dismissive glance over Levet. "She doesn't have time to be pestered by an interloper."

"Hey, I am no antelope."

Troy shook his head, turning toward Inga. "How do you bear him?"

Inga hunched her shoulders. "He grows on you."

"Like lichen?"

Levet cast a discreet glance over his toes and up his legs. There might be a little lichen. It wasn't his fault. He was a gargoyle. They were supposed to be mossy.

Hearing Troy's chuckle, Levet lifted his head with an annoyed frown. "I am going to turn you into—"

"Perhaps you can help us." Inga abruptly interrupted his threat, stepping toward the imp.

Troy strolled to stand directly in front of the ogress. "Of course I can. I am a handy sort of fellow. I have talents most males can only dream of possessing."

"You told me you were a diplomat," Inga said.

Levet snorted in disbelief. "Troy? A diplomat?"

"I was. A thankless job," Troy answered, his gaze never wavering from Inga. "Who wants to be polite to a tribe of evil-tempered trolls?"

"I wish they had eaten you," Levet muttered.

Inga pointed a finger at the book. "Do you recognize this?"

Troy stepped forward, brushing Levet aside to study the strange glyphs. "It's dragon," he at last announced.

"*Pfft.*" Levet flapped his wings in disgust. "I would recognize dragon."

"Ancient dragon," Troy insisted. "I recognize it from a vase I—" He bit off his words before clearing his throat. "From a vase I acquired from a lovely jinn who claimed that it had been in her family since the birth of this world."

Levet wanted to argue, but he kept his lips pressed together. The aggravating imp seemed to know what he was talking about.

"What does it say?" Inga demanded.

"Hmm." Troy's lush, fruity scent filled the air as he concentrated on translating the symbols. "Something about protecting the door that is no door."

"Door that is no door?" Levet scoffed. "That doesn't make any sense."

Troy pointed toward the book. "I'm just reading what's on the page. You can discuss your confusion with the dragon."

Levet sniffed. "I might very well do that," he said. "As it happens, I am a close personal friend of Baine."

"Go." Troy waved his hand in a shooing motion. "Tell Baine I said hello."

"That is it." Levet gathered his magic. Perhaps a large wart on the end of Troy's nose would wipe away that smug smile.

His glorious plan was interrupted as Inga abruptly headed out of the room. Was the female angry? Probably. And it was all Troy's fault.

Stupid imp.

With a curse, Levet jumped off the desk and hurried after the ogress.

"Where are you going?" he demanded as he scurried to keep up with her long strides.

"I've seen that symbol before."

Ah. She wasn't angry. *Good.* He didn't care what others might think of him. But he didn't like the thought that she found him annoying.

"Where?" he asked, doing his best to ignore the imp following them.

"The treasure room," Inga said, leaving the library and heading toward the royal chambers.

Several guards patrolled the hallways wearing the odd armor that looked like metal scales and carrying tridents. Inga waved them away, waiting until she, Levet, and Troy were alone before she halted in front of a door with a heavy lock.

Holding out the Tryshu, she touched it against the wood. Instantly it slid open. Levet was impressed. And a little jealous. He wished he had a magical trident.

Inga entered the room, followed by Levet and then Troy. A soft glow of fairy lights filled the space at their entrance. The delicate balls of light floated above their heads, reflecting off the precious gems that encrusted the ceiling. The walls were covered from floor to ceiling in vivid, magnificent frescos. And the floor was pure marble flecked with gold.

But it was the stacks of chests that were the most impressive.

They were stuffed with coins, jewels, carved coral, and rare magical artifacts. The place looked like a dragon's hoard. Only with an excess of pearls.

Troy whistled as he picked up a golden nugget the size of a football. "Well, well. You have a substantial dowry for when you decide to claim a consort, my dear."

Inga scowled. "This belongs to the mer-folk."

Troy shrugged. "And you're the queen."

Inga's eyes flashed red. "If I have to buy a consort, I don't want one."

Levet stomped to stand at her side. The mere idea that she might purchase a mate was...outrageous. Unthinkable.

Completely, utterly, absolutely unthinkable.

"You are so rude. Any male would be fortunate to be chosen by Inga," he informed the imp. "Besides, she has no interest in taking a consort."

Inga sent him an odd glance before sharply shaking her head.

"It's over here," she muttered, leading them to a distant corner.

Levet ignored the priceless treasure stuffed into the room. He had no interest in riches. Yet another reason he'd been voted out of the Gargoyle Guild. He was far more intrigued by the paintings that covered the walls.

"Did your grandfather paint all of these?" he asked.

Inga nodded. "Yes."

"It is easy to see who gifted you with your own talent," he told the ogress.

Inga blushed, clearly pleased by his words. "I'm discovering there are many hidden frescoes that tell the history of the mer-folk," she said, halting to push aside several treasure chests that must have weighed a ton. Then, bending down, she pointed at the wall. "You see?"

Levet and Troy stepped forward to study the painting. Surprisingly it represented two massive dragons in the middle of an epic battle. They were both an iridescent green with leathery wings, and both had flames shooting out of their mouths as terrified sea creatures fled in panic.

Levet shivered. He could almost feel the heat from the flames and the fear of the hapless victims caught in the middle of the battle. The fresco didn't just tell the story. It captured the feelings of the moment.

A rare talent, indeed.

Then Troy broke into his bemusement by reaching out to lightly brush his finger along the bottom of the wall. "It does look like the same symbol," he murmured, tracing the intersecting ovals that looked like a sideways 8.

"I've been studying the frescoes over the past weeks. I hoped they would give me a better understanding of my people. When I saw this one I just assumed this picture represented the dragon battles that nearly destroyed the mer-folk," Inga said, referring to the war that had massacred a frightening number of mer-folk and sent them into hiding in this isolated lair. "I noticed the symbol, but I didn't know what it meant."

"Perhaps the dragons were fighting something that was trying to get out of the door," Levet suggested.

Inga's features twisted with dislike. She was never going to be a fan of dragons. Or ogres. Or vampires...

"It's just as likely that their battle damaged it and released the evil," she muttered. Then, without warning, she squared her shoulders. "I will see if I can discover the doorway."

Levet and Troy stiffened, staring at Inga in horror. Then they spoke in unison.

"What?"

Inga looked confused by their outrage. "I've also studied the histories of the dragon wars. I think I can find this place."

"We do not even know if it is connected to the fog," Levet pointed out.

Inga shrugged. "There's one way to find out."

Troy clicked his tongue. "At least assure me that you're not planning to go alone?"

Inga looked offended by the question. She hadn't been raised to be a royal. She was a strong, fierce warrior who was used to taking care of herself.

"I'm not risking my guards," she protested.

"That's what they are for, my queen," Troy reminded her.

Inga shook her head. "It's my decision to go into danger. I want them to stay here and protect my people."

Levet's heart felt as if it was somewhere in his toes. He recognized that tone. Inga was going to look for the door. End. Of. Story.

"I will go with you," he said, his wings drooping.

Troy stared at him with blatant incredulity. "You?"

Levet puffed out his chest. "Why not me?"

"You will sink like the proverbial stone."

"I have magic," Levet protested. "Besides, it is none of your concern."

Inga cleared her throat. "Levet."

Suddenly angry, Levet planted his fists on his hips. "You can take me with you, or I can follow."

Inga blinked, seemingly confounded by his determination. "Fine," she at last muttered, her cheeks flushed. "I need to put on my armor."

Moving with remarkable speed for a demon of her size, Inga scurried from the room. Levet watched her depart, not entirely certain what had just happened.

Granted, he was a hero. And a Knight in Shining Armor. It was only natural he would offer his services.

But, quite honestly, the thought of traveling to some remote location at the bottom of the ocean to confront an evil capable of infecting magic…

Well, it was enough to dampen even his formidable courage.

He was jerked out of his dark thoughts when he felt a hand clamping down on his shoulder.

"Try to keep her from getting killed," Troy drawled. "I have plans for that female."

Chapter 13

Ulric was lost.

Standing in the thick mist, he struggled to recall how he'd gotten there. Something that would have been easier if his brain didn't feel as if it was stuffed with the same fog that swirled around him.

He had a vague memory of running through the desert. He'd felt hot and sweaty and gloriously free. He'd even howled at the moon. All right, it was cliché, but what the hell. It satisfied the heart of his animal.

And after that he'd returned to Dreamscape. He wanted to be in the hotel before Chiron disappeared into his private rooms. Then what? He'd strolled into the main casino and...

Ulric's heart slammed against his chest. Of course. He remembered now.

Brigette.

The female Were had been walking across the floor as if she had no idea that she'd just turned his world upside down.

His family hadn't been utterly destroyed, he'd realized with a flare of elation. At least one member had survived. So where was she? And how had he gone from the casino to this gray nothingness?

Forcing himself to stand still, Ulric closed his eyes. Then, he concentrated on his wolf. The animal's senses were far more acute than his human half. He waited for the familiar surge of raw, primitive power, but it never came. Ulric's breath lodged in his throat.

He could feel his beast. It was curled deep inside him. But he couldn't touch him. As if there was a mysterious barrier between them.

Clenching his hands into tight fists, Ulric refused to give in to the temptation to panic. His wolf was there. It was just muffled.

A hint of musk suddenly teased at his nose. Whirling around, Ulric watched as the fog thinned and then parted to reveal the female Were.

Brigette.

His heart swelled with joy. Thank the goddess. She hadn't been a figment of his imagination. She was real.

His avid gaze swept over her, absorbing the long crimson hair that framed her familiar features. It wasn't until she was standing directly in front of him that he noticed the smudge on her cheek and the dust that marred her long robe.

A strange unease tainted his euphoria.

He didn't know why. Were's weren't like vampires—they didn't mind a little dirt and grime. In fact, when he was in his animal form he loved to roll in the warm desert soil.

Still, the sight sent a chill creeping down his spine.

"There you are, Ulric." Brigette smiled, but it oddly didn't reach her eyes. "I've been searching for you."

"Where am I?"

"Lost."

He frowned. He already knew he was lost. "But…" His words faded away as a burning sensation drew his attention. Peeling up his shirt, he studied the deep scratches on his side. They were leaking blood. Why weren't they healing? He glanced back up. "How did I get here?"

"You wandered away from me."

"Hmm." That seemed…unlikely. Why would he wander away? He had so many questions to ask her. They were spinning through his head so fast they were making him dizzy.

Why would he leave?

"Ulric?"

Brigette's voice clawed at him. He felt unmoored. As if he'd been cut off from the links that bound him to reality.

"Yeah?"

"We need to go."

Go. His sluggish brain tried to grapple with what she was asking of him. "Go where?"

"Home."

"You mean the hotel?"

She shook her head with obvious impatience. "No, *our* home."

Ulric flinched. He didn't like to think about his village. Not after the massacre. "It's gone."

"We're going to rebuild it." She held out her hand. "Together. Isn't that what you want?"

It should be, right?

"Yes." He forced out the word.

"Then follow me," she urged.

He was stepping forward when he caught the sudden scent of a summer mist. It stirred a memory. A pale face surrounded by sleek black hair and wide gray eyes. His heart quivered with longing.

He couldn't leave her behind.

"Wait," he breathed.

Brigette's growl of frustration echoed through the fog. "What's wrong?"

"There's someone…"

"No." Brigette's tone was urgent. "There's just you and me."

"Rainn." The named reached out to wrap around his heart. Anchoring him in place.

Brigette cursed, glancing over her shoulder. What was she looking for? Then without warning the fog thickened in his mind. As if someone had opened the top of his skull and was pouring it in.

The name disappeared, along with the pretty face.

Nothing remained but Brigette.

"Come, Ulric," she urged. "Let's go home."

"Home."

He walked forward.

* * * *

Rainn had intended to leave the bed as soon as Ulric fell asleep. Instead, she'd cuddled close, trailing her fingers over his face, which was flushed with fever.

Worry had gnawed inside her like a cancer. Along with an aching sense of regret.

She hadn't meant to hurt Ulric. That was the last thing she would ever want. But he'd caught her off guard with his sudden claim that she was his mate. What woman's brain wouldn't have turned to mush? It wasn't like gorgeous, sexy males told her every day that she was the eternal love of their lives. Plus, he'd already started the brain-mushing process with his soft caresses and the press of his lips against her forehead. Her body had been on fire. And it hadn't been caused by a magical fever.

Just good, ol'-fashioned lust.

She'd planned to calmly explain that she couldn't risk making any decisions for her future until she'd finished her quest. That had to take precedence. But she completely and utterly bungled it.

Her stomach had instantly twisted with sick remorse at the sight of the raw pain that had flared through his eyes. She might as well have taken a knife and stuck it in his heart. But even as she'd tried to clarify that her people were depending on her, he'd closed his eyes and fallen asleep.

Or perhaps he was unconscious. Either way, she'd found herself unable to leave the bed. Not only did she have to wait for the sun to set so she could track down Tarak and ensure he found someone to heal Ulric, but she didn't want to return to battle Zella without the opportunity to make him listen to her explanation.

Unfortunately, she'd miscalculated her level of weariness. Even as she'd rehearsed exactly what she would say when he awoke, she was drifting into a deep sleep.

It wasn't until she heard the sound of a voice echoing through the cavern that she was jolted awake.

Blinking in confusion, she sat up. How long had she been asleep? A few minutes? Hours? Not that it mattered. She was more interested in why Ulric was standing in the middle of the floor. And why he was talking to himself.

"Ulric?"

He ignored her, his gaze focused on the far wall as he muttered something about home.

Rainn climbed out of bed, heading toward the male. Then abruptly she halted, a burst of fear exploding through her. Either his wound was causing Ulric to hallucinate, or he was talking to someone she couldn't see.

Both scenarios terrified her.

"Ulric." Jumping forward, she grabbed his arm as he started walking toward the tunnel. "What's going on?"

Nothing. He didn't even glance in her direction. Then, without warning, he simply disappeared.

A portal?

She stood in the center of the cave.

Why hadn't she sensed it was there? Even if she couldn't make a portal, she could tell when one had opened.

Then realization hit her with the force of a freight train.

Zella.

Just for a second, she was frozen in place. What did she do? There was no way for her to follow through the portal. And while she might be certain they were headed back to the burrow, it would take her hours to get there.

Too long to prevent Ulric from being sacrificed.

Muttering a string of curses, Rainn dashed out of the cavern and through the tunnels that were still half-filled with tidewater. Once on the beach, she glanced around, realizing that the sun had just set beyond the horizon. Dammit. She'd had no idea that so much time had passed.

Wading through the water to the pathway, she gritted her teeth and began the steep climb to the top of the cliff. She didn't have time to think about her fear of falling. Or even the futility of her swift scramble up the damp rocks. She was going back to the village to destroy Zella.

One way or another.

Awkwardly pulling herself over the edge of the cliff, she was still in the process of standing upright when she felt herself being lifted off the ground.

She screeched in frustration more than fear as she watched a dark-haired vampire step out of a portal, followed by a much larger leech and two females.

She didn't have time for this. Gathering her power, she struck out, slamming the air sharply against the vampire's chest. He grunted in surprise, stumbling back as he released his hold on her.

Rainn felt herself falling, but she didn't bother to ease her landing onto the hard ground. She'd already been forced to waste enough of her strength. And with the massive, golden-haired vampire charging toward her, she didn't have to guess whether or not she was going to need it.

But before the male could take more than a few steps, the other vampire abruptly stepped in his path.

"No, Cyn," the male rasped. "This must be Rainn." He waited for her wary nod. "I'm Tarak," he told her, waving his hand toward the female with long, pale hair with blue highlights. "This is my mate, Waverly." He gestured toward the large male. "This is Cyn, the clan chief of Ireland, and his mate, Princess Fallon." He took a step toward her. "How did you get here?"

Rainn battled back the urge to ignore the question and make a mad dash for the truck. Although she'd never met Chiron's master, she knew he could be trusted to help her. And more importantly, that his mate had an ability to open portals.

Exactly what she needed.

"We managed to escape from Zella," she muttered.

The four demons frowned in confusion. "What's a Zella?" Tarak demanded.

"The dark spirit that destroyed Ulric's village." Rainn waved an impatient hand. "She's working with Brigette to open a doorway."

CONQUER THE DARKNESS 123

Tarak's expression remained confused, but he latched on to the most pertinent point of her rambling. "A doorway to what?"

"Evil."

"Evil?" The large vampire made a sound of disgust. "That's a little vague."

Rainn clenched her hands into tight fists. She couldn't afford to waste her energy just to topple the clan chief of Ireland on his ass. "All I know is that they need Ulric's blood to open it."

Tarak glanced around, easily capable of seeing through the shadows that now draped the landscape. "Where is he?"

Her heart twisted with pain. "Gone."

Something that might have been suspicion tightened Tarak's features. "But he was here. I sensed him triggering the alarms I set around the lair, but I couldn't return until the sun set."

"He disappeared."

"How?" Tarak demanded.

"We were asleep in the cavern under the cliff. I woke up when I heard Ulric talking to someone I couldn't see."

She was still babbling, but who could blame her? She could physically feel each second ticking past.

She had to get to Ulric.

"They were invisible?" Waverly asked, her tone perfectly serious. As if she wouldn't be surprised to discover they had enemies who could hide their presence.

She forced herself to take a deep breath. She was only making matters worse. "Either invisible or on the other side of the open portal."

"Impossible," Tarak snapped. "I have layers of magic around the lair, including the cavern. They prevent any unwanted guests. It was only because of Ulric's intimate connection with Chiron that the spell didn't prevent him from entering."

Rainn was shaking her head before Tarak finished speaking. "The spirit has powers that none of us understand. I doubt any traditional magic could halt her."

There was a short silence as they absorbed the impact of her words. It was Waverly who at last asked the obvious question.

"They took Ulric?"

"Yes." Rainn wrapped her arms around her waist, suddenly chilled by the brisk breeze blowing off the ocean. "I tried to stop him, but he looked like he was in some sort of trance."

"Damn." Tarak squared his shoulders. "We need to get back to the village."

"I can take us there," Waverly offered.

Relief crashed through Rainn, along with a fresh batch of impatience. It was almost as if she could feel Ulric deep inside her, urging her to hurry.

"I'll go with you," Cyn offered.

"No." Tarak shook his head. "Levet might actually find something that will help us defeat the...whatever the hell it is," he said. "He'll be returning to your lair to find us."

Cyn didn't argue. "Okay. Take care."

Rainn's eagerness to leave was briefly overshadowed by her concern for the tiny gargoyle. "Where is Levet?"

Tarak grimaced, as if the mere mention of the gargoyle gave him a sour stomach.

"He's searching the libraries in the mer-folk castle," Waverly answered. "We believe there is a book that might offer information about what caused the decay that consumed Ulric's village, but most copies have been magically destroyed. We hope that the protection that surrounds my homeland will have preserved the book if it's there."

"Oh." Rainn wasn't sure she entirely understood. And right now, she really didn't care. As long as Levet was safe. "We need to go."

Waverly lifted her arm, then waved it in a swooping motion. Rainn felt the familiar tingle of magic wash over her as the air was split to reveal the narrow opening. She hurried forward, despite Tarak's warning to allow him to go first. She didn't have time to deal with his male ego. The need to get to Ulric was an overwhelming compulsion.

Still, she wasn't completely out of her mind. Once she was through the portal she waited for Tarak and Waverly to join her. Once they'd rescued Ulric, she was going to depend on them to get the injured Were to safety while she found a way to destroy Zella.

Tarak moved to stand beside her, muttering a curse. Whether it was at the sight of the thick fog that boiled just ahead of them, or because Rainn had refused to let him play the role of the big, bad male, she didn't know.

A second later, Waverly was joining them.

"I can't get us through the barrier," she said, her pretty face twisting with distaste at the foul smell.

"I can," Rainn announced. "Follow me."

Jogging at an angle away from the fog, Rainn headed for the edge of the cliff. She could only hope that the opening was still there. Otherwise they were screwed.

They'd inched along the edge for several feet when the fog finally thinned. Rainn released a shaky breath of relief.

Thank the goddess.

Tarak peered into the darkness, his face tight with concern.

"You can stay here if you want," Rainn offered.

She understood that the vampire wasn't worried for himself. It was the beautiful mermaid that was obviously causing him to hesitate.

Tarak continued to study the rotting landscape visible through the swirling mist.

"We can't be sure that Ulric is inside. This might be a trap."

Rainn shook her head. As soon as she'd stepped out of the portal she'd been able to feel Ulric. It was as tangible as if he was physically reaching out to touch her.

"He's in there."

Tarak sent her a glance that was more curious than suspicious. "How do you know?"

"I can sense him."

"You're sure?"

"Yes, he…" Her words trailed away, a blush staining her cheek.

It was idiotic, but the thought of discussing Ulric's most private emotions felt like a betrayal.

She sensed a gentle touch on her arm as Waverly stood next to her. The mermaid's soft scent wrapped around her, easing the foul odor that was putrefying the air.

"Rainn?" she prompted.

Rainn grimaced. She had to explain. These two were risking their lives. They deserved the truth.

"Ulric is convinced that I'm his mate."

Tarak and Waverly looked more baffled than shocked.

"Should I offer my congratulations?" Tarak demanded.

She waved away the question. "I can sense his wolf. It's reaching out to me."

Tarak nodded. As if suddenly understanding. Then, he glanced at his mate. "Waverly—"

"Are we a team?" she interrupted. Clearly she knew exactly what he was about to say.

His jaw tightened, but he was wise enough not to speak the words that were clearly on the tip of his tongue. "Yes, we're a team."

Rainn arched her brows. The vampire was smarter than she expected.

"Good." Waverly reached beneath her sweater to pull out a small trident.

Rainn had never seen anything like it, but she could feel the magic that hummed around the weapon.

"I'm ready," Waverly announced.

Rainn nodded, then without giving herself time to consider what was waiting for them, she entered the fog.

Chapter 14

Warily, Brigette watched as Ulric stepped out of the portal. She clenched the silver dagger she'd stolen from her father just before the mongrels had attacked the village. It was magically enhanced to ensure the blade would penetrate even the thickest armor. And while it had been created to battle trolls and orcs, it was equally lethal to Weres.

It was all well and good for Zella to claim that she had complete control over the dangerous male, but Brigette knew who would pay the price if the old woman was wrong.

Zella had no concern for anyone or anything beyond her own single-minded obsession with destroying the barrier that kept her trapped.

Of course, if Brigette were being honest, she would admit that she would destroy Zella in a heartbeat to achieve her own goals. She'd already sacrificed her family. Clearly, she hadn't been cursed with the tedious need for loyalty. Or morality. Only fools allowed such weaknesses to rule their lives.

Now she braced herself. One hint that Ulric was about to come to his senses, and she was sinking the blade into the center of his heart. She believed in killing first and asking questions later.

"Tell him to lie on the altar," Zella commanded.

Zella had used a portion of the rocks that had fallen during the cave-in to create a long, four-foot-wide platform. She'd even forced Brigette to help her arrange it directly in front of the skeleton. As if it wasn't bad enough that her hands were still raw from clearing the tunnel.

Once the woman was satisfied with the stupid thing, she'd created the portal. But obviously she wasn't as clairvoyant as she liked to pretend.

The opening had led them to Ulric, but neither of them could penetrate the magic that was surrounding him.

It'd been left to Brigette to try and coax him into the portal. And now she was still expected to get the Were into place.

Really, what was the point of Zella if Brigette was expected to do all the hard work?

"Ulric, I need you to lie down," she commanded between clenched teeth.

He swayed, gazing at her with clouded eyes. "Why?"

Good question. She didn't bother to glance at Zella for the answer. Although the older woman easily adapted to look and sound like a modern-day human, there was always something "off" about her. Brigette didn't want the woman alerting Ulric that he was walking into a trap.

"Because you're tired," she said in a cooing voice.

He swayed as if he was about to collapse. "I am."

"Then lie down."

There was a long silence as he continued to sway from side to side.

"No," he at last rasped. "Rainn. Where is she?"

Zella clicked her tongue in annoyance. "The hold of the female is greater than I expected."

Brigette frowned. Zella was right. After the portal was closed behind Ulric, any hint of the mysterious female should have disappeared. But the misty, summer scent remained embedded in Ulric's skin.

"I can smell her. As if…" Brigette's words ended with a low hiss.

"What?" Zella demanded.

"She's his mate."

Zella sent her an aggravated glance. "This would have been a lot easier if you'd killed her like you were supposed to."

Anger boiled through Brigette. She wasn't sure why the knowledge that Ulric had found his mate was pissing her off. She'd decided a long time ago she didn't want to be permanently tied to any male.

It had to be the fact that this male had been out there living his life, having a great time with his precious friends, while she'd been…A humorless laugh was wrenched from her throat. *Just be honest.* She'd been a damned servant to the crazy bitch who was glaring at her as if she was a bug.

"Why didn't *you*?" she challenged.

Flames danced around Zella's hands. "You forget your place, servant."

Brigette tilted her chin, refusing to back down. "Are you going to finish this or not?"

There was a dangerous silence before Zella was turning her attention back to Ulric. Heat surged in the already smothering cavern as she intensified her hold on the male.

"Ulric, you must lie down," Brigette said, her tone firm. "It's the only way to save the village. To save your family."

Sweat dripped down her face as he unconsciously battled against Zella's magic.

"No. They're gone." He lifted his hand to press against his side. Brigette could smell the blood of his open wound. "It's all gone."

"Listen to me." Brigette cautiously moved forward. Then, when he didn't shift into his wolf and tear her to shreds, she placed a hand on his arm. "You can prevent the massacre. All you have to do is lie down."

He released a low growl as she steadily pulled him toward the altar. In the grips of Zella's power, he stiffly climbed onto the flat rock and lay down. Brigette shuddered as the musk of his wolf filled the air. It was muted. A caged, wild animal who was furiously trying to get free.

Just like her own...

Another burst of anger flared through her. So much sacrifice.

She held the dagger over her head, needing a means to release her fury.

"Shall I do the honors?" she demanded.

Zella moved with remarkable speed, pushing Brigette to the ground. "Don't be an idiot," she snarled.

"What the hell?" Brigette surged upright, trying to dust the new layer of filth from her robe.

"His blood is the key to unlocking the door."

Brigette squashed a crazed impulse to slam the dagger in the woman's throat. Nothing could kill Zella as far as she knew—the spirit was impervious to weapons.

Besides, she needed the woman. At least until she got the powers she'd been promised.

After that? All bets were off.

"That's what I just offered," she snapped.

Zella moved forward, ripping off Ulric's shirt to reveal the deep gashes. Blood sluggishly dripped down his side, hitting the altar with a loud sizzle.

"We can't kill him until the spell has been destroyed."

"How long will it take?"

"As long as it takes."

Brigette glared at Zella. Dammit, she was tired of waiting. For over five hundred years she'd been told to do as she was commanded. To be patient. To wait for her ultimate prize.

It was one excuse after another.

She was done, done, done.

"And then?"

"And then what?"

Brigette hissed with rage. "You've promised that once the doorway was opened, I would be given the power to rule my own pack."

Zella shrugged. "In time."

"No, I'm tired of waiting." Brigette held the dagger over Ulric's chest. "I want to be away from this place."

Flames danced in Zella's eyes. But even as Brigette braced herself for her inevitable punishment, the woman's head swiveled toward the cleared tunnel.

"Perhaps you're right," she murmured.

Brigette lowered the dagger. "You're going to give me the magic?"

"Yes."

"Seriously?"

"Don't you trust me?" Zella taunted.

Brigette laughed. Was that a joke? "No, I don't trust you. Why now?"

Zella waved a gnarled hand. "We're no longer alone."

Brigette stiffened, tilting back her head as she drew in a deep breath. "The zephyr," she rasped. "How did she get here so fast? You said she couldn't create a portal."

Zella closed her eyes, no doubt reaching out with her senses. "She isn't alone."

She wasn't. Brigette finally caught the scents of the approaching demons.

"A vampire." Her stomach twisted with dread. "And something else." She frowned. The smell was…salty rather than fruity. "Another sprite?"

An emotion that might have been genuine fear darkened Zella's eyes. "A mermaid."

Mermaids were real? And more amazing, Zella was obviously afraid of them.

Damn. Why hadn't she known about the fishy demons? Any creature that had the power to unnerve Zella was worthy of her interest. After all, she'd been desperate to find some sort of leverage over the woman for centuries. Just to ensure that she wasn't cheated.

"You can deal with the intruders," Zella announced.

"Me?" Brigette jerked in shock. "Alone?"

"It should be simple enough once I've given you the power you've been so eager to acquire."

Brigette stared at the woman in outrage. She knew the woman was evil. That had been obvious from the day they'd first met. But now she was beginning to suspect that she was also a total whack job.

"I'll be able to defeat a vampire, a zephyr, and a mermaid?" she demanded, her voice dripping with sarcasm. "At the same time?"

The woman shrugged. "That's what I just said."

Brigette snorted. "When I agreed to this partnership, I accepted the sacrifice of my family. I even accepted the endless years of searching for the pack mate who'd escaped. But I'll be damned if I'm going to become cannon fodder just so you can escape your prison."

Zella looked confused. "Cannon fodder?"

"An expendable casualty in your personal war."

Zella waved her hand in a dismissive motion. "Don't be stupid. Why would I allow you to be killed now? I still have need of you."

Brigette faltered. "I'll be able to defeat three powerful demons at the same time?" she pressed.

"There will be nothing you can't destroy."

She should be thrilled. Hell, she should be doing cartwheels. Zella had promised her power, but the old woman had never said that she could turn Brigette into a killing machine.

Instead raw fear pounded through her.

She wanted power. Desperately. But she didn't want to be turned into some sort of freak show. Hey, she might be a demon, but she had her standards.

"I..." Brigette stopped and licked her lips. How did they get so dry?

Zella's creepy laugh echoed through the cavern. "You're not going to chicken out, are you? After waiting so long for your reward?"

Brigette backed away. "What's this power going to do to me?"

"Ah." Zella reached out. "A question you should have asked a long time ago."

"Wait." Brigette held up her hands, but they were no protection against the wave of flames that rose from the ground. She cursed as they encircled her, spinning faster and faster. The heat seared her skin, making it feel as if she was melting. And the smell. It was like having her face shoved in a cesspit.

But none of that compared to the agony of having her insides ripped apart as a molten lava poured through her veins.

Brigette tilted back her head and screamed.

* * * *

Rainn stopped in her tracks as the sound of a scream penetrated the fog. It was filled with a pure agony that raised the hairs on the nape of her neck. It sounded like a dog in its death throes.

Tarak stood at her side, trying to peer through the gray mist. "What the hell?"

"Brigette," Rainn breathed. She didn't know how she could be so certain. But she was.

Tarak frowned. "I thought she was working with the spirit?"

"Maybe she hit her expiration date," Rainn said.

The screams abruptly ended, leaving behind a heavy silence. Then, an unexpected howl vibrated through the air.

"Or maybe she's just pissed off," Tarak muttered.

Rainn grimaced. As much as she might want to personally kill the treacherous female for betraying Ulric, she couldn't deny that her destiny would be considerably easier without having to worry about the female Were.

"The burrow is this way," she muttered, leading her companions toward the center of the fog.

Their feet crunched over the brittle ground, sending up puffs of smothering dust. Around them an occasional tree could be glimpsed through the miasma, the trunks twisted and the branches rotting. Even the puddles of water were green and brackish.

"Dammit," Tarak ground out. "This is worse than I imagined. How could one creature create such damage?"

Rainn felt an icy breeze brush over her as Tarak took in the broken landscape. But it was swiftly smothered by the claustrophobic heat.

"She's much more than just a creature," Rainn reminded him.

"It has to be stopped," Waverly said, her voice thick with disgust.

Tarak reached to grab his mate's hand, tugging her closer to his tense body. "Agreed."

"First we rescue Ulric, and then I'll deal with the spirit," Rainn assured them.

"Wait." Tarak reached out to halt Rainn's brisk jog. "Is that Brigette?"

It took Rainn a second to make out the form that had suddenly appeared. She didn't have vampire-vision, but as the mist swirled, she could make out the tall, muscular form and the brilliant red hair.

"Yes," she said, her eyes narrowing. What was pulsating around the female Were? "Something's different about her," she muttered.

"You mean the fact that she's glowing?" Tarak demanded.

Rainn shook her head. Brigette wasn't glowing. Instead there seemed to be a living force that moved and crawled over her skin.

"It's an aura," she at last said.

Tarak sent her a confused frown. "Magic?"

"Darkness." Rainn had a bad taste in her mouth. As if the taint in the air was becoming a tangible force. "I've never felt anything like it."

"Stay back," Tarak commanded. "I'll get rid of her."

Rainn ignored his arrogant assumption that he should be the one to take charge. It wasn't because he was male. It was because he was a vampire. They were almost as bad as Weres. She was far more concerned that he was about to do something idiotic.

Before she could protest, however, Waverly had moved to stand directly in front of her mate. "No, Tarak." She placed her hands flat on his chest. "You can't touch her."

The vampire was instantly offended. "I can handle a Were. Even if she is glowing."

Waverly glanced over her shoulder, her expression troubled. "I think the darkness around her is..."

Tarak pulled back his lips, revealing his massive fangs. "What?"

"Poison," Rainn answered.

Tarak shrugged. "I'm impervious."

Rainn shook her head. "Not to this. It's not just a poison, it's..." She struggled for a way to explain the evil she could feel surrounding Brigette. "It's a mystical toxin."

"She's right," Waverly insisted, clearly capable of sensing the same darkness as Rainn. "You can't touch her."

Tarak glanced toward Rainn. "What is it?"

"I don't know, but it feels the same as whatever is annihilating this land," she said.

"How is that possible? A Were doesn't possess magic." Tarak's features twisted with disgust. "Or toxic auras."

It was the same question nagging at Rainn. Brigette might have been a smug bitch when they'd been trapped in the burrow, but she hadn't been coated in evil.

"I have no idea," she confessed. "She wasn't like this earlier."

Waverly looked worried. "Maybe we're too late."

"No." The denial burst out of her with shocking force, echoing eerily through the thick air. With an effort, Rainn regained her composure. "Ulric is still alive," she insisted, her voice low. "The spirit must have some method of sharing her power with Brigette."

Rainn was making a wild guess, but it was the only thing that made sense. Tarak hissed in annoyance. "Great. If we can't touch her, how are we supposed to kill her?"

Rainn considered the question. If she was right, and the aura was a result of Zella's powers, then there seemed only one logical way to get rid of her.

"The aura should disappear if we destroy the spirit," she told her companions.

Yeah, yeah. It was a lot of guessing and finger-crossing that she wasn't making a terrible mistake. But what choice did she have at this point?

"Right, and I could walk in the daylight if only I could get rid of the pesky sun," Tarak said in dry tones. "How do you intend to destroy the spirit?"

"There has to be away," she hedged.

"The first thing we need is reinforcements," the vampire announced. Waverly sent him a startled glance. Rainn assumed that Tarak was the sort of male who never asked for help. The vampire pointed toward a nearby bush that had shriveled to a brittle, charred pile of sticks. "Anything that can create this sort of devastation is too powerful for us to defeat without assistance," he said. "Cyn can gather his clan and Fallon can bring them here."

"I'm sure my people will help as well," Waverly added.

Rainn waved away their offers. "No. We can't wait."

"Rainn, I know you're worried about Ulric. We all are." Tarak's expression was somber. "It will destroy Chiron if something happens to his favorite wolf."

"This isn't about Ulric." Rainn held up a hand as Tarak's lips parted to argue. "Or at least, not entirely," she conceded. "I have to stop the spirit from fully entering the world."

Waverly stepped toward her, her luminous beauty oddly muted in the fog. As if her fey blood was being weakened by the dark magic. "You don't have to do it alone," the mermaid assured her. "We're in this together."

Rainn's lips twisted into a humorless smile. "Actually, it's my destiny to confront the evil."

"Destiny?" Tarak studied her, as if trying to decide if she was being sincere or just melodramatic.

Rainn swallowed a sigh. So much for her hope to keep her obligation a secret.

"The Oracles chose me at birth," she reluctantly admitted, holding out her arm to reveal the mark. "It's my duty to bring an end to the evil."

Tarak didn't bother to hide his surprise as his gaze flicked over her. No doubt he was wondering how a tiny sprite with little magic and no weapons intended to battle the most powerful creature on earth.

It was exactly what she was wondering.

"So you know how to kill the spirit?" he demanded.

She wrinkled her nose. "Not exactly. The Oracles didn't give me instructions."

"Typical," Tarak snapped. "From what little I know about the all-powerful beings, they tend to be—"

He bit off his words and glanced around. Almost as if he was afraid one of them might be hiding in the fog.

"Yeah," she agreed, equally reluctant to say anything bad. At least not out loud. Inside her head she was cursing the omniscient creatures for sending her to fight a war without a clue how to survive.

It was one thing if she died. But this wasn't about her. Or Ulric. If she failed, she didn't doubt that the darkness would consume the world.

"What do you want from us?" Waverly asked, thankfully interrupting her grim thoughts.

Rainn reached out to lay her hand on the female's shoulder. She hadn't been alone in her journey. She'd had her family. And then Chiron. And, of course, Ulric. But still, she'd carried a burden that she hadn't been able to share.

Now she realized it felt good to ask for help.

"I need you to distract Brigette long enough for me to get into the burrow," she said.

The vampire frowned, clearly intending to insist that they all stay together. Then, Waverly firmly grabbed his arm and tugged him away.

"We'll take care of her," she promised Rainn. "Good luck."

Rainn shivered. She didn't need luck.

She needed a miracle.

Chapter 15

As the two demons jogged away, Rainn captured what little wind could penetrate the fog and wrapped it tightly around her. Instantly, she regretted the need. Yuck. It was like being cocooned in filth.

How had Brigette endured spending endless centuries in this place? It would drive anyone mad.

She clenched her teeth, refusing to give in to her primitive urge to release her magic. Right now, she had to concentrate on disguising her presence. Once this was over she'd take a long, hot shower. For a decade. Maybe two.

Once she was hidden by the air, she watched as Tarak and Waverly headed directly toward Brigette. The female Were sniffed the air as they neared, howling in anticipation. But strangely, she didn't shift into her wolf.

Why not? Had the spirit done something to the animal inside her? The thought made Rainn's stomach clench in horror.

She had to get to Ulric.

Now.

On cue, Brigette charged forward, the creepy darkness swirling around her. She moved with the powerful grace of all Weres. And, as if she wasn't dangerous enough, she had a dagger clenched in her hand that had a blade that shimmered like pure silver despite the fog.

Raising the dagger over her head, Brigette prepared to strike. But with blinding speed Tarak and Waverly abruptly veered away, heading toward the destroyed village.

Brigette turned to follow, before she abruptly hesitated. Why? Did she sense Rainn hiding in the distance? Or did she fear she was being led into a trap? Whatever the cause, she at last tilted back her head to release a howl and chased after the intruders.

Rainn hissed out a breath she hadn't known she was holding.

It'd worked. Brigette was gone. Which meant that there was nothing between her and the burrow.

She didn't know whether to be happy or horrified.

"This is it, Rainn," she muttered. "Do or die."

Grimacing at the unfortunate choice of words, Rainn crossed the chalky ground. Then, slipping through the entrance of the burrow, she released her magic that hid her presence. In the cramped quarters, there would be no way to make herself invisible. Besides, she was going to need her magic for more important things.

Saving Ulric. Killing an unkillable spirit. And preventing Armageddon. No biggie.

Rainn swallowed the hysterical urge to laugh and forced herself to concentrate on the stairs crumbling beneath her feet. The cave-in had caused even more damage than she'd expected. The floor was shattered, and the walls were scarred and gouged from the rocks that had collapsed from the ceiling.

Who'd cleaned out the tunnel? Brigette?

Rainn grimaced. There had to be a ton of rocks the female Were had to remove. No wonder she'd been in such a foul mood.

Inching forward, Rainn felt a pulse of evil crawling over her. It was more than the gut-churning stench. Or the wind that whispered a shrill warning.

It was the darkness that clung to her skin like a parasite, sucking at her soul.

Nasty.

With a shudder Rainn halted at the entrance to the cavern. Her mouth was dry, and her heart was lodged in her throat. Not the most comfortable sensation. But miraculously, her courage never wavered.

She was determined to complete her duty. Come hell or high water. Well, there probably wouldn't be high water. But there was most certainly the potential for hell.

Rainn bent forward, glancing toward Zella, who was standing across the cavern with her back turned toward her. Like Brigette, the older woman had changed since Rainn had last seen her. Not so much physically. There was still the gray hair and softly rounded body. But there was a fuzziness to her. As if she was having difficulty holding her human form.

Or maybe she was so jam-packed with her dark magic that it was overflowing.

Great. Just what Rainn needed.

Squaring her shoulders, Rainn stepped forward. She allowed her gaze to briefly skim over Ulric, who was lying on a low, stone altar. Just long enough to reassure herself that he was capable of escaping once she managed to distract the spirit.

Her heart skipped a painful beat. His face was terrifyingly pale, and there were thick rivulets of blood that dripped down his side to pool on the stone beneath him. But she could see his chest moving up and down as he sucked in tortured breaths. And just as importantly, he appeared to be unrestrained.

That was the best she could hope for right now.

"I know you're there, zephyr." Zella suddenly broke the silence, turning away from the scrolls she'd been studying.

Rainn felt a ridiculous stab of annoyance at the woman's dismissive tone.

"I have a name. It's Rainn."

Zella tilted her head. Like a bird. A super-powerful, crazy-ass bird. "Such a strange habit," she murmured.

"Names?"

"Yes. Why seek to be an individual when you are stronger as one power?"

Rainn took a step back. Not because she was scared. Okay, that wasn't entirely true. She was terrified out of her mind. But she was hoping to lure the spirit out of the cavern.

"One power?" she demanded.

"Many who become one," Zella said, the hem of her gray gown brushing the floor as she moved to the center of the cavern. Seeing Rainn's confusion, she made a sound of frustration. "You will learn."

"Actually, I came here to teach *you* a lesson," Rainn retorted. Did she sound like a badass? Or a blathering idiot?

Not that it mattered. Her only concern was keeping the woman talking as she backed her into the tunnel.

Zella clicked her tongue, but she took a step forward. And then another.

"I sent Brigette to kill you and she failed," she said, shaking her head. "Again."

Rainn took two steps backward. "What did you do to her?"

Zella smiled. Or rather she stretched her lips into a creepy replica of a smile. "I've given her what she so desperately desired."

"Is that why she was screaming?" Rainn demanded.

"Power comes with a price," Zella's smile widened. Clearly, she'd taken a vicious pleasure in Brigette's pain. "At least for creatures of this world."

Rainn took another step back. "Does that mean you're not from this world?"

Either unaware or uncaring of the fact that she was being led into the tunnel, Zella moved to stand directly in front of Rainn.

"I am a part of all worlds." The woman waved her hands, sparks dancing around her fingertips. "All beings."

"Well, we don't want you here," Rainn taunted, not having to pretend that she was retreating to avoid the touch of the spirit.

Just the thought was enough to make her shudder in horror.

"Too late. Your mate is ensuring that I can fully return."

"Return?" Rainn demanded in sharp tones. She didn't want the spirit to glance back and realize how far they'd drifted away from Ulric. "You've been here before?"

Zella hissed with impatience. "I have just told you that I have been everywhere."

"And you have the ego to prove it," Rainn taunted.

Okay, provoking the evil spirit wasn't the best idea, but she didn't know how else to keep the woman following her as she at last reached the staircase. Once they were out of the burrow...

Well, she didn't know what happened then, but it would give Ulric the opportunity to escape. That was the only certain way to keep his blood from breaking the spell. Later she would figure out how the hell she was supposed to kill the spirit.

One desperate gamble at a time.

"A shame I am in a hurry," Zella murmured, speaking more to herself than Rainn. "I would enjoy watching you suffer."

"The feeling is mutual," Rainn said, her voice throbbing with a raw honesty. She wanted to see this creature suffer. Not only had she caused the death of Ulric's pack, but she was corrupting the earth with her foul magic. "You're an obscene insult to my world. The sooner you're destroyed, the sooner I can forget you ever existed."

"Enough." Zella scowled, almost as if Rainn had wounded her feelings. Could an evil spirit be insulted?

Coming to a halt, Zella pointed her finger at Rainn. Instantly a bolt of fire seared through the air.

Muttering a curse, Rainn leaped to the side. She slammed against the wall as heat sizzled against her skin and then exploded at the exact spot where she'd been standing.

Horrified, she watched the stone melt and an acrid smoke fill the air.

Crap.

She'd expected the spirit to have magic. And she'd assumed it would have something to do with the sparks she'd seen dancing around her body and smoldering in her eyes.

But she hadn't known she was a freaking flamethrower.

Gathering her own power, Rainn sent a blast of air at Zella. Not as scary as fire, but it had the benefit of being invisible. Which meant Zella wasn't ready for the punch in the center of her chest. She grunted in shock as she was knocked on her ass.

"You should be more careful," Rainn taunted, trying to distract the spirit long enough to catch her breath. "You're going to hurt someone."

Zella slowly shoved herself upright.

Rainn shivered. Zella's eyes were pure fire. And even more disturbing, the strange blurriness that surrounded the woman had intensified. As if she was somehow out of focus.

Did it have something to do with sharing her power with Brigette? Or was it connected to Ulric and his blood?

The thought sent a jolt of urgency through Rainn. She had to end this. Now.

"What are you?"

Rainn's lips twisted. That was a question she was only now starting to consider. Perhaps too late. "So far I've been an obedient daughter, and a weapon for the Oracles," she admitted, gathering her power as she watched the sparks begin to dance around Zella's fingers. "I'd like to discover if I can be more."

"You can be dead," Zella hissed.

"I don't think so," Rainn rasped, wrapping bands of air around the spirit.

She'd intended to slam the creature against the wall, but without warning, her magic went right through her. As if she was an illusion.

Dammit.

Zella smiled, waving her hand to shoot a tsunami of flames toward Rainn. There was no leaping out of the way this time. Instead, Rainn frantically wrapped the air around her as the fire roared through the tunnel.

Pain seared through her. Even with all her efforts, she couldn't deflect the nuclear-level heat. She had to stop it.

Desperately, Rainn diverted a portion of her magic. Bending the air, she used it to dislodge a large rock from the ceiling. She didn't have the strength for another cave-in, but as the rock hit Zella on the head, it managed to disrupt the flames.

Zella hissed, glancing up in annoyance. Clearly she was bracing for the ceiling to collapse on her.

Rainn used the momentary reprieve to try and connect with Ulric.

She had the ability to enter humans' minds and manipulate their thoughts as well as erase their memories. It was a trick that had come in handy since she'd started working at Dreamscape Resorts. Occasionally one of the guests would have the ability to detect that a staff member wasn't human. Rainn would tweak their memory to ensure they either dismissed their fears or forgot all about them.

Unfortunately, her power didn't usually work on demons. They had a primitive defense against mind control. But if Ulric truly was her mate, it should create a connection to allow her to reach him.

Using the last of her strength, she called out to the male who was the only hope she had to save the world.

* * * *

Ulric was lost in the fog.

Where had Brigette gone? She'd been standing directly in front of him and then she'd disappeared.

He tried to move. A mistake, as a vicious pain ripped through his side. It felt like a wild animal was clawing through his flesh.

Something bad had happened. Something really bad. Reaching for his wolf, Ulric growled in frustration.

Nothing.

His connection to his animal was blocked. Fury pounded through him as he battled against the gray shroud that clouded his mind. It was a spell. And he knew only one creature who had magic that turned to fog.

Zella.

But knowing what was happening to him didn't do a damned thing to help. Not even when he caught Rainn's misty scent.

Deep inside, his wolf howled with longing. The animal was desperate to reach her. Did he smell her blood? Was she injured? The fear was maddening.

At the same time he heard the distant sound of her voice urging him to get up. To flee.

Fiercely he latched on to her voice. He had no intention of fleeing. But it was like a lifeline leading him through the thick, gray clouds.

Vaguely he was aware of the hard stone beneath his back and the terrible stench of decay.

He was back in the burrow. He didn't know how he'd gotten there. The last thing he remembered was being in Chiron's old lair beneath the cliffs. He'd been lying on a bed…

"Ulric." Rainn's urgent voice sliced through his clouded memories. *Dammit.* He had to reach her.

Ignoring the pain in his side, Ulric struggled against the invisible bonds that held him hostage.

"There's a better way," a husky female voice whispered in his ear.

Ulric warily stilled. The voice wasn't in his ear, he abruptly realized. It was in his mind. "Who's there?"

"Chaaya," the voice answered. "The Gatekeeper."

Gatekeeper? What did that mean? Ulric shoved aside the question. It didn't matter. Not now.

"Get out of my head," he rasped, trying to block the female's voice. "Stop that."

Ulric felt a mental slap. As if there was someone actually inside his skull capable of physically whacking his brain.

It didn't hurt, but it was creepy as hell.

Inside, his wolf growled, but before he could threaten her with a bloody dismemberment, she was once again intruding into his thoughts.

"Do you want to rescue your female or not?" she demanded.

Ulric forced himself to take a deep breath. Obviously the mystery voice wasn't going to leave him alone until he'd heard what she had to say. "Why would you help?"

"I died to remove the beast," she told him.

Ulric frowned. He couldn't smell the female, but he could sense her essence. It was strange. Almost ephemeral.

"You're not a Were," he announced with absolute certainty. "You're a human."

"I was," she admitted.

Ulric sucked in a sharp breath, hit by a sudden suspicion. A human who died to remove a beast? Could the voice belong to the skeleton discovered in the burrow?

It seemed crazy, but no more crazy than anything else that'd happened since he returned to his homeland. "How do I know this isn't a trick?"

"You have no choice but to trust me," she said.

"Wrong," he growled, squeezing shut his eyes as he strained to shove her out of his mind.

"Demons," she muttered. Then, without warning, a vision of Rainn filled his thoughts. She was pressed against the side of the tunnel, trapped by a torrent of fire. "She's going to die if you don't listen to me."

Terror ripped through Ulric. Rainn was obviously wrapped in her magic, but the fire was creeping closer and closer. At any time she was going to be consumed by the evil.

"If something happens to her, human..."

"What part of *listen to me* do you not understand?" Chaaya interrupted. "I swear, dogs are the most thick-skulled demons ever created."

Ulric clenched his hands. When he finally got his powers back he was going to ensure he was treated with proper respect. For now, however, he had no choice but to grin and bear the constant insults.

Okay, he wasn't grinning, but he was bearing.

"What do you want from me?" he demanded.

"Your blood is destroying the barrier," Chaaya said. "You have to heal yourself."

"I can't."

"Just shift."

Ulric hissed in frustration. "The fog is interfering."

"Shit," the female muttered.

Rainn's voice abruptly echoed in his head. "Hurry, Ulric," she cried out. "You have to get out."

He grimly reached out to the stranger. "Do something."

His words were met by silence. Ulric cursed. Had the human disappeared? Or worse, had she been a figment of his fevered imagination?

"There's only one option," the female at last responded.

Ulric released a shaky breath of relief. She was still there. *Thank the goddess.* "What?"

"I have to get you out of there."

"Can you open a portal?" he eagerly asked.

She snorted. "How many humans do you know who can open a portal?"

"How many humans can use telepathy? Or hang around a burrow after they die?"

"You don't think that was my choice, do you?" she demanded. "If it was up to me, I'd be lying on a beach in the Bahamas."

Ulric bit back his angry words. If he didn't need the snarky female...

But he did, he sternly reminded himself. At least until Rainn was safe.

"Just get us out of here," he said between clenched teeth.

"I don't think you're in a position to be giving orders."

"Chaaya."

"Fine." He heard her click her tongue. "God, men are such drama queens."

He ignored her insult. "What are you going to do?"

"Get you out of there," she said.

Could she be any more vague? "How are you going to get us out?" he pressed.

He'd decided since Brigette's arrival in Vegas to be careful what he wished for. It too often bit him in the ass.

"I have to bring you to me," the female said.

"Where are you?"

"On the other side."

Still too vague. "The other side of what?"

"Hold on."

Ulric parted his lips to protest. He had no idea what the human thought she could do. She'd already admitted that she couldn't open a portal. And even if she was a witch, she couldn't teleport people.

But before he could demand a detailed explanation of what was about to happen, the world went dark.

It wasn't like entering the fog. Or even the few times that he'd traveled through a portal. This was an utter and complete nothingness. As if he was floating somewhere out in space.

Then he was whirling in a dizzying circle. He felt like he was being sucked down a drain. His stomach heaved and the pain in his side was excruciating. He was being ripped apart and there wasn't a damned thing he could do to stop it.

At last the swirling stopped and Ulric was dumped onto a hard patch of ground. He grunted, his hand instinctively pressing against his wound. He was still bleeding, but right now he was more focused on his new surroundings than his injury.

Forcing himself to his feet, he glanced around.

Where was he? He was no longer in the burrow. But that was all he could say for sure. There was nothing to tell him where he'd landed. The ground was a dull brown and extended as far as the eye could see. There were no trees. No vegetation. No buildings. Nothing.

Overhead the sky was a weird greenish-gray shade. There was light, but no sun or moon. As if the glow was simply a part of the air.

He stood still, sucking in a deep breath. Hell. There wasn't even any smell here.

It was empty.

Not sure whether to be relieved he was out of the burrow or terrified that he was someplace worse, Ulric felt a tingle of magic. Turning, he watched as Rainn appeared out of thin air.

"Rainn."

Leaping forward, he grasped her as she tumbled toward the ground. Then he squeezed her tight against him. Thank the goddess, she was alive. And in his arms. In this moment that was all that mattered.

She lifted her hands, using the tips of her fingers to trace his face. He shivered at her light touch, joy racing through him. But even as he started to lower his head and claim a long overdue kiss, she was turning her head to glance down at his side.

"You're still injured," she breathed.

About to assure her that he would eventually heal, Ulric was interrupted by the mysterious female voice.

"Can we postpone this touching reunion until we have some space between us and the pissed-off beast?"

Ulric tightened his arms around Rainn even as there was another tingle of magic and Chaaya appeared.

He didn't know what he'd expected. A gnarled old woman with a hunchback. Or a walking skeleton that rattled with every step. Instead there was a tiny female who didn't look more than twenty-one in human years.

Astonished, he allowed his gaze to roam over her slender body, which was covered by a pair of leather pants and a matching leather jacket. She had a perfect oval face with large dark eyes and soft pink lips. Her skin was a rich shade of bronze and her dark hair was cut short, almost buzzed to the skull. He assumed it was to reveal the Celtic tattoos that started behind her ears and ran down the sides of her neck.

She could have walked into his casino and he wouldn't have batted an eye. Well, except for the short spear she had belted around her waist.

"Who are you?" Rainn demanded in confusion.

"Not now," the girl snapped. "Follow me."

Rainn sent him a searching gaze. "Ulric?"

Ulric hesitated. None of this made sense. The young woman who claimed to be human was striding away without bothering to glance back at them. How had she brought them to this place?

More important, *what* was this place?

Then he gave a sharp shake of his head. He wasn't stupid. He knew that they'd fallen down the rabbit hole. Still, they were out of the burrow. And the fog was gone.

For now, he was going to take that as a win.

"She calls herself Chaaya. I think we have to trust her," he muttered. "For now."

"Okay."

Something inside Ulric melted at Rainn's ready willingness to follow his lead. She might not accept him as a mate, but...

No. He slammed the door on that painful thought.

He wasn't going to dwell on Rainn's rejection. Not now. Hopefully not ever.

Keeping his arm wrapped around the sprite's shoulders, Ulric followed Chaaya. He was careful to keep a reasonable distance between them. If this was a trap, he wanted time to react.

They traveled over the empty landscape, the dull ground absorbing the sound of their footsteps. Everything here was muffled. As if they were stuffed in some gigantic closet.

Then the girl in front of them gave a wave of her hand. "In there."

Ulric blinked. Just ahead of them was a small, thatch-roofed cottage. Had that been there before? No. Surely, he would have noticed it?

Perhaps it was an illusion.

Giving a shake of his head, he slowly approached the structure. The white paint was peeling off the sides of the cottage, and the narrow windows were clouded with age. Even the front door was weathered.

"Is this real?"

Chaaya shrugged. "As far as I can tell. It's the one place in this hellhole that the beast can't enter."

"The beast." Rainn glanced at the girl in confusion. "Is that Zella?"

"It has a thousand names and a thousand faces," the girl said.

Ulric grimaced. He was beginning to suspect he'd seriously underestimated the scope of Zella's immense power.

"What is it?" Rainn demanded.

Chaaya paused, as if not sure how to explain.

"Corruption," she at last said.

"I don't understand what that means." Rainn furrowed her brow. "Is it a demon? A spirit?"

"It's the darkness that corrupts the soul and taints the magic," Chaaya tried to clarify.

"Evil?" Rainn pressed.

"It gave birth to evil," Chaaya said.

That was a conversation ender. Nothing like the knowledge they were being chased by the mother of all evil, to terrify them into silence.

At last Ulric forced himself to clear the lump from his throat.

"And this place is its lair?" he asked.

"No." Chaaya glanced around. "It's more like a foyer to our world."

Ulric didn't entirely understand, but he stored away the information and moved on. "And who are you?"

"The Gatekeeper."

"You keep using that word," Ulric complained. "What does it mean?" The girl's features abruptly hardened. "It was my death that created the barrier."

Ulric heard Rainn suck in a sharp breath as she realized who this girl must be. Or at least who she *had* been.

"You were the one sacrificed," she said.

Chaaya pressed her lips together. "Yep."

"How did you end up in that burrow?" Ulric demanded.

"The witches came to my village, demanding a sacrifice. I was chosen." Something that looked like pain smoldered in her eyes before her snarky defiance returned. "Lucky me."

Rainn made a soft sound of sympathy. The zephyr no doubt understood Chaaya's sense of betrayal better than anyone. She might not have been offered up by her tribe as a sacrifice, but her duty to the Oracles might easily be a death sentence.

Even Ulric couldn't deny a small amount of pity. "When?"

Chaaya squared her shoulders, as if slamming the door on her painful memories. "I don't have an exact date. Long before you were born."

Long before? That meant she had to be well over a thousand years old. Probably several thousand. "So if you're the skeleton—"

"Rude," Chaaya scolded.

Ulric plowed ahead. "Then what are you now?"

"I don't know. I suppose I must be a ghost. After I was...well, you know." She ran a finger across her neck, indicating someone slicing her throat. "I woke up in this place. Thankfully, I'm able to glimpse the world." She moved her hand from her throat to wave it above her head. Instantly a small square appeared. It looked like a window, and Ulric had a glimpse of a busy city street. New York? Paris? Maybe London. "I've watched generations come and go." She lowered her hand and the window disappeared. "It relieves the tedium."

Ulric glanced around. This strange place just kept getting stranger. And Chaaya...

He'd never encountered anything like her.

Right now, however, he needed to focus on protecting Rainn. A job that would have been a lot easier if he wasn't weak, bleeding, and incapable of shifting into his wolf. "You're here alone?"

"Just me and the beast." She glanced around the empty landscape. "The other demons battled against the darkness, but I was the only one actually sacrificed. Again"—a humorless smile twisted her lips—"lucky me."

"What other demons?" Ulric demanded.

"All of them." Chaaya waved a hand in an inclusive motion. "The fey, the Weres. Even the dragons. Everyone except the vampires."

"Dragons?" Ulric arched his brows in surprise.

The dragons had retreated from this world a very long time ago. Although he'd heard rumors that they'd started to return. At least for short visits.

Chaaya nodded. "They used their fire to seal shut the door that the mermaids created."

Ulric exchanged a confused glance with Rainn.

"There were mermaids in the burrow?" he demanded, returning his attention to Chaaya.

The girl sent him a frown that implied she couldn't believe he was so stupid. "The doorway isn't in the burrow."

Ulric blinked. Okay. That was a shock. After all, everything connected to Zella had been happening in the cavern beneath his old village.

"Then why is your skeleton there?"

Chaaya narrowed her eyes, but she didn't reprimand him again. Clearly, she was touchy about the whole skeleton thing.

"My blood was used to provide a barrier in case the door was somehow damaged," Chaaya told him. "You could say I'm the backup plan."

"And the scrolls that were in the burrow?" he pressed.

"They were placed there on the day I was sacrificed. They were part of the barrier," Chaaya told him. "The magic is a mystical blockade. It didn't physically have to be next to the doorway." She held up a hand. "And before you ask, I have no idea why that precise spot was chosen."

Rainn leaned against Ulric, clearly weary from her battle with Zella. "Why have a doorway at all?"

This time it was Rainn who got the *Are you stupid?* glare.

"Because there was a gaping hole from where the beast clawed its way into the world the first time. They couldn't repair the damage, so they had to put a patch over it." Chaaya paused, sucking in a deep breath as if trying to keep control of her temper. Obviously, spending so many years alone in this place did nothing to improve her people skills. "Then they created a second layer of protection."

Rainn appeared indifferent to the girl's mounting impatience. "With all that protection, how did Zella manage to get through?"

Chaaya took another deep breath, but she answered the question.

"It started with the Dark Lord," she said, referring to the godlike creature the vampires had destroyed only a few years ago. "His disciples released his evil into the world. The beast used them as anchors to sneak small portions of itself through the doorway," she explained, nodding toward Ulric. "It was your father who recognized the danger. He tried to stop her with a new layer of magic, but..."

"He was too late," Ulric breathed, suddenly understanding why his father had been so obsessed with the burrow. He'd known something was wrong. The girl nodded. "Yes."

Ulric felt a pang of self-loathing. Why had he so childishly run off to London? He should have been here helping his father. And even if they couldn't have halted Zella, at least he wouldn't have come bumbling back here, allowing his blood to destroy the barrier.

Damn.

Chapter 16

Brigette snarled in frustration. How long had she been chasing the intruders? A half hour? More? It felt like an eternity.

And still they managed to elude her.

She needed her wolf. In her animal form nothing could outrun her. But no matter how hard she strained, she couldn't reach the elusive creature.

Damn Zella.

For centuries the old woman had kept Brigette as her personal slave. Over and over she'd promised that Brigette would have her rewards, but each passing year she'd found some excuse to keep Brigette trapped.

Now, at last, she had her power. It coursed through her like a river of fire. But it didn't make her faster or stronger. In fact, she didn't know what it was doing beyond causing her wolf to retreat even deeper inside her. As if it was terrified of the evil magic flowing through her veins.

She wanted to howl in misery.

Once she received her gift, she was supposed to flee this rotting pile of crap. She would have a new home. And her awesome powers would attract the strongest of Weres to form her new pack. And, in time, she'd intended to challenge Salvatore, the current King of Weres. Why not dream big?

Instead she was stuck chasing a vampire and mermaid across the barren landscape. She didn't know where the zephyr was, and she didn't care. She didn't even care that she was being led away from the burrow.

It was as if she was being compelled to finish the hunt.

And perhaps she was. Zella had possessed control over her since the first day they'd met. Brigette might have been vain and hungry for power, but she would never have agreed to the atrocities that'd destroyed her family.

And certainly she wouldn't have wasted the past centuries, either scouring the world for her missing pack mate or stuck in this disgusting fog.

But now it was more than the mental prodding that had urged her to give in to her worst impulses. It was a ruthless compulsion that she couldn't battle against.

Dammit. She'd leaped from the frying pan directly into the fire.

Maybe Ulric would kill the bitch, she told herself. Now that she realized the power she'd been promised was a hoax, she was even more eager to see the woman destroyed.

She wanted to be free.

A grim smile twisted her lips as she recalled her brief visit to Vegas. She hadn't wanted to admit it to herself, but she'd savored the glitz and glamour of Ulric's life. It'd been a stark contrast to her own barren existence.

Unfortunately, right now she had no choice but to give in to the brutal demand that she hunt down her prey.

Jogging over the rocky ground, Brigette scanned the empty landscape. She could still smell the mermaid, but the vampire had disappeared. Not totally unexpected. Vampires didn't leave a trail. Even a Were had to be within a few feet to actually catch their icy scent.

Which meant there was always the danger that he could circle around and attack her from behind.

Remaining on high alert, she continued along the edge of the cliff. She was not only worried about the vampire and mermaid, but there was a strange sensation starting to ripple through her.

As if...

Stumbling to a halt, Brigette concentrated on the power that was churning inside her. What was happening? It didn't feel the same as when Zella had shoved the magic inside her. That had been like swallowing lava. This was more a wavering in the power. Like a loose light bulb that was flickering on and off.

Was it possible that Ulric had shaken off the mind control around him and was battling against Zella? Or was it the zephyr?

Maybe something else.

Fear shot down Brigette's spine. It was one thing to fantasize about Zella's death and another to consider it a reality.

Not that she cared about the bitch. Her only concern was for herself. As always.

What happened to her if Zella was somehow killed? Or even if her physical form was destroyed? Could their connection somehow pull Brigette into the evil cesspit Zella had crawled out of?

That would be disappointing as hell. Literally.

And even if her bond with Zella was broken, she was far too close to Ulric and his bizarre collection of friends. She didn't doubt for a second that killing her would be on top of his to-do list.

She needed to get away from there. ASAP.

Busy struggling against Zella's lingering compulsion, Brigette failed to pay attention to the scent of salt. Not entirely her fault—she assumed it was coming from the ocean breeze. It wasn't until she heard the sound of footsteps that she recognized the danger. Stiffening, she watched the mermaid appear out of the darkness.

Why wasn't she still running away?

Did the fey creature sense that Brigette was losing the dark power she'd been given?

Clutching the dagger, Brigette muttered a string of curses. She wasn't scared of the mermaid. She didn't need extra powers to kill a fey creature, although she would prefer to do it as a wolf. But she wanted to disappear before Ulric could come looking for her.

"Go away, mermaid." She made a warning gesture with the dagger. "Or die. Your choice."

She expected the female to dart away. She had to know that she was no match for a pureblooded Were. Instead, she stood her ground.

"Do you think you're scary?"

Brigette stepped forward. She could rip the tiny female to shreds, but she didn't want to waste the energy. "Obviously I am," she growled. "You're the one who has been running away from me."

"Not running," the mermaid denied. Then she smiled. "Leading."

Brigette tried to laugh. The female was bluffing. She had to be. But the laugh stuck in her throat.

"Leading me to what?" she demanded.

"Away from the fog."

Any fear that had started to form in the pit of Brigette's stomach disappeared. The mermaid was an idiot if she thought the fog provided her power.

"Why? I can kill you as easily here as surrounded by Zella's magic." Brigette took another step forward. "Perhaps easier."

"Ah. But I couldn't do this." The mermaid lifted her hand.

Brigette braced herself. She didn't know what kind of magic the mermaid might have. Most fey creatures were prey, not predators, but that didn't mean they couldn't hurt other demons.

When nothing happened, Brigette frowned. Then, suddenly she felt herself being tugged forward.

"What the hell—" Her words were cut off as she watched a gaping portal being opened directly in front of her. *Oh shit.* She dug in her heels even when she knew it was futile. "No."

* * * *

Rainn studied Chaaya, her heart heavy with sympathy. The girl looked like she'd barely been more than a teenager when she'd been sacrificed. And if that hadn't been awful enough, she'd been trapped in this skeevy foyer between dimensions. It was no wonder she was a little...short-tempered.

Rainn might have resented the Oracles and the knowledge that she would eventually be called to fulfill her destiny, but at least she hadn't had her throat slit and her bones hung in a dirty burrow.

"Where is the beast?" Ulric demanded, breaking into her dark thoughts.

Chaaya tilted back her head, as if she was sniffing the stale air. With a grimace, she glared at Ulric.

"She followed you here," she said.

Ulric countered her glare with one of his own. The two obviously weren't about to become BFFs anytime soon. "She's here?"

Chaaya pointed toward Ulric's wound. "She still needs your blood."

Ulric scowled, pressing his hand over the scratches. "How do we stop her?"

"You have to heal," the girl insisted.

A flare of heat pulsed through the air. Ulric was always hot-tempered. After everything they'd just endured, his mood was set to volcanic.

"I can't," he said between clenched teeth. "Not without my wolf."

Chaaya turned her attention to Rainn. "There's another way."

Rainn blinked in confusion. Did the girl think she had the healing magic? Some fey creatures did. But not zephyrs. "What are you talking about?"

"I don't have to be a Were to know he's in the middle of his mating madness," Chaaya drawled.

"Hey," Ulric muttered even as Rainn slowly realized what the girl meant.

Ulric's weakness wasn't caused just by his injury. It was her refusal to accept the mating bond. Regret twisted her heart. Along with a completely inappropriate flare of anticipation.

Chaaya flashed a deliberately provoking smile toward Ulric. "Are you blushing, dog?"

"You..." Ulric stepped forward, but Rainn quickly grasped his arm.

"Don't, Ulric."

Chaaya's smile widened. "Go in the cottage and put this male out of his misery," she commanded, her smile fading as she glanced toward Rainn. "And don't come out until he's healed."

"I'll take care of Ulric," Rainn promised.

Ulric narrowed his eyes as Chaaya took a step back. "Wait. What are you going to do?"

The girl grabbed the spear holstered at her side. The blade looked like it'd been made out of copper and the ebony handle was decorated with strange markings.

"I'm going to keep the beast entertained."

Chaaya was jogging away before Ulric could protest. Then, she simply disappeared. As if the strange, stagnant air had swallowed her.

Rainn grimaced, then tugged Ulric toward the nearby cottage. "Come on."

Ulric allowed himself to be led up the pathway. Rainn pushed open the door, her eyes widening in surprise.

The cottage had looked traditional from the outside, but she hadn't really expected the old-fashioned style to be reflected inside. After all, Chaaya didn't seem like a chintz and lace sort of gal. She was more leather, guts, and pointy weapons.

Of course, this house might very well have been created long before Chaaya was condemned to stand guard in this place.

"It feels different here," Rainn murmured, relieved at the warm, fragrant air that wrapped around them.

Her gaze moved over the flagstone floor that was covered by hand-woven rugs, and the low, open-beamed ceiling. Next she took in the carved wooden furniture that was piled with bright cushions.

Ulric's expression was oddly wistful. "Like home."

Rainn's heart squeezed with sympathy. Did the place remind him of his parents' cottage?

"Yeah," she softly agreed. Then, tightening her grip on his arm, she urged him toward the opening across the room.

They were wasting time. As much as she wanted to wrap her arms around Ulric and urge him to reminisce about his childhood with his pack, they needed him strong and healthy.

And there was one way to accomplish that task.

A renegade excitement tingled through her. It had nothing to do with her duty to the Oracles. Or the fear that the world was in danger until Zella was destroyed.

It was entirely focused on her selfish desire to get her hands on Ulric. Not just on, but all over. Head to toe and all the delicious spots in between.

"Stop," Ulric protested, clearly sensing Rainn's ruthless determination to seduce him.

"Don't be stubborn," she chided.

Ulric muttered a curse, but he readily allowed himself to be led into the bedroom. "You call *me* stubborn?" he groused. "You could give lessons to a mule."

She shrugged. "It's part of my charm."

"Yes."

Rainn's heart fluttered. Really and truly. Just like a butterfly trapped in her chest.

Unnerved by the sensation, Rainn glanced around the snug bedroom. Once again, she was astonished by the homey feel to it. There was a stone fireplace with a heavy mantel that was lined with delicate pottery. The windows were covered by lacy curtains, and a hand-stitched quilt was spread across the brass bed set in the center of the floor.

Suddenly Ulric swayed from side to side, as if he was on the point of collapse. Rainn chided herself for her momentary distraction, firmly pulling Ulric toward the bed.

"Lie down before you fall down," she ordered.

Ulric grimaced, collapsing on the mattress. He rolled onto his back, gazing up at her with pain-filled eyes. "I don't suppose there's anything to eat here?" he demanded. "I'm starving."

A toxic combination of fear and regret swirled through Rainn. Taking care not to jostle him, she crawled onto the bed and stretched out next to him.

"I'll look," she promised, turning to the side to face him. "Later."

His head swiveled on the pillow to study her with a wary gaze. "Rainn—"

"Ssh." She pressed her fingers to his lips. "I need you to listen to me."

He arched a brow. "I always listen."

"You promise?" she pressed.

He paused before giving a nod of his head. "Okay. I promise."

Rainn's fluttering heart went into overdrive. Why was this so difficult? It felt like that moment she'd been swept over the canyon, frantically trying to float before she was plummeting toward the ground.

"When you confessed that I was your mate—"

"Don't, Rainn," he interrupted in harsh tones.

She scowled at him. This was hard enough without him making it more difficult. "You promised to listen."

"There's no need to discuss this."

"There's every need," she insisted.

He turned his head to stare at the open beams above them. His body was stiff and a fine layer of sweat coated his skin. He was in far more pain than he wanted her to realize.

"Rainn, I'm as anxious as you are to find a way to destroy Zella, but you can't force yourself to become my mate. It doesn't work that way."

"I know how it works, Ulric. I don't have a wolf, but I have this. She reached to grasp his hand, pressing it to the center of her chest.

A prickling heat filled the room. Ulric could never hide his emotions. They spilled out of him like a furnace.

"What are you talking about?" he rasped.

"My heart."

He sucked in a pained breath. "You made your feelings clear earlier."

"Actually, I didn't," she insisted. "I made a mess of everything."

"I don't blame you," he assured her, his jaw tight as if he was clenching his teeth. "We aren't in charge of destiny. No matter how much we might want to be."

"Trust me, I know. Probably better than anyone." She abruptly wrinkled her nose, remembering her earlier decision that her fate hadn't been nearly as bad as others'. "Except for Chaaya. And that's why I reacted like an idiot."

"You were honest." The words were bleak. As if he was talking about a death. "And that's the end of the story."

She clicked her tongue. Was he deliberately making this difficult?

"You keep forgetting that whole listening thing."

"I'm listening."

"No, you're deflecting." She held his gaze. "It's hard enough for me to share what I'm feeling. My people aren't like most fey creatures, who are always spewing their emotions around. We are a secluded, private tribe."

He moved his hand to stroke a path up the side of her neck, tucking her hair behind her ear. "Your ability to stay calm no matter what is happening has always impressed Chiron."

"And infuriated you."

He wrinkled his nose. "I thought it was because I was so impulsive and hotheaded. You made me look like a raving lunatic in comparison."

Rainn's lips twitched. Ulric had never been a raving lunatic. He was too disciplined. But he was much more...expressive with his feelings than her. Or Chiron.

Oddly, his temperamental style made him a favorite with the Dreamscape staff. Most of them were terrified of Chiron, and they found Rainn aloof, but they would readily go to Ulric if they had a problem.

"But?" she prompted.

His fingers brushed over her cheek, the heat of touch branding her with pleasure.

"But now I suspect I wanted to rip through your composure to find the woman beneath," he admitted. "My wolf already sensed you were special." Rainn shivered. She was making her own realizations. Like why she'd gone to such lengths to avoid spending time alone with Ulric. And why she'd evaded his touch.

Just the light brush of his fingers was causing complete chaos. Her heart banged against her ribs and her breath tangled in her throat.

She forced herself to continue. "Once I was taken to the Oracles I only became more determined to bury my emotions." She needed him to understand. "My people were depending on me to fulfill my duty. I couldn't risk being distracted."

"That's what I am?" His fingers drifted along her jaw. "A distraction?"

"At first," she murmured, tilting back her head as his hand wrapped around her throat. It wasn't threatening. It was a gesture of delicious possession. "A very sexy, occasionally charming distraction."

His eyes darkened, the heat in the room ratcheting up several more degrees.

"Sexy," he growled. "I like the sound of that."

Rainn swallowed a groan, her gaze skimming over his hard, chiseled features, and down the muscular chest that was emphasized by his tight T-shirt. Sexy was actually an understatement. He was...well, she didn't know what was sexier than sexy. All she knew was that he was a loyal, gorgeous male who came complete with a wolf.

What could be better?

"But I had to stay focused," she said, reminding herself she *still* had to stay focused. "And then Brigette made her appearance in the casino."

"Brigette." His expression hardened with fury at the mention of his cousin. "She's going to pay for what she did."

Rainn refused to think about the treacherous female. This moment was about Ulric. And their bond. And all the delicious ways she intended to prove to this male that she was completely on board with the whole mating thing.

"She'll pay," Rainn assured the male, using the tips of her fingers to smooth away his frown. "But not until you have your strength back."

"Rainn."

She once again pressed her fingers to his lips. She wanted to finish her story. Once they were done with the past, they could concentrate on the present.

A warm bed. Some temporary alone-time. And the urgent desire to mate.

"Once I recognized the evil was centered on the female Were, and ultimately Zella, I became even more determined to fulfill my duty," she said.

"I understand," he insisted. "I truly do."

Rainn made a sound of impatience. "I didn't. When you confessed that I was your mate, I panicked. I told myself that I had to concentrate on battling the evil. That I couldn't allow myself to be diverted from my quest. Even if..." A sudden lump of anxiety lodged the words in her throat.

"Even if what?"

"Even if it meant denying what was in my heart."

He stilled, almost as if he was expecting a blow. "What was in your heart?"

She swallowed the lump. This was it. Now or never. "The knowledge that you belong to me."

Chapter 17

Ulric sucked in a sharp breath. Somewhere in the back of his mind was an urgent voice whispering that they couldn't be sure the cottage was safe.

Chaaya had given them a fanciful story about being sacrificed and endless centuries of battling the beast. But what if she was just some weird manifestation of evil? And what if she'd urged them to stay in the cottage until Zella could travel to this place and destroy them?

Still, it was remarkably easy to ignore the voice.

He was too weak to fight. Or even run. Hell, he wasn't sure he could roll out of the bed at this point. And besides, he was willing to risk death if it meant he could savor the feel of Rainn's fingers gently stroking his face.

"You said you couldn't be my mate," he forced himself to remind her.

He'd been deeply hurt by her rejection. It wasn't easy to open himself up to another disappointment.

She flinched, as if disturbed by his accusation.

"Because I feared it might jeopardize my people," she insisted. "It was only because I agreed to the Oracles' demands that they continue to offer their protection. How could I choose to follow my heart if it meant putting my family in danger?" Her fingers lingered against his cheek, the warm mist of her breath brushing his lips. "It didn't occur to me that I could find my true love and still battle against Zella."

A shudder of anticipation rippled through him. "True love?"

Her eyes darkened to smoke, her scent drenching the room. "Mmm."

There was a stirring deep inside him. Something familiar and wonderful.

"Does that mean mate?" he demanded. He wanted it spelled out in black and white.

"It does."

The words were simple. *It does.* But they sent an avalanche of sensations cascading through him.

Still, his animal remained wary. "What about the Oracles?"

"They told me I had to destroy the evil," she said, her voice husky. "They didn't say I had to do it alone."

"Alone is a very bad thing," he agreed.

"Yeah. I like together better."

He hesitated, his gaze anxiously scanning her face. Once he committed, there was no going back. "Are you sure?"

A slow, wicked smile curved her lips. "I'm happy to convince you."

Ulric growled. He liked the sound of that. "How?"

"I could do this." Inching closer to his tense body, she nipped the lobe of his ear.

Ulric jerked, his cock hardening in anticipation. "That's a good start."

Using the tip of her tongue, she traced a wet path down the length of his jaw. "And this."

"An even better start," he rasped, the fingers that had instinctively cupped around her throat skimming up to grasp her chin. "Rainn."

"Has anyone told you that you talk too much?" she murmured, cutting off his last demand to be sure she knew what she was getting into.

He arched a brow. "Not and lived."

She gave his ear another nip. "My big, bad wolf."

Ulric rolled to his side, facing her. A sensation far too big to fit into his heart swelled through him at the sight of her flirtatious smile. He'd tried so hard to accept that this female would never be his mate.

Even though it'd nearly destroyed him.

Now, his body tingled with life, as the soul-numbing grief was replaced with joy.

"You tease me at your peril, zephyr," he warned in soft tones.

She arched toward him in silent invitation. "What are you going to do to me?"

He bent his head to brush a soft kiss over her lips. "Everything I've been fantasizing about."

Her eyes darkened with the same erotic need that churned inside him. Reaching up, she smoothed her hands over his chest. "That sounds promising."

He growled low in his throat, tugging her sweater over her head. Then, tossing it aside, he once again sought her mouth with his own.

"Not a promise," he assured her, using the tip of his tongue to lap the moisture from her lips. "A pledge."

He heard the erratic beat of her heart, but even as his hand curved around the delicate mound of her breast he felt a breeze brush over him.

Ulric lifted his head, blinking in surprise. "Is that you?"

A blush touched her cheeks. "My powers are a little…unpredictable when I'm excited."

A raw desire blasted through him, combined with an intense need to protect this female. Lying next to him she looked so tiny. So vulnerable. But there was a sensual hunger smoldering in her eyes.

"Ah," he rasped, his fingers gliding downward to discover the crest of her nipple.

She sucked in a sharp breath. "What?"

"A challenge," he murmured, lowering his head to skim his lips over the upper curve of her breast.

"A challenge? Oh." Her words were lost on a sigh as he sucked her nipple between his lips.

"I intend to ensure you lose complete control," Ulric warned.

Her nails dug into his chest, and with a greedy haste he was tugging off her remaining clothes before shedding his own. Once they were both naked, he crouched above her, relishing her beauty.

It was more than the slender body, or the finely chiseled perfection of her face. It was the luminous essence that glowed around her like a halo.

It was mesmerizing.

Suddenly he could feel his wolf pressing against his skin. Ulric hissed as utter joy surged through him. Dear goddess, until this moment he hadn't realized just how terrified he was that his animal would never fully return.

Now he wanted to tilt back his head and howl in ecstasy.

Easily catching the scent of his musk, Rainn reached up to frame his face in her hands.

"There you are," she whispered, gazing into his eyes.

His wolf took a deep breath of Rainn's misty fragrance and settled back in satisfaction. Now that this female had accepted the mating, the animal was content to leave his human side in control.

"You made me whole again," he said, his voice husky with emotion.

"We made each other whole," she countered, her hands drifting down the rigid muscles of his stomach. Taking care, she touched the wound on his side that was beginning to heal. "Someday I might even thank the Oracles for sending me to Vegas."

"We'll send them a gift basket." Planting his hands flat on the mattress, Ulric lowered his head to press his mouth between her breasts. "One after each litter."

"Litter?"

He laughed at the shock in her voice. Then the sensation of her satiny soft skin beneath his lips drove all thought from his mind.

"Spring mist," he whispered, kissing a slow, lingering path down her body.

She lifted her head off the pillow. "What do you mean by litters?"

"Mmm." Ulric tugged her legs apart. "Weren't you just complaining about too much talking and not enough action?"

Her lips parted, but before she could continue her argument, he turned his head to nuzzle the soft skin of her inner thigh.

She made a strangled sound, flopping back on the pillow. Ulric was going to take that as a *yes, please.*

Nipping at her tender flesh, Ulric teased and tormented her until Rainn reached down to position him at the spot that ached for his touch.

Ulric chuckled. "Bossy."

"Desperate," she rasped.

"Good."

Satisfaction warmed his heart. He wanted her desperate for his touch. He wanted her trembling and melting and begging...

Slipping his hands beneath her bare butt, he tilted her hips toward his mouth. Then, breathing deeply of her sweetness, he licked through her moist slit.

Rainn's hands moved to clench the patchwork quilt. Her breath rasped loudly in the silence as Ulric devoured her with a steady rhythm.

Lust thundered through him. Along with something else.

Power.

Even more power than he had before Rainn had accepted him as her mate.

Intoxicated by the sensations cascading through him, Ulric delved his tongue deep into her body. Rainn groaned her approval, moving against his tongue as he lapped at her with increasing urgency.

But even as she neared her climax, he could sense her holding back.

"Ulric, I want you with me," she breathed.

He shuddered with longing. *Yes.* He ached to be deep inside her.

Scattering kisses over the soft curve of her stomach, Ulric made his way back up her body. He paused to taste the temptation of her rosy nipples. Using his tongue, he teased the tips to tight points of need.

Mmm. His wolf growled in delight. She tasted...right. His glorious mate.

He lifted his head to simply cherish the sight of her lying beneath him.

Her hair fanned from her face, the strands as glossy as a raven's wing against the white pillow. Her cheeks were flushed, and her eyes were smoky with primitive hunger.

Then, with a mysterious smile, she reached to curl her fingers around his erection. Ulric jerked as pleasure blasted through him.

"It's my turn to play," she murmured.

Keeping her touch frustratingly light, Rainn traced the quivering length of his cock. Ulric's back arched in a silent demand for more.

He forgot the evil darkness that lurked just outside the cottage. And the knowledge that Rainn had offered her heart, but not her future.

Right now, there was nothing but his female, and the soul-shattering pleasure of her touch.

"You're killing me, my love." The words were forced through his clenched teeth.

"I'm just getting started," she murmured.

Her fingers glided to the tip of his cock, exploring the crown before moving back down. Ulric forgot how to breathe as she continued to stroke him. Up and down. Her touch as soft as a summer breeze.

"Enough," he finally rasped, reaching down to gently tug her hand away. "You can play later."

She smiled, clearly pleased by her bewitching power over him.

"Not such a big, bad wolf after all," she teased.

Ulric lowered his head to nip at her bottom lip. He wasn't bothered by her taunt. He fully intended to have the last laugh.

Settling between her legs, Ulric claimed her mouth in a sizzling kiss. Rainn moaned and twined her arms around his neck. The movement pressed her soft breasts against his chest and allowed the top of his cock to slide into the entrance of her body.

The last thread of Ulric's control snapped.

He had to have her.

Now.

Fiercely reminding himself she was considerably smaller than he was, Ulric pressed his erection deeper into her silken heat. She sighed, her legs lifting to wrap around his waist.

Heat spiked through him. Nothing had ever felt so good. Nothing.

With a groan, he started to move. Slow and steady, then faster and faster.

Beneath him the wind whirled like a tiny tornado. Something shattered. Maybe a window. And then a chair smashed into the fireplace.

Rainn's power.

The furious tempest was echoed inside Ulric as the pressure of his looming climax clenched his muscles. He was close. So close. Still, he continued to pump deep inside her, waiting until she cried out in ecstasy before he at last crested in one explosive burst of bliss.

A howl was ripped from his throat as the orgasm roared through him. Then, bending his head, he allowed his fangs to lengthen before he was sinking them into the tender flesh of her throat.

The bite would heal, but she would carry his mark for the rest of eternity.

Mine.

Chapter 18

Levet nervously paced from one end of the treasure room to the other. Inga had been gone forever. Or at least it felt like forever.

Where was she? Had she changed her mind? *Non.* Levet shook his head. He'd seen that stubborn expression on her face before. It meant that nothing was going to stop her from charging into danger.

He couldn't even hope that she was busy gathering her royal guards. Inga hadn't been raised as a queen who depended on others to willingly bow and scrape and rush to do her bidding. She had survived her grim life by taking care of herself.

Levet spun on his heel and marched back across the room. He barely noticed the piles of gems and stacks of gold. Instead he brooded on what could have distracted the ogress.

Or who.

Troy had disappeared shortly after Inga. Was it possible he was responsible for her tardiness? The thought burned like acid through Levet.

What was wrong with him? It was almost as if he was jealous. Which was ridiculous, of course. Completely locomotive.

He was Levet.

The Prince Charming of gargoyles.

The ladies adored him. And he adored them. But he didn't allow his heart to become involved. After all, there were plenty of mermaids in the sea.

He was still brooding on his stupid fear that Troy was keeping Inga entertained when the ogress stomped into the room.

Levet's breath caught in his throat. She was always an impressive sight. Now she was magnificent.

Her gown had been replaced with the mer-folk's strange, pliable armor. The small, overlapping scales were as tough as steel and shimmered with an iridescent rainbow of colors beneath the muted fairy lights. She'd scrubbed the makeup from her face and combed the curls from her fiery tufts of hair. In her hand, she proudly clutched the mighty Tryshu.

A glorious warrior preparing to go into battle.

It wasn't until Levet waddled toward her that he noticed the color staining her cheeks.

"What's wrong?" he demanded, inwardly promising to throttle Troy if he'd upset this female.

Inga ground her pointed teeth together. "I don't understand why my guards insist on treating me like I'm some delicate flower."

Ah. She hadn't been with Troy.

Something that might have been relief flowed through Levet.

"You are their queen," he reminded the ogress. "It is their duty to protect you."

She snorted. "I'm a grown demon who can make my own decisions. I don't need them fussing over me while I'm putting on my armor. Or trying to convince me I'm supposed to sit on the throne, twiddling my thumbs, while they decide what threats are worthy of the mer-folk's attention."

"They will eventually learn that you are not the twiddling type."

"I most certainly am not."

Levet studied her flushed face and the hint of crimson in her eyes. Inga might be half mermaid, but right now she was full-on, pissed-off ogress.

"Did you injure any of them?"

"Nothing serious." Inga hunched a shoulder. "One guard tried to block me from leaving my rooms. And another threatened to contact Rimm. They will heal."

Levet started to wince in sympathy for the hapless warriors who had no doubt been pulverized by Inga, only to find himself distracted by the familiar name.

"Rimm is still alive?" he demanded in surprise. Rimm had been Riven's most loyal servant.

Inga nodded. "He's the captain of my royal guards."

"I thought you planned to kill him."

Inga glanced away, as if hiding her expression. "I did, but my mother convinced me that a male capable of such unwavering loyalty to the throne was worth keeping."

Levet parted his lips to protest, only to snap them shut. He was not the most insightful demon. In truth, he found it difficult to comprehend the complex emotions that tormented so many demons. His own were less complicated.

If he was alive, it was a good day. Or rather, a good night.

But with surprising ease, he realized why Inga had allowed Rimm to stay on as the captain of her guards. The male hadn't been devoted to Riven. Just the opposite. But he'd been devoted to his people, and to performing his duty to the best of his ability.

That's exactly what Inga had been doing when she'd agreed to help Riven hold Tarak as a prisoner. She'd been a victim of the merman's evil manipulations.

No doubt her decision to offer Rimm forgiveness was a silent plea for her own past to be absolved.

"Your mother sounds like a wise female," he assured the ogress.

"Yes."

Levet cleared his throat and squared his shoulders. The reminder of Inga's painful past only intensified his urgency to rattle some sense into her thick skull. "Now about this foolish journey—"

"Shit."

With amazing speed for a female her size, Inga spun in a half circle and headed toward the door.

Levet blinked in shock. Had he offended her? *Non.* He had said far worse things to her without her storming away.

He waited for her to explain, but without even glancing back at him, Inga left the room and hurried down the corridor.

"Wait." Levet scrambled to follow her. Something that would have been a lot easier if she didn't have legs that were far longer than they needed to be. "You are not going without me," he called out. She turned the corner and headed up a pair of wide stairs. "Inga, did you hear me?"

"I'm not leaving yet," she muttered.

They climbed two flights of stairs, racing toward the private wing of the castle. Levet's concern was drowned by confusion. "Then where are you going?"

"Waverly's rooms."

They dashed down the wide hallway lined with brilliant frescoes and marble columns. More than one guard appeared to investigate the sound of running footsteps, only to duck out of the way. Anyone stupid enough to get in the path of a charging ogress deserved to be squashed like a bug.

"Is Waverly here?" he asked.

"I can't tell. I felt something." Inga gave a frustrated shake of her head. "But it's muffled."

They skidded to a halt in front of the heavy wooden door. Inga tilted her head to the side, listening for any sound that would indicate the young mermaid had returned. Silence. Inga frowned, lifting her hand.

"Wait, Inga," Levet rasped, grabbing Inga's arm.

Making a sound of impatience, she glared down at him. "What?"

Levet glanced toward the door. He wasn't afraid. He was a hero with nerves of...Well, he couldn't remember what they were supposed to be made of, but they ensured he was never scared. But he'd survived on his instincts for centuries. He wasn't going to ignore the unease that was prickling over his skin like a nasty rash.

"Are you sure we should rush in without allowing your guards to check it out first?" he asked.

Inga glanced down at him, something that might have been disappointment in her eyes. "Not you too?"

Levet squeezed her arm. He didn't want to hurt her, but he would say or do whatever necessary to keep her from rushing into danger.

"I am just suggesting we not be overly hasty," he assured her. "Once we know what is inside, then you can go in and kill it with your big fork."

She shook her head. "We can't wait. I need to make sure there's nothing that's going to harm my people." She sent Levet a stern frown. "Stay behind me."

Levet sniffed in outrage. He did not cower behind females. "Hey."

Inga waved the Tryshu. "Who has the big fork?"

Levet grimaced. No arguing with that.

Returning her attention to the door, Inga was reaching toward the knob when there was a tingle of magic, quickly followed by a warm, salty scent. Levet turned to watch as a portal formed in the center of the hallway and Waverly stepped out.

"Inga, stop," the young mermaid called out.

Freezing in place, Inga glanced over her shoulder. "Waverly?"

"What are you doing here?" Levet demanded. The female was supposed to be helping Ulric escape.

A tall, dark-haired vampire stepped out of the portal, lowering the temperature as he glared at Levet. "I could ask you the same question. You were supposed to find the book."

Levet sniffed. He was happy enough to see Waverly, but she could have left her walking-dead mate in Ireland. "I did find it," he announced.

Tarak looked caught off guard by Levet's response. "Where?"

"Not now," Inga snapped, pointing the Tryshu at the nearby door. "I sense something entered your rooms," she said to Waverly.

The mermaid nodded. "Yes, I know. I sent her there."

Inga looked confused. "Her?"

"Brigette," Waverly said.

Levet's unease solidified into fear. "Bad Brigette?"

"Yeah. Only now she's badder than before." Waverly shuddered. With lightning speed Tarak had moved to wrap a protective arm around her shoulders. "She's been infected with Zella's poison."

Inga huffed out a shocked breath. "She's infected and you brought her here?"

"She's trapped in the safe room that my father created when he built the castle," Waverly said in soothing tones. "There's no way for her or her toxin to escape."

Inga glanced toward the door, her jaws clenched. "You're sure?"

Waverly moved to place her back against the wall, as if she was on guard duty.

"I'll keep watch until we know that Zella is destroyed," she assured her queen. "Then we can move her to the dungeons."

Inga remained unconvinced. "And what if Zella isn't destroyed?"

Tarak took a position next to his mate. "Then Brigette will be the least of our concerns."

A bleak silence followed his words. The thought of a world covered by the nasty fog was enough to make Levet's heart sink to his toes.

"We will stop her," Levet said, his tone not as certain as he wanted it to be.

As if sensing his dark warning was threatening to paralyze them with fear, Tarak glanced toward Levet. "Tell me about the book."

For once, Levet didn't bristle at the commanding tone. He was as eager as the vampire to concentrate on how they could defeat the darkness rather than the nightmare awaiting them if they failed. "It was written by various demons who all warned of a corruption of magic," he said.

Tarak and Waverly exchanged a glance.

"We saw it for ourselves." Waverly's face paled, her eyes darkening with revulsion at the memory. "It was horrifying."

Levet didn't ask for details. His fleeting brush with Zella had been enough.

"It also revealed an ancient dragon symbol that translates to 'a doorway that isn't a doorway,'" he continued.

"Doorway?" Tarak appeared disappointed by the explanation. No doubt he was hoping for step-by-step directions to defeat the darkness. "The one in Ulric's village?"

"*Non.* This one is under the ocean," Levet said.

Tarak glared at Levet, as if it was entirely his fault that the book hadn't provided the answers they needed.

"Then why is the creature holding Ulric captive in the burrow?" Levet snapped his wings. "How should I know?"

"I'm about to find out," Inga announced, halting the brewing squabble. Tarak reluctantly shifted his attention to the ogress. "How?"

Inga jutted her chin. "I'm going to find the doorway that's not a doorway." "You know where it is?" the vampire demanded.

"There's a fresco in the treasure room that has the same symbol that we found in the book," Inga revealed. "There are also two dragons sealing a door shut with their fire."

"Oh." Waverly widened her eyes. "I remember seeing that painting. I thought the dragons were fighting."

"Me too," Inga admitted. "But if we believe the book, then it suggests they were holding back the darkness. I need to find the doorway and see if it's been opened."

Waverly stepped away from the door, reaching out to grasp Inga's hand. At a glance the two females couldn't look more different. Waverly was a typical mermaid: a slender, golden beauty with the long, pale hair that was tinted with blue. Inga was...Inga. A massive warrior with the features of an ogress.

But they possessed the same soft, salty scent and the aura of ruthless determination. These were two females who'd sacrificed everything for their people in the past. And would do so again if necessary.

"You can't go there alone," Waverly said. It was a command, not a request. Levet sent Inga a meaningful glance. "See?"

The ogress flushed. "Why does everyone assume that I'm suddenly helpless?"

Waverly refused to back down. "You're our queen."

"I know that," Inga muttered.

Waverly held the ogress's gaze. "Do you?"

Inga lifted up the Tryshu. "It's hard to ignore."

"The mer-folk were terrorized by Riven for centuries." Waverly continued to press. "They need a leader they can depend on. Someone who puts their people's needs ahead of their own."

Inga released a harsh sigh. "That's what I'm trying to do."

"No." Waverly planted her hands on her hips. "Putting their needs first means that you don't risk your neck chasing after danger."

Inga pressed her lips together, sparks of crimson in her eyes as she struggled to control her quick temper. "I'm only going to see if I can find the location of the door and if there's anything leaking out of it," she said, the words no doubt intended to be soothing. Instead they were a fierce warning that she wouldn't be talked out of her foolish decision.

Waverly gave one last effort. "The guards—"

"Need to stay here and make sure we're not attacked by the darkness," Inga interrupted.

"She's not wrong." Tarak intruded into the argument, glancing toward the door. "Zella might come in search of her pet Were."

There was a tense pause before Waverly at last heaved a resigned sigh. She turned her head to send Levet a warning glance.

"Don't let her get hurt."

Levet could have pointed out that it wasn't his duty to protect the female on her foolish quest. Inga wasn't his queen. But he didn't. In fact, if he was being honest with himself, he would acknowledge that he would have battled anyone who tried to keep him from standing at Inga's side as she went into danger.

Placing a hand over his heart, he offered a formal bow. "You have my pledge."

Chapter 19

Rainn released a deep sigh of satisfaction.

The sex had been great. No, not great. Earth-shattering. Better than any fantasy that had filled her dreams. But as much as she savored the climaxes that were still quaking through her body, it was the bundle of awareness that was tucked in the center of her soul that was responsible for her current state of utter bliss.

Ulric.

It felt as if the wolf was entwined with her heart. As if they truly had become one.

Drifting her fingers over his bare chest, Rainn relished the rich musk that drenched the air.

"I feel your wolf," she murmured. It wasn't a physical touch, but the sensation of his animal reaching through their bond to connect with her.

It was astonishing.

Ulric rolled to the side, balancing on his elbow as he gazed down at her with smoldering eyes. "He's eager for another bite."

Rainn shivered, hot anticipation clenching her stomach. "Insatiable."

"Absolutely." Ulric swooped down, nibbling a path of kisses along the side of her neck. "He's waited his entire life to find you."

Sharp prickles of pleasure darted through her as he reached the spot where he'd bitten her. The skin had healed, but it remained exquisitely sensitive. The lightest brush of his lips was enough to make her back arch in silent invitation.

"And the man?" she asked.

His lips moved to explore the tender line of her jaw. "The man is utterly enchanted."

Enchanted. Yes. That perfectly captured what Rainn was feeling.

"Mating magic," she whispered.

"Mmm. My tasty zephyr," he rasped, placing a lingering kiss on her mouth. But even as her lips parted, he was lifting his head. Then, without warning, he grabbed her arm and turned it over to study the mark that revealed the Oracles' ownership. "Mine," he growled. "I don't share."

Rainn's euphoria dimmed. When she was young she'd bitterly complained about her fate. Why was she the one who had to battle evil?

But over time she'd come to accept her duty. She still didn't know why she'd been chosen, but it didn't matter. The Oracles had ordained her destiny, and that was that. She would protect her people, no matter what the cost.

She'd never really considered the fact that someday she might have a mate. And that he would be forced to share her fate.

Now she studied his fierce expression with a pang of regret. "Ulric."

"Once we've destroyed the beast, I want this mark removed," he insisted.

"It will vanish when it passes to another," she told him, torn between the hope that she would someday be free, and dread at another of her people being forced to shoulder the burden. "I have no idea how the Oracles will decide if I've fulfilled the bargain."

He studied her in silence, as if trying to read something on her face.

"How did you become indebted to the Oracles?" he demanded, frowning as her lips parted to offer the glib explanation her people always used. "It has to be more than the fact that you are not the most powerful fey creatures," he contended. "Dew fairies aren't offered protection, and they are by far the most fragile creatures in the demon world."

Rainn grimaced. "It's a history we don't like to remember."

"Can you tell me?"

She hesitated. It was a tightly held secret. Then again, Ulric was destined to be a part of her life for the rest of eternity. She couldn't keep it from him forever.

"I suppose you have a right to know now that you're my mate," she conceded, trying to ignore the bad taste in her mouth. It happened every time she forced herself to consider her ancestors. "But I hope you don't think badly of my people."

He arched a brow. "I'm a Were. Our history is about as bloody as it gets."

That was true. Werewolves had a long tradition of death and destruction. Still, she had to force the words past her stiff lips.

"A very long time ago we weren't weak."

Ulric snorted, deliberately glancing around the room. "I would never call you weak."

Heat crawled beneath Rainn's cheeks as she belatedly realized the extent of the damage she'd caused to the room. The windows were shattered, the pottery tumbled off the mantel and the firewood splintered across the floor. Her blush deepened. She'd sensed she was losing control of her magic.

But...wow.

Giving a shake of her head, Rainn pushed away her embarrassment. She wanted to tell her story and be done with it. Like ripping off a bandage. Quick and painless as possible.

"Our powers were far greater than they are today," she told him.

"What sort of powers?"

"We could build lairs out of air, which were impenetrable. For a long time we lived among the clouds," she said.

Ulric's eyes widened in shock. Rainn didn't blame him. It truly must have been an amazing sight.

"Like angels?" he asked.

She wrinkled her nose. "We were no angels."

He brushed his finger over her cheeks. "Tell me."

"We could also use our minds to enter the thoughts of others."

He frowned in confusion. "You can still do that."

"Only on humans," she corrected. "And while I can wipe memories, or even *encourage* them to obey me, I don't have any ability to force demons to bend to my commands. And I certainly never enslaved anyone."

"Slaves?"

Rainn flinched at the edge in his voice. Ulric had every reason to look disgusted. He better than anyone understood the horror of being held hostage by another demon.

"Unfortunately." She glanced away, unable to watch his reaction. "And there's worse," she warned in harsh tones. "There were a few zephyr sprites who were capable of becoming the wind."

She felt him stiffen, almost as if preparing for a blow. "Becoming the wind. What does that mean?"

Rainn considered the best way to explain the unique talent. It was difficult for someone who wasn't a zephyr.

"They could turn their corporeal form into a mist," she said.

His brows snapped together. "That's worse than having slaves?"

"They were completely invisible to their enemies. And they could approach without making a sound."

A slow comprehension spread over Ulric's face. "Invisible and silent warriors?" He grimaced. "I wouldn't want to fight against them."

"There's more," she said.

"More?"

Rainn nodded. Although the history of her people was nothing more than stories to her, she still felt guilt. How could you claim pride in your ancestry without also acknowledging their faults?

"My mother told me that her father could travel through a demon's body and appear on the other side holding its heart in his hand."

Ulric hissed, no doubt imagining an enemy that could approach without any hint and rip out his heart. Or throat. Or any other vital organ. "Hell."

"Or he become a blade and cut off a vampire's head," she continued.

"Dangerous."

"Not in the beginning." She heaved a regretful sigh.

Everything would have been different if her forefathers had been content with their peaceful lives. There would have been no Oracles, and no need for Rainn to leave her home to battle evil.

Of course, that would have meant she would never have met Ulric…A sharp pain sliced through her, making it hard to breathe. *No, no, no.* The thought was unbearable.

She instinctively reached out to place her hand against his bare chest. The steady beat of his heart beneath her palm helped to ease her sudden burst of panic.

Taking a deep breath, she forced herself to continue her story.

"Zephyrs always preferred to live in isolation. Our warriors were trained to defend us, not attack others. But eventually the leaders became greedy." Revulsion curled through her stomach. Her grandfather had been destroyed centuries ago, but his legacy of violence still haunted her people. "They began to crave the same things other demons possessed. Land. Wealth. Power."

Ulric smoothed a strand of hair behind her ear. "Did they start a war?"

She shook her head. "They became assassins. They killed whenever and wherever they wanted, terrorizing anyone who refused to give in to their demands."

Ulric pointed out the obvious. "I doubt that made them popular with the other demons."

Rainn grimaced. That was the understatement of the millennium. According to her mother, their ancestors would sweep through a territory, murdering indiscriminately until the leader of the local population would offer up obscene amounts of treasure to get them to leave. Sometimes they would simply drive every creature from the area, keeping the land for themselves even if they had no intention of living there.

"Eventually the demons banded together and put a bounty on our heads," she told him. "And it wasn't just warriors. Males. Females. Even children were targeted. They paid vast rewards for each kill." A cold chill wiggled its way down her spine. Although she'd been born after the purge, the zephyrs never forgot how close they'd come to utter devastation. "We were nearly exterminated."

Ulric leaned down to brush his lips over her forehead. "No one deserves that."

Rainn blinked back tears. She'd expected Ulric to recoil in horror at her story. Or at least look at her differently. Instead, he offered her the comfort that she needed to continue.

"As our numbers dwindled, so did our powers," she confessed. "No one knows if it was the result of some divine punishment, or simply the death of our warriors, but we were no longer capable of maintaining our lairs in the clouds, so we retreated to hidden caverns in the middle of the desert."

Ulric lifted his head to study her with a somber expression. "A heavy price to pay."

It had been. And it had only been the beginning of the cost.

"We hoped we were finally safe, but the other demons refused to withdraw the bounty. We were constantly in danger, with no true power to protect ourselves."

Ulric's lips twisted into a wry smile. "I suppose that's when the Oracles made their appearance?"

"Yes." Rainn shivered. She'd known about the Oracles since her birth. After all, she carried their mark. And she'd been warned that they would eventually demand she fulfill her duty. But thinking about the all-powerful beings and actually being in their presence had been two different things. She hadn't come close to anticipating the crushing fear when she'd actually been standing in front of them. "They promised to keep us from annihilation if we agreed to their demands. Ironic, I guess, considering that's what my ancestors did to other demons."

Easily sensing the guilt that had been a part of her from the day she'd been told of their past, Ulric sent her a chiding frown. "None of this was your fault, Rainn."

"The sins of the father," she murmured, using a human quote she'd overheard. "Or in my case, the sins of my grandfather."

"No." Ulric gave a sharp shake of his head. "You may be forced to pay the price for the sins of your people, but you weren't responsible for the carnage."

She moved her hand to brush her fingers over his cheek. "Neither were you," she said in soft tones.

He flinched, his wounds still raw despite that it'd been over five hundred years since his village was destroyed.

Some pain never healed.

"Touché," he murmured. "Clearly, we were destined for one another."

* * * *

Ulric stared down at his mate.

It amazed him to think that all those years of working with her at the casino, he'd never realized the fierce emotions that churned beneath her calm façade. The guilt, the ruthless sense of duty, the fear that she might fail her people...

Or maybe he had sensed the turmoil and had been unconsciously drawn to her. His wolf had certainly accepted that they were two kindred souls.

On the point of wrapping her in his arms so he could convince her to forget the past and concentrate on the future, Ulric was distracted by a prickle of evil in the air.

There was no other way to explain it.

The sensation crawled over him. Like a cobweb clinging to his skin.

"As much as I want to stay here and forget the outside world, I'm afraid we've pressed our luck far enough," he rasped.

Rainn gave a shaky nod, scurrying out of the bed to pull on her clothes. Ulric did the same, shoving his feet into his boots before he led her into the living room.

With a soft gasp, Rainn came to a halt, glancing around the floor that was littered with glass and bits of pottery, along with slivers of wood from the overhead beams.

"Oh," she breathed in horror. "I've made a mess."

Ulric chuckled. The tempest that had swirled around them as they'd made love had only added to the intensity of his pleasure.

"*We* made a mess," he corrected, bending down to place a soft, lingering kiss on her lips.

"Yes." She pushed him away with a teasing smile. "It really is your fault."

"I'm good with that," he assured her. "It lets me know when I'm doing things right." He paused, pretending to consider the hazards of a lover who could cause complete chaos. "Of course, I need to make sure I clear out any projectiles from our lair. I'd hate to be skewered while I was—"

She pressed her fingers against his lips. "Ulric."

He savored the sight of her rosy blush. His wolf wanted to nuzzle against her cheeks, absorbing her delightful heat. Instead he settled for one last kiss.

"We'll finish this later," he promised.

She nodded. "After I've destroyed Zella."

Ulric frowned at her choice of words. "After *we've* destroyed her," he corrected.

"Ulric, it's my duty—"

"You're wasting your breath." He overrode her words. "We're in this together."

"Like the Justice League?" she demanded in wry tones.

He tapped the end of her nose. "Yeah, but I refuse to be Wonder Woman."

"*Pfft*. You should be so lucky. *I'm* Wonder Woman."

He gazed down at her, refusing to be distracted. "What do you need from me?"

"I need you to get out of here."

He shook his head. "Not happening."

"I'm serious, Ulric," she insisted. "If Zella gets her hands on your blood, she can destroy the last barrier. We can't let that happen."

He refused to consider what would happen if Zella managed to burst through the barrier and fully enter the world. He wasn't leaving Rainn. End. Of. Story. "We're partners."

Her eyes darkened to a steely gray, her hair floating around her face as her powers leaked out.

"We are, but nothing is more important than preventing the darkness from infecting the magic."

Ulric stiffened as he caught the sound of running footsteps outside the cottage.

"Too late," he muttered.

"Dammit." Rainn sent him a frown of frustration before the door was shoved open and Chaaya rushed inside.

"Showtime, kiddies," she announced in breathless tones. As if she'd just run a marathon. Then, with a frown, she glanced around the living room. "What the freak did you do to my house?"

Rainn ignored Ulric's stifled laugh. "Sorry. Things got a little…"

"Catastrophic?" Chaaya suggested when Rainn's words trailed away.

"Energetic," Ulric corrected.

"Eww." Chaaya wrinkled her nose. "TMI."

Ulric returned his attention to his mate, reaching out to grasp her hands. They felt as cold as ice despite the heat that lay thick in the air. "Are you ready?"

She forced a smile to her lips. "I don't think it matters."

"What are you going to do?" Chaaya demanded.

Rainn shrugged. "Wing it."

Chaaya blinked. "That's the plan?" Her voice dripped with sarcasm. "Winging it?"

"Do you have a better one?" Rainn challenged.

"I'm just the sacrifice." The girl glanced toward Ulric. "I guess we're both sacrifices."

"Which means you should both get out of here," Rainn reminded them.

Chaaya shrugged, holding Ulric's gaze. "She's not wrong."

He sent her a glare that would have made a full-grown troll cower in fear. Predictably, the aggravating girl blew him a kiss of complete indifference.

He muttered a curse and forced himself to concentrate on his mate. "You can't kill her on your own," he insisted. "You need me."

"Hmm." Chaaya tapped the spear in her hand against the side of her leg. "Maybe you don't have to kill the beast."

"What are you talking about?" Rainn asked.

"If you can seal the doorway again, it will lock the beast in this place."

Ulric snorted. "I forgot to bring my dragon with me."

Chaaya narrowed her eyes, turning toward Rainn. "How can you stand the mutt?"

"He's an acquired taste."

"Doubtful."

Ulric made a sound of impatience, glaring at Chaaya. "Can you take us to the doorway?

"Yeah. But first." The girl picked her way across the littered floor to pull open a closet door. Reaching inside, she pulled out a spear identical to her own. Then, making her way back across the room, she tossed the weapon to Rainn. "Copper is the only thing I've found that the beast doesn't like."

Rainn nodded, clutching the weapon. "Let's go."

Chaaya headed toward the open door. "This way."

Chapter 20

Levet intended to spend the journey to the doorway that wasn't a doorway urging Inga to return to the castle. It was madness to face whatever was down there without a shoal of mer-folk warriors at their backs.

But as soon as they stepped out of the portal, the words died on Levet's lips.

He'd expected to be at the bottom of the ocean. A cold, dark place that could crush lesser demons. Instead they were floating in a ball of magic created by the Tryshu.

The shimmering sphere was clear enough to reveal the fish swimming past them, as well as providing a soft glow of light. Astonished, Levet reached out to place his hand against the bubble, pleased by the effervescent magic that tingled against his palm.

"I did not know you could do this," he breathed.

Inga's features twisted into a wry smile. "Neither did I," she admitted. "It has to be coming from the Tryshu."

"Amazing." Levet jumped as if he was on a trampoline, delighted as the ball bobbed up and down even as it continued to zoom through the water. "We should float away."

"Don't think I'm not tempted," Inga muttered.

Levet swallowed a small sigh, a portion of his delight vanishing. Slowly he turned to study his companion. "I am sorry."

She looked surprised by his soft words. "Sorry for what?"

"I had hoped that discovering the truth of your parents and being reunited with your family would bring you happiness."

"Is that why you abandoned me?"

Abandoned her? Levet slammed his fists on his hips. "I left because I was angry. You had violined with my mind."

Inga's brittle defenses shattered as her shoulders slumped and a deep sadness rippled over her face.

"Fiddled," she absently corrected him. "And you're right. I don't blame you for leaving."

Levet waved away her apology. He'd been furious at the time. What demon wanted to be manipulated by magic? But over the past weeks he'd come to accept that Inga had been desperate. And desperate demons sometimes did stupid things.

Not himself, of course.

"It will get easier," he said, patting her arm.

"Will it?" Inga released a bitter laugh. "I don't know how to be a mermaid, let alone the Queen of the Mer-folk."

"You have your mother to help you," Levet pointed out. "That's more than most of us have."

His own mother had tried to kill him. More than once.

Inga's features softened. Well, as much as ogress features could soften. "It's...nice to have her in my life."

Levet tilted his head to the side. "Just nice?"

"Wonderful," Inga admitted. "For so long I believed she'd considered me a blight. And that she couldn't bear to have me in her life."

Levet gave her arm another pat. "Just as you fear your people will not accept you. Once they realize who you are—"

"Who am I?" Inga interrupted in harsh tones. "A slave who helped their crazy-ass king stay in power for centuries."

Levet refused to be silenced. Inga wasn't angry. She was afraid.

"He deceived you just as he deceived everyone else. There's no shame in that."

She scowled. "You don't understand."

"Probably not. I rarely do, for some odd reason," Levet agreed. "Explain it to me."

She clicked her tongue. As if Levet was being deliberately dense. Then, thrusting out her arm, she pushed up the armor to expose her wrist.

"I'm a slave," she said, flashing the ugly tattoo that marred the skin. "Not a queen."

Levet shrugged, even as he inwardly seethed. He wanted to track down the stupid mer-folk who dared to make Inga feel unworthy, and...Okay, he did not know precisely what he wanted to do to them, but it would certainly include boils and pus and seepage.

For now, he gently tugged the armor back over the tattoo. "Have you ever considered the fact that the Tryshu chose you because you have been forced to battle to survive from the day you were born?"

Inga stilled, like a dog waiting to be kicked. "Why?"

"The mer-folk were isolated and abused by Riven," Levet reminded her, his voice low and solemn. "Then they were forced to accept he was a fraud. Now they need a leader who understands how to crawl out of a shattered past and create a new future."

"That's…" Inga's voice cracked, then she gave a loud sniff.

Levet studied her in confusion. He'd tried to help, but now he worried that he'd only made matters worse. "Are you crying?"

"Don't be stupid." She turned away, still sniffing. "I have something in my eye."

"Oh. I can help," Levet assured her. He stepped forward only to be tossed against the side of the bubble as it jerked to the side and then began to sink at an alarming speed. There was another jerk and Levet struggled to stay upright. "What are you doing?"

"Nothing." Inga glanced downward, her face paling. "We're being pulled down."

Levet followed her gaze, belatedly noting the black, inky liquid swirling around them.

"What is that?" Levet dropped to his knees, trying to peer through the darkness. He was surprised to discover they'd nearly reached the ocean bed. And that the entire area looked as bleak and desolate as the land around Ulric's old village. There were no fish, no coral, or even rocks. The only thing that remained was a large crack that was leaking the oily darkness. "I think we found the doorway that isn't a doorway."

Inga knelt beside him. "Or it found us."

They shuddered in unison.

* * * *

Rainn hissed as they stepped out of the cottage. Her sensitivity to the wind made the thick, tainted air even worse. It was like being shrouded in a blanket of sheer filth.

Easily sensing her distress, Ulric stepped toward her. She waved him away, grimly concentrating on keeping pace with Chaaya. She could physically feel Zella out there, just waiting to attack. Rainn wanted to get Ulric to the doorway before the fighting started.

She didn't know how she was going to force the stubborn Were to leave without her. But that was a worry for later.

As if sharing her urgency, Chaaya picked up speed. Rainn did the same, her feet pounding against the hard ground to send up puffs of powdery dirt. She coughed, her eyes watering, but she never slowed.

She didn't have a clue how Chaaya knew where they were going. Everything looked exactly the same to her. A flat, endless hellscape.

Chaaya, however, never hesitated as she led them forward. Or maybe they were standing still, and the weird space was moving around them. Hard to tell.

It was equally hard to determine how much time was passing. They might have been in this place for a couple hours or days.

The sensation was unnerving.

Clutching the spear that Chaaya had tossed to her before leaving the cottage, Rainn glanced over her shoulder.

There was a pressure building behind them. Like the pulse of lava before a volcano erupted.

"The beast is coming," Chaaya muttered.

Rainn scanned the horizon. "I can't see her."

"She won't be in her human form," Chaaya warned. "Hurry."

Rainn didn't need to be coaxed. Swiveling her gaze back to the empty land in front of her, she ran as fast as her feet would carry her.

The swelling sense of doom followed closely behind them, the stench of evil washing over the land like a wave. Rainn gagged, then skidded to a halt as she nearly smacked into Chaaya's back. "Why are you stopping?" she rasped.

Chaaya sent her a puzzled frown. "This is it."

Ulric stood next to Rainn, scowling at the girl. "Is what?"

"The doorway," Chaaya said in impatient tones.

Rainn and Ulric glanced around. There was nothing to see beyond the empty landscape.

"Is it invisible?" Ulric snapped.

Chaaya appeared genuinely confused. "You can't see it?"

Ulric snorted. "I see a big crack," he said, pointing toward the wide fissure that split the powdery ground.

Chaaya nodded. "That's it."

"That?" Ulric demanded in disbelief.

"What did you expect?" Chaaya sent him a mocking smile. "The Pearly Gates?"

Ulric glanced toward Rainn, his teeth clenched. "This place truly is hell."

"It's about to get a whole lot worse," Chaaya warned.

"Zella," Rainn breathed without bothering to turn. She could feel the malevolent heat blasting against her skin.

Chaaya paled. "Yep."

Rainn reached out to grasp her mate's arm. "Ulric," she pleaded in soft tones, glancing toward the crevice. The male could easily fit through the opening. Hell, a tribe of trolls could squeeze through.

"No." Ulric jutted his chin to a stubborn angle. "It's not happening."

"Listen to me." She dug her fingers into his arm, as if she could force him to listen. "If we both die, there will be no way to warn the world about the danger."

He shrugged. "Screw the world."

Stubborn, aggravating male. She barely resisted the urge to poke him with her spear.

"And what if we don't die?" She tried a new tactic. Anything to convince him to leave. "We might destroy Zella and then be trapped here. If you go now, you can return with the dragons to get me out."

"No."

Rainn glanced toward the crevice. If she wrapped Ulric in her magic, she might be able to stuff him into the—

"Too late." Chaaya intruded into her frantic thoughts. "It's time for you to wing it."

"Great," Rainn muttered, forcing herself to turn and confront her destiny.

Her entire life had been waiting for this moment. This was why she'd been born with the mark on her skin. And why she'd been whisked to the meeting with the Oracles. And why she'd been sent to Vegas.

This…

Her mouth went dry as she watched Zella approach. Only it wasn't Zella. The old woman was gone and in her place was a towering nightmare of flames.

Sweeping forward like a tornado, it sent a choking cloud of dust swirling around them.

"Rainn." Ulric grasped her shoulders, turning her to meet his glowing golden gaze.

"I know," she whispered, lifting her hand to lightly touch his cheek. "I love you too."

"Aw." Chaaya intruded into their brief moment of intimacy. "Group hug?"

Ulric snarled in frustration, but Rainn turned toward the girl. "You said copper can hurt the…" Her words trailed away. She didn't know what to call it. A fire spirit? A creature from her deepest nightmares? "Beast," she settled on. "How?"

"Watch."

With blurring speed, Chaaya abruptly charged toward the fire creature, waving her spear in front of her. The flames veered away, as if afraid of the weapon. Then, spinning on her heel, Chaaya was racing back to stand next to Rainn.

"Does it actually injure the thing?" Ulric demanded.

The girl grimaced. "I think so, but I'm usually just trying to run it off, not kill it. I don't know how much damage it actually does."

"Let's find out," Rainn forced herself to say, annoyed when her voice quavered.

She wanted to confront her fate with the sort of bravery that was worthy of her people. If she was going to die, it would be with her dignity intact.

Her lips twisted into a wry smile. At least she hadn't run away in terror. Maybe that would have to be enough courage for today.

"I'll keep her distracted," Ulric said, brushing his lips over hers before he stepped back.

Magic swirled around him, the sparkles dulled by the strange air. Rainn heard the sound of bones snapping and muscles stretching before there was a howl that was a cross between pain and ecstasy. A few seconds later the large wolf was bounding toward the fire.

Rainn lifted a hand, as if she could call him back, but before she could say a word, an arm wrapped around her shoulder.

"Ready?" Chaaya demanded.

A lump formed in Rainn's throat. "No."

"Yeah, me neither." Chaaya dropped her arm, giving her spear a twirl. "Let's do it."

With a cocky grin, the girl dashed forward, releasing a war cry as she headed toward the side of the beast.

Rainn sucked in a slow, deep breath, forcing herself to ignore the sound of Ulric's snarls as he slashed his claws through the flames, and Chaaya's grunts as she stabbed at the beast on the other side.

Instead she gripped the spear in a sweaty hand and charged forward.

As if sensing her approach, the fiery spirit spun to the side. Exactly what she wanted. She gathered in the stale air, using it to catapult herself upward at a sharp angle. At the same time, she slashed her arm from side to side, slicing the spear through the outer flames.

Rainn thought she heard a scream. Not with her ears, but inside her head. Startled, she dropped back to the ground and hastily glanced toward

Ulric. The wolf was busy nipping and clawing at the trailing tendrils of fire, while Chaaya was slashing and dashing with her spear.

The scream had come from the beast.

Which meant it could be hurt.

Squaring her shoulders, Rainn once again used the wind to launch herself upward. This time, unfortunately, the beast wasn't so easily fooled. Even as Rainn jabbed the spear into the flames, it whipped out to smack her across the chest. The blow sent her flying backward, and she lost control of her power. Flailing her arms, she plummeted downward, hitting the ground hard enough to crack a rib and rattle her brains.

She blacked out for a minute before struggling back to consciousness. Distantly she heard Ulric howl in fury, but before he could rush to her rescue, Rainn forced herself to her feet. She groaned as pain shot through her body. Every instinct told her to curl into a ball until she healed, but instead she stiffened her spine and held up a hand. Ulric snarled, but he returned to badgering the spirit.

On the other side, Chaaya had attached a leather strap to her spear and was whirling it over her head, tossing it into the flames before yanking it back.

Even at a distance Rainn could tell the girl was growing tired. Her movements were slower, and her shoulders were beginning to slump. She wouldn't be able to continue at this pace for much longer. Neither would Ulric. They were both risking everything to allow her the opportunity to strike the killing blow.

A damned shame she didn't have a clue how to do that.

Squashing the urge to panic, Rainn studied the swirling fire.

There had to be a way to destroy it. There *had* to be. Otherwise they might as well lie down and die.

No. That wasn't going to happen.

Fiercely she concentrated on the flames that swayed and twirled in front of her. She could see a lingering slash where she'd struck it with her spear.

It had not only been injured, but it was taking time to heal.

The thought had barely formed when there was the sound of a sharp yip. Jerking her head to the side, Rainn was horrified as she watched Ulric being circled by a wall of flames.

Shit. He was trapped. She had to—

Before she could move, Chaaya was leaping over the barrier of fire and landing on top of the wounded wolf. She stabbed the looming flames with her spear, trying to keep them at bay.

Rainn fiercely turned her back on her companions, even when the stench of burnt fur assaulted her nose. Every second that passed made it more likely they were going to die.

She had to do something.

Now.

Concentrating on the beast, Rainn battled back the bleak despair. There had to be a weakness, so what was it?

Her gaze lingered at the very center of the beast. There was something there. A dark core. Or a black hole. No, wait. Not a hole. As she studied it, she realized it was pulsing.

The heart of the beast.

If she could stab the copper spear into that place, it might actually damage the spirit. But how did she reach it?

There was no way she could throw the spear hard enough to prevent the creature from slapping it away. Not even Ulric would have the strength. And she would be fried to a crisp if she tried to force her way to the center.

A strangled laugh was wrenched from her throat. For the first time in her life, she regretted not possessing the power of her ancestors. Not to conquer or terrorize, but to save the world from evil.

All very noble. Unfortunately, the magic had been lost long ago...

Or had it? Surely magic didn't disappear? It was a part of who she was as a zephyr. What had faded was the power necessary to tap into the ancient gifts.

Power that Ulric possessed.

Rainn sucked in a slow, deep breath. Was it possible? Only one way to find out.

Gripping the spear, she allowed the sensation of the mating bond to flow through her. She urgently latched on to his presence that was nestled in her heart, using it to pull at his power. There was a mere trickle at first, as if Ulric was fighting against her. Or perhaps he simply didn't understand what was happening.

Then, as if sensing her need, he abruptly halted his struggles. Instead he fiercely shoved his power through the bond.

Rainn gasped, shocked by the force of the raw animal energy. It surged through her body and heated her blood. *Holy crap.* No wonder Ulric was so eager to shift into his wolf. The power was intoxicating.

Wishing she could simply savor the sensations that were supercharging her, Rainn instead concentrated on her magic. She allowed it to tingle through her, as soft as a breeze. It felt even...lighter than usual, and Rainn started to panic.

Was Ulric's power not enough to stir her most ancient gifts?

Then, without warning, she felt the ground dissolving beneath her feet. No wait. It wasn't the ground dissolving. It was her.

It was the weirdest thing she'd ever experienced. It felt like she was turning to mist. No, that wasn't quite right. She wasn't a cloud. It was more that she'd become a part of the air. Or the air had become a part of her.

She could still feel herself. The beat of her heart, her legs that seemed to dangle off the ground, and her jagged breath. But at the same time, she was as weightless as a summer breeze.

Amazing.

Clutching the spear in fingers that shouldn't be capable of holding the weapon, Rainn returned her attention to the dark core at the center of the beast. Awkwardly she drifted forward. It wasn't like floating. She lurched to the side, buffeted by the wind. *Crap.* She was drifting away from the beast. Frantically she used her magic to take command of the breeze.

Inch by inch she managed to spin herself back around and even started to pick up speed as she glided closer to the flames. She held the spear in front of her, allowing the copper blade to pierce the fire.

Heat seared through her. Hotter than anything she'd ever felt before. But while the pain was grinding, it didn't halt her forward momentum. In fact, she was going even faster.

As if the flames were sucking her in.

Imagining herself as an arrow, she held the spear in front her. Then, with a last burst of her magic, she headed toward the dark center.

She heard the screams again. So loud and piercing that they threatened to shatter the earth. This time, however, they held more than pain. There was fury and hunger and…

Fear.

Chapter 21

Ulric was melting.

Not figuratively. Literally.

The intensity of the flames that surrounded him had reached a thermonuclear level. The only reason he hadn't been utterly consumed was Chaaya's frantic efforts to keep the fire from sweeping over him.

Still, as much as he appreciated her efforts, he knew it was a losing battle. The girl was swiftly weakening. Within a few minutes the flames were going to overwhelm them both.

Using the last of his strength, Ulric turned his head toward Rainn. If he was going to die, he wanted her to be his last thought. But even as he caught sight of her on the other side of the beast, he felt the tug on his waning strength.

Instinctively he tried to fight against the leeching. It was only when he sensed the soft, misty presence of Rainn that he realized she was pulling at their mating bond.

She needed his power.

Without hesitation, Ulric lowered his barriers and shoved every last ounce of his strength through their mystical connection.

He wasn't sure what he'd expected. Perhaps for her to use the energy to throw the spear. Instead she…

Disappeared.

What the hell? His eyes had to be playing tricks on him. Or maybe he was going blind from the agonizing heat.

No. He could see the spear. It was darting directly into the center of the fiery beast.

Rainn.

She was invisible. Which meant she'd somehow called on her ancient magic. It was the only explanation.

Then all thoughts were wiped from his mind and he howled as he felt her pain drill through his body. She was being obliterated by the creature.

No, no, no.

He attempted to stand. He had to get to her. Chaaya obviously had the same impulse as she slashed through the flames and tried to take a step forward. At the same time, the spear that Rainn was holding penetrated the dark core of the creature.

The world came to a complete and utter halt. As if they were all frozen in place. Ulric didn't dare to breathe. Even his heart stopped beating. Then the air pressure thickened, a weird buzzing ringing in Ulric's ears before a violent explosion sent him flying through the air.

He hit the ground with a heavy thud, knocking the air from his lungs. But thankfully he'd been tossed away from the flames, allowing him to slowly regain his strength.

Once the most dire injuries had been healed, he scrambled to his feet. Glancing around, he wasn't surprised to discover the scorched pit that had been gouged into the ground. It'd felt like he'd been hit with a bomb.

But what he hadn't expected was the realization that the towering inferno was gone. As if Rainn had managed to blow the creature to smithereens. Whatever smithereens were.

Was it possible?

Ulric gave a shake of his head.

He didn't care what had happened to the fiery bitch. All he wanted was to find Rainn.

Remaining in his animal form, Ulric loped across the shattered landscape. For a frantic few minutes he couldn't see her. In fact, it was only because he could sense her through their mating bond that he wasn't in an instant frenzy. She was alive. And nearby.

After what felt like an eternity, he finally caught her scent. Digging his claws into the dirt, he leaped over a pile of jagged rocks that had been blown out of the pit, landing next to her unconscious body.

With a shimmer of magic, he was shifting into his human form and kneeling next to Rainn. She didn't look injured. Hell, he would assume that she was sleeping if she hadn't just battled an evil spirit that had nearly roasted them into the netherworld.

Gently he reached out to touch her cheek. It was pale but warm beneath his fingertips, and he could hear the steady beat of her heart.

So why didn't she wake up?

The wolf in him wanted to stretch out beside her and pull her close against his body. The man, however, understood that the only way to protect her was to get her out of there.

He had no idea if the evil spirit was dead or just regrouping, but he didn't intend to stay around long enough to find out.

Scooping Rainn's limp body off the ground, he pressed her against his chest. He cast a quick glance around, trying to orient himself. This weird-ass place screwed with his senses. Where was the doorway?

His breath abruptly caught in his throat at the small form sprawled near the edge of the pit.

Chaaya.

He told himself to ignore the sight. Chaaya had been sacrificed endless centuries ago. This was now her domain, right? It was quite likely he would destroy her if he took her out of here.

Trying to force himself to turn away, he realized that his feet wouldn't obey. They were glued to the ground, refusing to budge.

Dammit.

The girl had saved his life. If she hadn't jumped in front of him to fight back the flames, he would have been destroyed.

He couldn't leave her here.

If she wanted—or needed—to come back to this nasty place, she could. For now, he was taking her with them.

Ignoring the inner voice that told him he was being an idiot, Ulric raced over the charred ground. Then, slinging Rainn over one shoulder, he bent down to grab the unconscious Chaaya and flung her over the other one.

Straightening, he grimly jogged in the direction that he hoped would take him to the doorway.

Dear goddess, let him be right.

He had a terrible premonition that their time was running out.

* * * *

Levet pressed his snout against the bubble, his wings fluttering with unease.

Why did Inga have to be so stubborn?

They were supposed to find the doorway that wasn't a doorway. Very well. They'd found it. Now they needed to return and warn everyone that it was broken.

But was that what they were doing?

Non.

Inga had regarded the inky sludge that boiled out of the crack on the ocean floor and announced that she was going to take a closer look. What did she need to see? A hole in the ground? Nasty black goop?

Before he could halt her, however, she'd somehow stepped out of the bubble and was bobbing along the crack.

Horrified, Levet banged his fist against the invisible barrier that surrounded him.

"Inga," he roared. "Get back in here."

She bounced along the edge of the opening, moving with astonishing ease through the crushing pressure of the water. With her ogress features it was easy to forget her mermaid blood until she was in this element.

"You don't have to shout," she said, her voice echoing through the bubble as if she was standing next to him. "I can hear you just fine."

Levet stomped his foot. He could feel the evil churning around her. What if it touched her? Or worse.

"I will shout when you are being a hog-headed idiot!"

She turned her head to send him an outraged glare. "Excuse me?"

"*Non*. I do not excuse you," Levet retorted, giving another bang on the side of the bubble. "It is time to return to the castle."

She stubbornly shook her head. "I think I can fix it."

Levet scowled. "What?"

"I think I can close the opening," she told him.

"How?"

She gave a wave of the Tryshu. "With this."

Levet wasn't impressed. Inga had been in control of the mystical weapon for a handful of weeks. Hardly long enough to have any idea what it could or couldn't do.

"Do you even know how to use that thing?" he demanded.

She puffed out her chest, her tufts of hair swaying as the current swept past her.

"I'm the Queen of the Mer-folk," she snapped. "Of course I know how to work it."

Levet held her crimson gaze. "Really?"

There was a long silence before she heaved a frustrated sigh. "Fine," she at last muttered. "I might not understand how the stupid thing works, but I don't need to. It…" She halted, as if considering her words. "It tells me what to do," she finally admitted.

Levet snorted. Big forks didn't speak to people. Even if they were magical. Then he realized there was a strange noise vibrating through the air.

"Is it humming?" he asked.

"Yes."

Okay. Perhaps it was talking to her. But that wasn't necessarily a good thing. "Inga."

She looked impatient. "What?"

"Have you considered the idea that the Tryshu might be in the control of whatever evil is leaking out of that hole?"

She frowned, studying the end of the trident as she released a burst of power. Sparkles swirled through the water.

"The magic is mermaid," she announced.

"But—"

"Shh," she interrupted. "I need to concentrate."

Levet stomped his foot in frustration. "If you get yourself killed I'll..."

"You'll what?"

"I will follow you to the netherworld and torment you for the rest of eternity," Levet warned.

A wistful smile touched her lips. "Would that be such an awful thing?" she whispered.

A funny, fluttery thing happened in the center of his chest. Was that his heart?

"Inga." He tried to force his way through the wall of the bubble. If she was going to put herself in danger, he needed to be at her side.

The humming intensified, and Inga pointed the Tryshu at the long crevice.

"I have to do this," she said, releasing the magic of the powerful weapon.

Levet watched as the sparkles shot directly toward the darkness. Astonishingly, the power of Inga's magic managed to drive the evil back into the crevice that it was boiling out of and, at the same time, pull the ground into a smooth seam, as if she was knitting the solid bedrock back together.

Stunned into a rare silence, Levet simply admired the female's outrageous display of power. He'd once seen a dragon in full-out battle mode. He'd assumed that nothing could come close to such raw strength.

Inga was every bit as powerful.

Sacré bleu.

Lost in awe, Levet nearly missed the strange scent that was suddenly teasing at his snout. What was that? And why was it familiar?

Oh no.

"Inga," he called out. "Wait."

She refused to glance in his direction. "What now?"

"Something is coming."

That got her attention. She darted her gaze from left to right while continuing to seal the crevice. "Where?"

"From the crack."

She tightened her fingers around the Tryshu. "Is it the corruption?"

Levet shook his head even though she wasn't looking in his direction. "It smells like werewolf," he told her. "I think it's Ulric."

He heard her gasp of surprise. "You're sure?"

"I'm certain," Levet said, bouncing on his toes. Now he could also get the scent of Rainn. Along with another female he didn't recognize. "Here they come," he warned.

The words had just left his lips when Ulric burst through the crevice with two unconscious females slung over his shoulders.

Inga grabbed the naked male and with one mighty heave shoved him into the bubble. Then, turning back, she used her magic to finish closing the crack.

Intent on Inga, Levet barely paid attention to Ulric, who was squatted on the other side of the bubble, both women still held in his arms.

"I've gone from one hell to another," the werewolf rasped before he collapsed with a soft groan.

"Stupid dog," Levet muttered, concentrating on Inga as she finished up her task. "Come on, come on."

Seconds later the ogress had shoved her way back into the magical sphere and was dropping to her knees in exhaustion.

"That's as good as I can do," she breathed.

Levet moved toward her, framing her face in his hands. "Take us home."

Chapter 22

Rainn snuggled next to Ulric, rubbing her nose against his chest. The warm musk of his wolf spread over her like a blanket.

She'd awakened when they'd arrived at the underwater castle. There had been a mass of folks talking and asking questions, but one growl from Ulric and they'd parted so he could carry her to a private bedroom.

They'd had a few minutes to discuss how the beast had exploded when she'd rammed the spear into its heart. And how he'd carried her, along with Chaaya, through the crack. She was still fuzzy on how they'd come to the castle. Something about an ogress and gargoyle and a floating ball.

At the time, she'd been too weary to care, tumbling into a deep sleep.

Now she allowed herself to stretch out her stiff muscles and relish the fact that she was alive.

Warm lips brushed the top of her head as Ulric's arms tightened around her.

"Good morning, sleepyhead," he said in a voice husky from sleep. "Or rather, good evening."

She tilted back her head to study his gorgeous male features. "Evening?"

"You've been asleep for over twenty-four hours."

"Oh." She was only mildly surprised. "I had a big day," she reminded him.

"You certainly did." His fingers skimmed up and down the curve of her spine. "You battled Zella, got sucked into another dimension, then turned into the Invisible Warrior Woman to destroy the fiery beast who intended to destroy the world."

"Invisible Warrior Woman?" She wrinkled her nose. "That's not nearly as good as Wonder Woman."

"It's exactly what we needed." He brushed a kiss over her forehead before studying her with a searching gaze. "How did you do it? I thought the ancient magic was lost?"

"It was." She lifted her hand to rub it over the center of his naked chest. Beneath her palm she could feel the steady beat of his heart. Nothing had ever felt so wonderful. Against all odds, they'd survived. A miracle. "Until I managed to boost it with Wolfman power."

"Wolfman?" He grimaced in horror. "Absolutely not."

"It's better than Invisible Warrior," she chided.

"Maybe we can just be Ulric and Rainn from now on."

A soul-deep longing twisted her heart. That's exactly what she wanted. No more fighting. No more evil. No more destiny hanging over her head like a guillotine.

"Do you think the beast was destroyed?" she asked.

"Either it was destroyed, or Inga managed to seal the door with enough power to block it from entering our world."

She blinked at the sheer confidence in his voice. "You sound very certain."

He smiled. "I am."

"How?"

"This." He reached to wrap his fingers around her wrist, holding up her arm.

It took her a second to realize what he was talking about. Then the breath was driven from her lungs.

"It's gone," she rasped, gazing at her skin where the Oracles' mark used to be.

"You're free," Ulric told her.

Joy raced through her. She'd never dared to think beyond her duty to the Oracles. It was too painful. Now...

Now she could barely contain her happiness. Twining her arms around Ulric's neck, she gazed at him in wonderment. This male had given her more than his heart. He'd given her a reason to fight for a future.

"Not exactly free," she murmured, tugging his head down to nip at his lower lip. "Now I have a mate."

Easily sensing her wakening passion, Ulric rolled on top of her, his eyes smoldering with a golden heat. "A very demanding mate."

She pressed a lingering kiss against his lips. "You talk too much."

Epilogue

Ulric and Rainn remained at the castle for another day, returning to Vegas just as the sun was setting. Escorting his mate to his private rooms, he left her to enjoy a hot bath, while he went in search of Chiron.

He found the vampire seated at his desk in his sleek silver-and-black office. Closing the door, Ulric watched as the vampire rose to his feet and crossed the carpet to stand directly in front of him.

"How is Rainn?"

Ulric wrinkled his nose. "Still exhausted, but delighted to be released from her duty to the Oracles."

"Hmm." Chiron studied him with a faint smile. "And you?"

Ulric felt a shiver race through him. Not one of fear, thank the goddess. But of anticipation.

"Ready to conquer the world."

"Yeah." Chiron slapped him on the shoulder. "A good female will do that to a male. You'll need a larger apartment. The penthouse suite is available."

"Actually, I think we might spend some time with Rainn's family," he said. Rainn had mentioned her desire to visit her parents shortly before they'd left the mer-folk castle. "She's been away from them for years. Plus, she wants to search for the child who will be marked by the Oracles. She doesn't want them to feel alone, as she did."

Chiron nodded. "How long will you be gone?"

"I'm not sure." Ulric glanced around the office, knowing he was going to miss this hotel. It'd been his home for decades. But now his place was at Rainn's side. "Don't worry. I'm sure that Waverly will be more than capable of helping with Dreamscape."

Chiron appeared oddly offended. "I'm not asking you as a business partner. I'm asking as your brother."

Brother. Warmth cascaded through Ulric. He'd grieved for the loss of his family for so long, always somehow blaming himself for their loss. Now, he was ready to put the memory of his pack to rest. He would always miss them, but he had a new family.

Chiron and Rainn. And even Waverly.

Then the thought of family triggered a less pleasant thought.

"We'll be gone a few weeks or so," he told Chiron. "At some point I'm going to have to return to the mer-folk's lair and make a decision about what to do with Brigette."

"A worry for later." Chiron squeezed his shoulder. "Go enjoy your new mate."

Heat prickled through Ulric. It didn't take much effort to imagine Rainn in his deep soaking tub, completely naked. In fact, it was harder *not* to keep imagining it.

But first he had to finish the task that had brought him to this office in the first place. "I do have one request."

"Name it," Chiron said without hesitation.

"Can Chaaya stay here until we know exactly how she's going to react to this world?" he asked. He'd brought the girl with him when they came to Vegas. Not out of choice, but because Inga had threatened to have Chaaya tossed in the dungeon if he didn't get her out of there. "I'd like to have her someplace where she'll be protected."

"Chaaya?" Chiron's brows snapped together. "The dead human who challenged the mer-folk warriors to a drinking contest and got them so trollied they were swinging from the chandeliers and running naked through the hallways?"

Ulric grimaced. "She's like a human teenager. All hormones and smartass mouth. But she did save my life, and she needs someone watching over her."

Chiron shuddered, but he offered a grudging nod. "Fine. But you'll owe me."

Ulric abruptly pulled the vampire into his arms for a rough hug. This male had rescued him from the slave pits, given him a purpose in his life, and filled the sense of pack that he'd so desperately needed. "More than I'll ever be able to repay."

Chiron returned the hug for the briefest moment, then he pulled back with a chiding frown.

"Okay, that's enough mush. Your mate's waiting for you." He waved his hand toward the door. "Go."

Ulric didn't have to be told twice.

Leaving the office, he sprinted down the hallway. He fully intended to rejoin Rainn before she left her bath.

He ignored the startled glances that followed his mad flight, his laugh of pure joy trailing behind him.

ONCE, SHE GOT AWAY

The body lying on a cold steel slab bears all the hallmarks of the Chicago Butcher. There's a cruel slash across her throat, deep enough to sever the carotid artery, and a small crescent carved into her right breast. Her delicate features are painfully familiar to Ash Marcel, once a rising star in the Chicago PD. But though the victim resembles his former fiancée, Remi Walsh, he knows it's not her.

BUT THIS TIME

Though Remi escaped a serial killer five years ago, her father died trying to save her. Grief and guilt caused her to pull away from the man she loved. Now Ash is back in her life, insisting that Remi is still in danger.

IT'S A DEAD END...

Someone is targeting women who look just like Remi. With or without a badge, Ash intends to unmask the Butcher. But the killer isn't playing games any longer. He's moving in, ready to finish what he started, and prove there's nothing more terrifying than a killer's obsession...

**Please turn the page for an exciting sneak peek of
Alexandra Ivy's**

THE INTENDED VICTIM

coming soon wherever print and e-books are sold!

Prologue

The sun was still struggling to crest the horizon when Angel Conway entered the small park next to Lake Michigan. Shivering, she hunched herself deeper in her heavy coat. Shit. Was there anywhere in the world colder than Chicago in the winter? She doubted even the North Pole felt as frigid. Especially this morning, with the wind whipping the icy droplets from the nearby lake. They stung her face like tiny darts.

Unfortunately, she had no choice but to drag herself out of her bed at such a god-awful hour to brave the cold. It was the same reason she snuck out every Friday morning.

When she came to Chicago, she'd intended to have a clean start. No drugs. No men. Nothing that would screw up her one opportunity to climb out of the sewer she'd made of her life. But after the operation, she'd been given painkillers, and the hunger had been stroked to life. Within three weeks of her arrival in the city, she was back to the same old habits.

Stomping her feet in an attempt to keep blood flowing to her toes, she scanned the shadowed lot. Where was her john? Usually she was the one running late. She did it deliberately to avoid being turned into a human popsicle. She wanted to arrive at the park, climb into the man's expensive Jag, do her business, and get her pills. No fuss, no muss.

And no frostbite.

"Come on, come on," she muttered, rubbing her hands together.

Maybe she should bail. She could sneak out this weekend and find a street dealer. Of course, what little money she had…

Her thoughts were shattered by the sharp snap of a branch. She frowned, glancing over her shoulder at the trees directly behind her. She'd chosen this spot because it gave her an open view of the lot, but at the same time offered her cover in case a cop decided to drive through the park. Now she felt a weird sense of dread crawl over her skin.

She was from the country. She knew the sound of a critter scrambling through the underbrush.

There was someone moving in the darkness. The only question was whether it was an early morning jogger. Or a pervert who was spying on her.

She never considered there might have been a third possibility.

Not until she felt the cold blade press against her throat…

Chapter 1

Dr. Ashland Marcel entered his office on the campus of Illinois State University. It was a small, dark space that had one window overlooking the parking lot. An office reserved for a professor who hadn't yet received his tenure. Not that the cramped space bothered Ash. As much as he enjoyed teaching criminal justice classes, he hadn't fully committed to spending the rest of his life in an academic setting. Especially after a day like today.

With a grimace, he dropped into his seat behind the cluttered desk. A sigh escaped his lips. It was only noon, but he was grateful he was done teaching his classes for the day.

The students weren't the only ones looking forward to the end of the semester, he wryly acknowledged. Early December in the Midwest meant short, brutally cold days. A bunch of twenty-somethings trapped inside for weeks at a time was never a good thing. His classroom was choking with their pent-up energy.

But it was Friday. And Monday the students started finals. Which meant that in less than seven days he could look forward to a month of peace and quiet.

Pretending he didn't notice the tiny ache in the center of his heart at the thought of spending the holidays alone in his small house, Ash opened his laptop. He needed to get through his email before he could call it a day.

He'd barely fired up the computer when the door to his office was shoved open. He glanced up with a forbidding glare. His students were told on the first day of class that they could come to him during his posted office hours. He'd discovered his first year of teaching that they would follow him into the toilet with questions if he didn't set firm guidelines.

His annoyance, however, swiftly changed to surprise at the sight of the man dressed in a worn blue suit who stepped through the opening.

Detective Jackson "Jax" Marcel.

At a glance, it was easy to tell the two were brothers. They both had light brown hair that curled around the edges. Ash's was allowed to grow longer now that he was no longer on the police force, and had fewer strands of gray. And they both had blue eyes. Ash's were several shades darker, and framed by long, black lashes that had been the bane of his childhood. And they were both tall and slender, with muscles that came from long morning jogs instead of time in the gym.

Ash rose to his feet, his brows arching in surprise. It wasn't uncommon for his family to visit. The university was only a couple hours from Chicago. But they never just appeared in his office without calling.

"Jax."

Jax stretched his lips into a smile, but it was clearly an effort. "Hey, bro."

Ash studied his companion. Jax was the oldest of the four Marcel brothers, but since they had been born within a six-year span they were all close in age. That was perhaps why they'd always been so tight. You messed with one Marcel, you messed with them all.

"What are you doing here?" Ash demanded.

"I need to talk to you."

"You couldn't call?"

Jax grimaced. "I preferred to do it face-to-face."

Fear curled through the pit of Ash's stomach. Something had happened. Something bad. He leaned forward, laying his palms flat on the desk.

"Mom? Dad?"

Jax gave a sharp shake of his head. "The family is fine."

"Then what's going on?"

"Sit down."

Ash clenched his teeth. His brother's attempt to delay the bad news was twisting his nerves into a painful knot. "Shit. Just tell me."

Perhaps realizing that he was doing more harm than good, Jax heaved a harsh sigh.

"It's Remi Walsh."

Ash froze. He hadn't heard the name Remi in five years. Not since he'd packed his bags and walked away from Chicago and the woman who'd promised to be his wife.

"Remi." His voice sounded oddly hollow. "Is she hurt?"

This time Jax didn't torture him. He spoke without hesitation.

"Her body arrived in the morgue this morning."

Morgue.

"No." The word was wrenched from Ash's lips as his knees buckled and he collapsed into his chair.

Jax stepped toward the desk, his expression one of pity. "I'm sorry, Ash."

Ash shook his head. "This has to be a mistake," he said, meaning every word.

It *was* a mistake. There was no way in hell that Remi could be dead.

"I wish it was a mistake, bro," Jax said in sad tones. "But I saw her with my own eyes."

Ash grimly refused to accept what his brother was telling him. He'd tumbled head over heels in love with Remi from the second she'd strolled into the police station to take her father to lunch. Ash had just made detective and Gage Walsh was his partner. Thankfully, that hadn't stopped him from asking out Remi. She'd been hesitant at first, clearly unsure she wanted to date someone who worked so closely with her father. But from their first date they'd both known the sensations that sizzled between them were something special.

That's why he couldn't accept she was gone.

If something had happened to Remi, he would know. In his heart. In his very soul.

"How long has it been since you last spent time with her?" he challenged his brother.

Jax shrugged. "Five years ago."

"Exactly. How could you possibly recognize her after so long?"

"Ash." Jax reached up to run his hand over his face, his shoulders stooped. He looked like he was weary to the bone. "Denying the truth doesn't change it."

Anger blasted through Ash. He wanted to vault across the desk and slam his fist into his brother's face for insisting on the lie. It wouldn't be the first time he'd given Jax a black eye. Of course, his brother had pounded him back, chipping a tooth and covering him in bruises, but it'd been totally worth it.

Instead, he forced himself to leash his raw emotions.

"It's official?" he demanded.

Jax gave a slow shake of his head. "Not yet. The medical examiner is overwhelmed, as usual. It will be hours before they can run fingerprints, even with me putting pressure on them."

The anger remained, but it was suddenly threaded with hope. Nothing was official.

The words beat through him, echoing his heavy pulse.

At the same time, he continued to glare at his brother. "Why come here before you're sure it's Remi?"

Jax coughed, as if clearing his throat. "I wanted you to be prepared."

Ash narrowed his gaze. The shock of Jax's announcement had sent his brain reeling. Which was the only explanation for why he hadn't noticed his brother's hands clenching and unclenching. It wasn't just sympathy that was causing his brother's unease.

"No. There's something you're not telling me," he said.

Jax glanced toward the window, then down at the scuff marks on his leather shoes. Was he playing for time? Or searching for the right words? "Let's go for a drink," he finally suggested.

"Dammit, Jax. This isn't the time for games," Ash snapped. "Just tell me."

Jax's lips twisted before he forced himself to speak the words he'd clearly hoped to avoid. "She was found with her throat slit."

Ash surged to his feet, knocking over the chair. It smashed against the wooden floor with a loud bang, but Ash barely noticed.

"Was there a mark?" he rasped.

It'd been only a few weeks after he'd started dating Remi that Gage had put together the connection that a rash of dead women was the work of a serial killer. They'd tagged him the Chicago Butcher since it was suspected that he used a butcher's knife to slice the throats of his victims. Only the cops knew that there had been a hidden calling card left behind by the killer: a small crescent carved onto each victim's right breast. No one knew if it was supposed to be a "c" or a moon or perhaps some unknown symbol. But it was always there.

"Yes."

"Like the others?" he pressed.

Jax nodded. Ash reached into his pocket to pull out his keys. He'd gone from white-hot emotion erupting through him like lava to an ice-cold determination.

The Chicago Butcher had destroyed his life five years ago. If the bastard was back, then Ash was going to track him down and kill him. He didn't care if he had a badge or not.

He tossed his keys to his brother. "Go to my house and pack a bag."

Jax caught the keys, his brows tugging together. "Ash, there's nothing you can do."

"I have to see her," Ash muttered, not adding his secondary reason for returning to Chicago. His brother was smart. He knew Ash would be hungry for revenge. "She was my fiancée."

Jax grimaced. "It was all a long time ago."

Ash snorted. It had been five years, not an eternity. And most of the time it felt like it had all happened yesterday. "We both know it doesn't matter how long ago it was, or you would never have come down here to tell me."

The older man hunched his shoulders. "I didn't want you to hear it on the news."

Ash didn't believe the excuse for a second. "Pack a bag," he commanded, reaching down to right his chair. "I'll be ready by the time you get back."

"What about your classes?" Jax tried a last-ditch effort to keep Ash away from Chicago.

"Finals are next week." Ash sat down and reached for the cell phone he'd left on his desk. He might be under thirty, but he held the old-fashioned belief that there was no need for phones in his classroom. Including his own. "I'll call the dean and warn him there's been a family emergency. If I'm not back by Monday, my teaching assistant can proctor the exams."

"Ash—"

"I can go back with you or I'll drive myself," Ash interrupted.

"Hell, I don't want you behind the wheel." Jax pointed a finger toward Ash. "Don't move until I get back."

Ash ignored his brother as he turned and left his office. He not only needed to contact the dean, but he wanted to make sure that his assistant knew he would be expected to take over his classes if necessary, as well as make his excuses to the dozens of holiday invitations that were waiting in his inbox.

He was back in his office and just finishing his tasks when his phone pinged with a text telling him that Jax was waiting for him in the parking lot.

Grabbing his laptop and the coat that hung in the corner, he stepped out of the office and closed the door behind him. Then, using the back stairs, he managed to avoid any acquaintances. Right now, he would be incapable of casual chitchat.

Pushing open the door, he stepped out of the building and headed for the nearby parking lot. The sun was shining, but there was a sharp breeze that made him shiver. Like all his brothers he enjoyed being out in the fresh air, either jogging or spending the weekend camping near the river. But with each passing year he found he was less willing to brave icy temperatures.

Soon he'd be spending the long winters sitting in front of a warm fire with a comfy sweater and his favorite slippers.

Shaking away his idiotic thoughts, he stopped next to his brother's car. Pulling open the door, he slid into the passenger seat and wrapped the seat belt across his body.

"Have you heard anything from the medical examiner?" he demanded as his brother put the car in gear and headed out of the lot.

"Not yet." There was silence as Jax concentrated on negotiating the traffic out of town. It wasn't until they reached the interstate that Jax glanced toward Ash. "Mom will be happy to have you home for a few days. She complains you never bother to come and see her anymore."

Ash pressed his lips together. It was that or snapping at his brother that this wasn't a damned social visit. Eventually, however, he forced his tense muscles to relax. He wasn't so far gone that he didn't realize that Jax was trying to distract him. And that there was no point in brooding on what he was going to discover once they reached Chicago.

"Mom's too busy planning Nate's wedding to notice whether I'm around or not," he managed to say.

Nate was the youngest Marcel brother, who'd moved to Oklahoma after leaving the FBI. He had proposed to his neighbor Ellie Guthrie a few months ago, and since she didn't have a relationship with her own parents, June Marcel had eagerly stepped in to act as her surrogate mother.

Jax released a short laugh. "She's been in heaven, running around the city to find the perfect flower arrangements and sewing the bridesmaids' dresses," he agreed. "The poor woman assumed with four sons she would never get the opportunity to be so involved in all the frou-frou nonsense that comes with a wedding." Jax set the cruise control and settled back in his seat. "Still, you must have been gone too long if you've forgotten Mom's ability to concentrate on more than one thing at a time. I remember her baking cupcakes for Ty's Boy Scout troop while helping Nate with his math homework and at the same time making sure I raked every damned leaf in the backyard because I missed curfew."

Ash's lips curved into a rueful smile. His mother was a ruthless force of nature who'd occasionally resorted to fear and intimidation to control her four unruly sons. Mostly she'd smothered them in such love that none of them could bear the thought of disappointing her.

"True. She has a gift." He felt a tiny pang in the center of his heart. It'd been too long since he'd been home. "I could use her in my classroom."

"Lord, don't say that. She'll be waiting next to your desk with a ruler in her hand," Jax teased.

Another silence filled the car, then Jax cleared his throat, and abruptly asked the question that had no doubt been on his lips for the past five years.

"I never knew what happened between you and Remi." Jax kept his gaze focused on the road, as if knowing that Ash wouldn't want him to witness the pain that twisted his features. "One day you were planning your wedding and the next the engagement was over and you were moving away."

Ash's breath hissed between his clenched teeth. "The Chicago Butcher happened."

He expected his brother to drop the issue. His breakup with Remi was something he refused to discuss. His family had always respected his barriers.

But whether he was still trying to keep Ash distracted, or if it was the shock of seeing a woman he believed to be Remi at the morgue, Jax refused to let it go. "You both suffered when she was captured by the Butcher and her father was killed trying to save her," he pointed out. "I thought it would draw the two of you closer together."

Ash turned his head to gaze at the frozen fields that lined the road. The memories of that horrifying night were firmly locked in the back of his mind. The frantic phone call from Remi telling her father that she was being followed as she headed home. Gage Walsh's stark command that Ash drive Remi's route in case the killer forced her car off the road on the way home, while he went to his elegant mansion on the North Shore to meet her. And then Ash's arrival at the mansion to discover that he was too late. Gage's blood had been found at his home, but his body had never been discovered. No one knew why the Butcher would have taken it, unless he feared that he'd left evidence on the corpse that he didn't have time to remove. The killing, after all, wouldn't have been planned, unlike the females he stalked and murdered. Thank God, Remi had been alive, although she'd been lying unconscious in the kitchen.

But while he wasn't about to go into the agonizing details, Jax deserved an answer. The older man had been an unwavering source of strength over the past few years. Whether it was to shut down his father's angry protests when Ash announced that he was leaving the police department, or driving down to the university and getting him cross-eyed drunk when he was feeling isolated and alone.

"After I brought Remi home from the hospital she started to shut me out," he said in slow, painful tones. "At first I assumed she would get her memories back, and that she would be able to heal from the trauma she'd gone through."

"But the memories never came back," Jax murmured.

"No, they never came back." Ash grimaced. He'd wasted a lot of emotional energy trying to convince Remi to get professional help to retrieve her memories. As if the return of them could somehow heal the growing breach between them. It was only with time and distance he could see that they were struggling with more than the trauma of her being attacked by the Butcher. "But it was the guilt that destroyed our hopes for the future."

His brother sent him a sharp glance. "Guilt for what?"

Ash gave a sad shake of his head. "Remi felt guilty for her father's death. She had a crazy idea that if she hadn't called to say she was being followed, her father would still be alive. And to be honest, it only made it worse that his body was never found. I think a part of her had desperately hoped that he would miraculously return. With each passing day, she blamed herself more and more."

"And your guilt?" Jax pressed.

"I should never have let Gage go there alone. I was his partner."

Jax muttered a curse. "His *younger* partner. Gage was your superior, and it was his call to split up so you could cover more ground. Just as it was your duty to obey his order."

Ash shrugged. Easy to say the words, it was much harder to dismiss the gnawing remorse. If only...

Heaving a sigh, he leaned his head back against the seat and closed his eyes. He'd given Jax the explanation he demanded. He didn't have the strength to argue whether it made any sense or not.

Ash kept his eyes closed even as the traffic thickened and they slowed to a mere crawl. He'd driven to the morgue enough times to know exactly when they were pulling into the side parking lot.

Lifting his head, he studied the long cement-block building with two rows of narrow windows. Nothing had changed in the past few years. Maybe the trees lining the street had grown a little taller, and they'd replaced the flags out front. Otherwise it was the same stark structure he remembered.

Jax switched off the engine, turning his head toward Ash. "I wish you wouldn't do this."

"I have to." Ash unbuckled the seat belt and pushed open the door before stepping out.

Behind him was the sound of hurried footsteps as Jax rushed to keep up. Not that Ash was going to get far without him. He was no longer a cop, which meant he would have to hang on to the hope that Remi still had him listed as an emergency contact to get past the security.

Much easier to let Jax do his thing.

Quickly at his side, Jax took charge as they entered the building. They were halted twice, but Jax flashed his badge and quickly they were stepping into a harshly lit room that felt ice-cold.

Ash shivered. He hated coming here. Even when it was a part of his job. Now his stomach was twisted so tight it felt like it'd been yanked into knots.

They were led by a technician down a long row of steel racks where bodies wrapped in heavy plastic waited for an official ID. Or perhaps for an autopsy. He'd tried not to really notice what was going on behind the scenes. Now he felt as if he was in a dream as the technician waved for them to stop and Jax wrapped an arm around his shoulders. No, it was more like a nightmare. One that wasn't going to end if it truly was Remi who was being slid out on a steel slab.

Taking care not to disturb the body any more than necessary, the technician slowly pulled back the plastic cover. Ash made a choked sound as he caught sight of the long black hair that was glossy enough to reflect the overhead light. It was pulled from a pale, beautiful face, just like Remi liked to wear it.

He swayed to the side, leaning heavily against his brother as pain blasted through him. "Christ."

"Steady," Jax murmured.

Ash's gaze absorbed the delicate features. They were so heart-wrenchingly familiar. The slender nose. The high, prominent cheekbones. The dark, perfectly arched brows. The lush lips.

"I didn't want to believe," he rasped, his voice coming from a long way away. As if he was falling off a cliff and was waiting to hit the bottom.

Would he die when that happened?

He hoped so.

What would be the point of living in a world without Remi Walsh?

"I'm sorry," Jax said, his own voice harsh with pain.

Ash's gaze remained locked on Remi's lips. It'd been five years but he still remembered their last kiss. He'd just told her that he intended to take a job at the university. Deep inside he'd hoped she would be furious at his decision. He wanted her to fight for their future together. Instead she'd offered a sad smile and leaned forward to brush her mouth over his in a silent goodbye.

He'd nearly cried even as he'd savored the taste of her strawberry lip balm…

Ash stilled. Lip balm. Why was there a warning voice whispering at the back of his fuzzy brain? Maybe he was going crazy. What the hell did her lips have to do with anything? He frowned, telling himself to turn away.

He'd done what he came there to do. What was the point of gawking at Remi as if he hoped she would suddenly open her eyes? It was time to go.

But his feet refused to budge. He knew Jax was staring at him in confusion, and that the technician was starting to shift from one foot to another, but still he continued to run his gaze over Remi's pale face.

Something was nagging at him. But what?

Then his gaze returned to her mouth and he realized what his unconscious mind was trying to tell him.

She was wearing lipstick. A bright red shade. And more than that, there was makeup plastered on her skin and what looked like false lashes stuck to her lids. The harsh lighting had washed everything to a dull shade of ash, which was why he hadn't noticed it the minute the cover had been pulled back.

"That's not her," he breathed.

"Ash." Jax's arm tightened around his shoulder. "I know this is tough, but—"

"It's not her," Ash interrupted, his heart returning to sluggish life.

How had he been so blind? Remi never wore makeup. Not even when her mother insisted on dragging her to some fancy-ass party. She claimed that it made her skin itch, plus she didn't feel the need to slap paint on herself to try and impress other people. If they didn't like her face, then they didn't have to look at it.

Her down-to-earth attitude was one of the things he'd loved about her.

Of course, as far as he was concerned she was gorgeous. She didn't need anything artificial to make his palms sweat and his pulse race.

"How can you be sure?" Jax demanded, his voice revealing his fear that Ash had gone over the edge. "Like you said, it's been five years. She could have changed in that time. Unless there's something you haven't told me?"

Ash jutted his chin. He wasn't going to explain about the makeup. Jax would tell him a woman might very well change her mind about cosmetics as she started to age. Or perhaps she had a boyfriend who wanted her to plaster her face with the gunk. Besides, now that he was looking at the dead woman with his brain and not his heart, he could start to detect physical differences. The nose was just a tad too long. Her brow not quite wide enough. And her jaw too blunt.

"I'm sure." His voice was strong. Confident. "It's not her."

"He's right." A new voice cut through the air, echoing eerily through the racks of dead bodies. "I just got the results back from the fingerprints."

They all turned to watch as Dr. Jack Feldman, one of the city's top medical examiners, stepped out of the shadows. A short man with salt and pepper hair and a neatly trimmed beard, he was wearing a white lab coat that didn't hide the start of an impressive potbelly. He'd been a good friend of Gage Walsh, and had extended that friendship to Ash when he'd become his partner.

He'd also adored Remi, treating her like she was his own child. It must have been a hideous shock to have a woman who looked so much like her show up in his morgue.

"Feldman," Ash murmured, stepping away from his brother so he could pull the older man into a rough hug.

They shared a silent moment of tangled emotions, then the doctor slapped him on the back and pulled back to study him with a sympathetic gaze.

"Good to see you, Ash, although not under these circumstances."

Ash cleared his throat, his attention moving toward the electronic pad clutched in Feldman's fingers. "Did you get an ID?"

Feldman held up a hand before he glanced toward the silent technician. "I'll take it from here, Jimmy," he told the young man. They waited until Jimmy turned and left the room before Feldman led them to a distant corner. His dark eyes rested on Ash's face. "I shouldn't be talking to you, but I'm pretty sure you'll get the information one way or another. Plus, you're one of us, even if you did jump ship for a while. Eventually you'll come back where you belong."

They were the words he'd heard from a dozen different lawmen when he'd announced his decision to leave the Chicago Police Department and take a job teaching. And in truth, a part of him had secretly agreed.

Being a detective was in his blood.

He shook away the thought, nodding toward the electronic pad. "Who is she?"

Feldman lifted the pad and touched the screen to call up a file. "Her name is Angel Conway. She's a twenty-five-year-old white female. Five feet, six inches tall. One hundred thirty pounds."

Ash frowned. "Is she local?"

"No." Feldman brushed his finger over the screen. "Her address is Bailey, Illinois. A small town fifty miles south of the city."

Ash glanced toward Jax, who gave a shake of his head. He'd never heard of it.

"Do you have any other info?"

Feldman was silent as he read through the short report. Ash knew Feldman must have shouted and bullied and called in every favor owed him to get any information so quickly. The Chicago coroner's department was notoriously understaffed and overworked. It was only because of their dedicated staff they weren't completely overwhelmed.

"It looks like she worked at a convenience store and has a rap sheet for petty crimes," Feldman murmured. "Mostly stealing and one count of prostitution."

Ash tried to process what he was being told. Not easy when his brain was still foggy from the extreme emotions that had battered him. Fear. Shock. Grief. Soul-shaking relief.

He did, however, tuck the information away so he could pull it out later and truly consider what it all meant. "Where did they find her?"

"Jameson Park," Feldman said.

Ash lifted his brows in surprise. Jameson Park was built along the shores of Lake Michigan, and popular enough to be crowded this time of year despite the frigid weather. Plus it would have a regular patrol officer who would do sweeps through the area.

A dangerous place to do a dump.

"That doesn't fit the pattern," he said.

"No. But everything else does," Feldman told him, turning around the pad so Ash could see the photos taken of Angel Conway's naked body.

For a second his stomach rolled in protest. It'd been a while since he'd seen death up close and personal. And the violence one person could inflict on another. Then he sucked in a slow, deep breath.

Shutting down his emotions, he studied the picture with a professional attention to detail. He'd learned as a detective it was too easy to get overwhelmed by death. He had to break it down to small, individual pieces to keep himself focused on what was important.

Leaning forward he studied the cut that marred the slender throat. It was thin and smooth and just deep enough to cut through the carotid artery. There were no hesitation marks, and no ragged edges to indicate nerves or anger. It was a precision kill that seemed to be oddly lacking in emotion.

Next his gaze moved to the small wound on the woman's upper breast. It was carved into a neat crescent shape. This was the one detail they'd never revealed to the public.

"Christ," he breathed as he straightened. "He's back."

Jax reached out to grasp his shoulder. "We can't jump to conclusions, Ash."

Ash understood his brother's warning. There was nothing more dangerous for an investigator than leaping to a conclusion, then becoming blind to other possibilities.

But he was no longer a detective, and his gut instinct was screaming that this was the work of the killer who'd destroyed the lives of so many. Including his own.

"There's more." Feldman cleared his throat, lowering the pad. "She's had plastic surgery."

"Not that unusual," Jax said, echoing Ash's own thoughts. "Lots of women, and men for that matter, think they need some nip and tuck."

Feldman grimaced. "This nip and tuck was for a particular purpose."

A chill crawled over Ash's skin. Not the frigid air of the morgue, but something else. Perhaps a premonition. "What purpose?" he forced himself to ask.

"If I had to make a guess, I would say it was to make Angel Conway look like Remi Walsh."

Printed in the United States
by Baker & Taylor Publisher Services